THE RETREAT

Conor Kostick

RED STAG

Published in 2020 by:
RED STAG
(a Mentor Books imprint)

Mentor Books Ltd
43 Furze Road
Sandyford Industrial Estate
Dublin 18
Republic of Ireland

Tel: +353 1 295 2112 / 3
Fax: +353 1 295 2114
Email: admin@mentorbooks.ie
Website: www.mentorbooks.ie

A CIP catalogue record for this title is available from the British Library.

ISBN 978-1-912514-56-4

CONTENTS

Dedication 4

1   Memories of Summer 5

2   The Decision 9

3   The Devil's Own 19

4   In the Name of Christ 31

5   They Shall Return at Evening 45

6   A Dream that Affrightens 55

7   Speeches and Exhortations 61

8   Beserkir 65

9   Thy Sleep Shall be Sweet 73

10 Bring Forth the Prisoner 79

11 Among my People are Found Wicked Men 89

12 An Empty Road 101

13 Lying Lips Put to Silence 109

14 He Soweth Discord 115

15 He that Provoketh a King to Anger 125

16 The Song of Count Stephen 133

17 Forest Beasts 143

18 I Will Track Them Down 151

19 Vengeance Rendered 157

20 Fly Away, Blackbirds 167

21 He that is Greedy of Gain 177

22 The Sons of Men are Liars 185

23 Feet Dipped in Blood 195

24 A Strength Laid Waste 203

25 The Path of Ages 211

26 Wrath, Devastation, Desolation, Bitterness 219

27 Keep Thy Money to Thyself 227

28 Arise, and Let Us Flee 235

29 The Red Horseman 243

30 Heaven Departed as a Book Folded Up 251

31 Conversation from a Child 257

32 There is no Covering for Destruction 265

DEDICATION

Did you grow up listening to tales of famous heroes? And were your daydreams filled with scenes of extraordinary bravery in which you were the knight who earned the cheers of the crowds? I did and mine were. From the age at which I could hold a practice sword — five years — I wanted nothing more than to be a knight whose deeds were acclaimed by the poets. And under the approving eye of my father and his soldiers, I worked hard to become as good as they at fighting and riding.

Now that I've achieved my goal and learned something about war, I feel a compulsion to write my story. I do so, not for the sake of other youths aspiring to be heroes. This is not a moral guidebook. Nor do I write it to ensure that the fate of Duke Shalk's army is known to all and for all time. This is not a history. I write because I feel a dark *geas* upon me: almost as though I have been condemned to search my own memories and relive these experiences. Cateline, Gerard, Rainulf. Talk to me again. By writing of you, can I come to properly understand you?

I'm told that it is customary to write a dedication before an account such as this begins. At first, I thought I would dedicate this narration to Count Stephen, a very worthy man whom I have come to love. Yet, there is a shadow over me and over my tale, which prevents me from making so obvious a choice. Instead, I dedicate the following story to Achilles. Yes, the most famous knight of all.

Achilles, listen to the following words and recognize the truth of them. I dedicate this to you, the slayer of brave Hector. You, who saved the Greek ships after the death of your beloved companion. You, who when filled with wrath caused havoc to the Trojan ranks. More than this, Achilles, hear me preach the same unbearable truth as you. Recall, as you read this, the answer your shade gave to cunning Odysseus: you told him to choose one day of life as a slave in dusty fields over an eternity of death as the ruler of Hades.

1

MEMORIES OF SUMMER

Perhaps I should start with my childhood at Castle Rocadamour. My father was lord of a mountain town in the most beautiful part of central France. Whenever I think of my youth, I think of the blue skies of long summer days and daily adventures with my friends. My friends and I had our own ponies from when we were eleven and we rode to fight in imaginary wars whenever we could. Each morning, I would wake with excitement, ready for the new day. Ignoring the complaints of my younger brother William, I'd jump from our bed and yell for the servants to come assist with my dress. Within the hour, I would have washed, eaten and had the stablehands prepare my pony. Then I was away, trotting down the mountainside, breathing in deep of the cool morning air, searching the horizon above the ochre hills for distant hawks and feeling like the happiest boy in creation.

It will be easy for the reader to understand how such a boy would become an impatient young man of sixteen. To appreciate how eager he would be to face real enemies, lance in hand. And to daydream that by defeating them, he would earn the accolades of the poets. Above all, I was impatient to impress Father and demonstrate to him I was a warrior who did not fear battle. Lord Rocadamour was a stern man, although his knights all loved him deeply. He had fought in four wars. He had nothing to prove to anyone about his bravery or skill at arms.

Sometimes, Father would take a direct hand in my learning. On such days, William and I sprang to our tasks like young lions. When I got the chance to display to Father my strength with a wooden practice sword, I would lash at him with blows so mighty as to break mountains apart. Or so I wished. Father would laugh (a flash of white teeth in a black beard) and deflect my sweeping cuts effortlessly. When he had enough of this play, he would suddenly move upon us both. Feint, jab, jab. And two winded boys would be sat on the ground, gasping and red faced, while Lord Rocadamour's knights laughed at us.

Naturally, when later that year word of the Holy Expedition came to us (we did not call it a *croisade* until it was under way), I was eager to go. Father, anxious for the future of his dynasty, or perhaps out of love of me, put up strong resistance to my joining the army. As for Mother and my sister Alice, you can picture the tears and the pleading as they clung to me; both with arms wrapped around me as if to protect me from arrows. They insisted I should not go. Not even for love of God (who I invoked, of course, though the truth was, I had only glory in mind).

Probably, I would not have been permitted to participate in the march to Jerusalem, but that Duke Shalk himself arrived at our castle, hoping to persuade the lords of southern France to join him. Full of passion and determination, the voice of the tall nobleman echoed powerfully in our hall, prophesying immortal fame for those who rescued Christ's church at Jerusalem from the heretics. Only after this direct appeal, although visibly reluctant, did Father grant me permission to join the departing army. O, what agony I could see in the sulks of William, since he was refused the same opportunity in no uncertain terms. At night, my younger brother would whisper to me of his plans to run away to join me. Knowing that they would come to nothing and knowing too how hurt he was, I indulged his wishful visions. As I lay in our bed, listening to him explain how his lot was nothing but injustice, my own heart was secretly aglow. At last, a worthy enterprise and one that would present many a chance to demonstrate that I was no coward.

It was in late summer, on the Feast Day of St Bartholomew, that I rode through the gates of Castle Rocadamour to take the northern road towards Rouen, where I was to rendezvous with Duke Shalk's army. Near the tip of my lance, the sunflower yellow and pale blue colours of our dynasty were fluttering as rapidly as my heart. Behind me were my two squires and somewhere above me, I knew, Alice was throwing rose petals (the wind took them away from our path). No doubt, Mother was fighting back the tears. And, no doubt too, for very different reasons, William was also teary-eyed as he watched me ride off.

In every way but one, this was a proud moment for me. The maggot in the apple of my life was the presence of one of Father's knights, a sergeant called Arnulf who had been assigned to guide me and bring me back safely. A chaperone. While Arnulf felt insulted that Father was willing to lose a man who in battle and counsel was one of his most reliable knights, I was equally annoyed that I was supposed to defer to Arnulf, 'in all matters of importance' as my father put it. Assigning this sergeant to guide me was an insult to my status as future lord of Rocadamour. It was as though I had never been knighted and was still a squire.

Even so, I was on my way. No longer the boy on the pony with the pretend weapons, daydreaming of adventures; now I was riding towards very real battles, with armour that glittered in the sunshine, an iron sword and with murderous intent.

2

THE DECISION

In that year, Shalk led a mighty army east across the Reiber to subdue the pagans. But Shalk's people did not cease from lust and greed and so incurred the wrath of God. Rightly, the expedition ended in shame and ignominy. The only man to emerge from the affair with any credit was Gerard and he but a poor footsoldier.

– Anonymous, The Deeds of Count Stephen

In the first weeks of the crusade to the Holy Land, I paid no attention to those who walked on foot and I'm sorry that I failed to take the opportunity to learn from a man whom I came to admire very greatly. It may well have been that I had ridden past Gerard at some point during the month that our army marched eastwards through a grim German forest, but he would have been beneath my notice. Gerard was a footsoldier, whereas I was a knight riding a warhorse that cost twenty pounds of silver.

I've since learned to not judge men or women by their birth or position. A bishop might be a coward and a fool, while a farmer's daughter might be as terrifying as a goddess from the ancient world. Back then, though it was not so long ago, I thought differently and despite the fact that I was surrounded by thousands of footsoldiers, farmers, cooks, washerwomen, ironworkers, carpenters and craftsmen of every kind, I gave them no heed.

Only when he grasped my foot did Gerard come to my attention. This incident occurred when we were in the central square of the city that our army had just sacked: Devinium. We should never have been there. These were Christians that our army had killed. Devinium was one of King Bratislav of Hungary's most important cities. Despite the reluctance of our leader, Duke Shalk, our army had thrown ladders up against the walls and captured the city. Utterly surprised, the defenders of Devinium had been overwhelmed by the assault. They had trusted fellow Christians not to harm them. Yet had they heard the vigour with which our soldiers cursed at the high price set on foodstuffs and had they known of the rumours that circulated, blaming Devinium for the murder and robbery of our poor, then perhaps the people of that city would have realised their danger.

Of course, I took no part in the looting and was as eager as anyone to leave a city on whose streets could be seen bloodstains that made me feel guilty. So as our people made preparations for departure, Arnulf and I were among the first to mount. Shalk's sergeants were ushering everyone towards the gates and as they did so, they explained to us all an agreement that had been reached between King Bratislav and the leaders of our army. We were to surrender our weapons and be escorted to the border of Hungary, where they would be returned to us.

Carts, creaking loudly each time they lurched forward, queued to pass under the great portcullis; soldiers hurried to find their places; all along the main street of the town, women – some with children, it was that kind of expedition – waited for their turn to join the slow-moving line. In the past, the assembly of our army was the occasion for a certain amount of ribald shouting from the women, along with cheers for their favourites (they had never cheered for me; perhaps that was just as well, for I would have blushed at some of the invitations they made). Today, however, the women were subdued and anxious. As well they might be. Could we trust King Bratislav after our people had looted one of his most important cities?

'Come on!' Arnulf, my sour-faced, moustached sergeant had spotted an opening in the queue and urged his courser onwards. Even without my bidding him to, my stallion – Tenebrour – stepped forward also. The whole journey thus far had been like this and it irritated me. I was a lord, well, eldest son of a lord, and (despite my promise to Father) felt that I should be making the decisions, not my sergeant and certainly not my horse.

So far this expedition had provided me with little excitement and a great deal of frustration. I had joined the army wanting to fight in epic battles so that I could prove myself and return home a hero. Instead, throughout our long journey in the German forest we'd seen nothing more dangerous than raids on our goods by vagabonds. These skirmishes were always over quickly and I had yet to draw my sword in anger. Nor had I done so when Devinium was taken. Yesterday's fighting was just butchery.

Barely had I joined the throng working its way towards the city gate, when I realised with a shock that my foot was in the grasp of a stout, balding man of about forty years. His was a fleshy face, one that made me think he was formed more by eating than fighting. His shoulders and arms were sturdy enough, clad as they were with thick layers of black leather armour on which were bolted strips of iron. The stranger looked up at me from beneath dark eyebrows that indicated with a ferocious scowl the passion of his feelings.

'Don't go. It's a trap.' His voice was deep, with a moving cadence to his accent that I later learned was Irish.

Involuntarily, I glanced across at Arnulf for guidance and then, annoyed at myself for having done so, looked back down at the footsoldier. 'What do you mean?'

'No one who leaves this town now will live to see the sun set.' He broke off, exasperated by the fact that horses and knights were beginning to push past us on either side. 'Stop! Don't go to your doom!' Now the full strength of his voice was to be heard and it was powerful. Nor was it a lone cry, other men too, lowly men of modest arms, were in and among the knights, urging us all to stay.

'Out of our way!' Although he was perfectly willing to give orders to me, evidently Arnulf was not going to allow a common footsoldier do the same.

Partly to stand up to my sergeant, I shook my head. 'Wait.' Then I turned to look back down at the stocky man at my horse's flank. He was balancing on his toes to survey the scene and on his face was such an expression of worry that my heart shrank a little. 'Explain yourself.'

The anxious eyes – surprisingly blue – of the footsoldier fixed on mine. 'If we surrender our weapons, they'll massacre us.'

'Come on!' Arnulf urged again. 'What right has this man, this commoner, to detain us?'

In that moment, I confess, I still had complete faith in Shalk and thought the footsoldier utterly mistaken to attempt to dissuade us to act against our instructions. At the same time, I was also in a mutinous state of mind and desired to send my sergeant a clear signal as to who was in charge. Arnulf had the advantage of many years over me and he had ridden in all four of Father's wars, nevertheless, I was the lord here and from now on I would choose my own destiny.

Such foolish, insubordinate and aristocratic feelings saved my life that day.

'Very well; we'll stay.'

Mouth open, his face longer than ever, Arnulf was shocked.

This time, when the footsoldier looked at me, he seemed to really see me. 'Good.' He took the bridle and pulled my horse across the street, out of the line. I could hear my sergeant behind me and sensed the fury of his stare upon my back.

'So, young knight,' asked the footsoldier. 'What's your name?'

'Guibert of Rocadamour.'

'You're a long way from home.'

'Aren't we all?'

'We are that. We certainly are.' Then he turned to look over at the crowds. 'Follow Lord Rocadamour! Follow Lord Rocadamour if you value your life!'

Perhaps it was the fact that my name was being shouted out along the nearby streets but I suddenly realised that this man had followers: officers or comrades of some sort. Looking past Arnulf's severe, angry expression, I picked out about a dozen men and, indeed, a few women, who were raising their voices and urging the departing army to turn back and follow me. Follow me! It was the first time a body of adults had claimed me as their leader. This was thrilling, albeit that I could see Arnulf growing red with frustration and anger. In the colour of his cheeks was shame too, perhaps, since the name of Rocadamour was now being used to encourage disloyalty to Duke Shalk.

All at once, my excitement collapsed into worry about the situation. Yet what could I do? Find my place among the departing knights again? To turn back now would be an even more shameful act than to allow our family name to be used in this disobedient action.

Still holding the bridle of my steed, the footsoldier led us out of the slow-moving files of people and carts to a small square. Tenebrour wanted a drink and pulled his head away from the footsoldier, to take me towards a trough. The reigns came free and panic flashed across the man's unshaven face, subsiding when he saw I was not leaving him.

'Wait here.' And he stepped hurriedly towards the street.

What was it about my demeanor that allowed those beneath me to give me orders? Yet my resentment was only short-lived. It faded fast against the fact that I was witnessing a crisis and a split in the army. Thus the determination of this man and the potential consequences of his actions (and mine too) overrode the lessons of my upbringing and I remained still, watching.

'Rainulf Bluetooth. Don't tell me you are fool enough to leave these walls?' My footsoldier was pointing and shouting at one of the *mutur* – a band of thugs without a palfry between them – a burly and heavily tattooed man, whose long, dark hair hung in tight braids.

'We aren't fools, Gerard, and we don't like it. But what else can we do?'

'Stay.'

The brute shrugged. 'Who else is staying?'

Glancing towards me, Gerard hesitated. 'Who knows? But if the *mutur* stay, maybe more will.'

Rainulf Bluetooth came to a stand and all around him other *mutur* did likewise. There was talking, but it was impossible to hear what they were saying over the excited cackle of chickens, the deep grunts of pigs and the other sounds of the peasants making ready to depart. Impossible, until Rainulf raised his voice again.

'Fall out!' The leader of the *mutur* gestured towards me and soon I was surrounded by the scum of the army. Maybe they were giving me curious looks, or maybe that was my imagination. But I felt out of place among these thick-bearded, unwashed men who stank of the horse manure they had been walking upon.

A group of a dozen knights fought clear of the crowds to our position.

'Who's in charge here?'

'The boy.'

'No.' I pulled the coif back from my brow so the newcomers could see me better, then I shook my head. 'He is. That footsoldier, Gerard.'

'Well, Gerard? What say you?'

'Count Stephen of Nangis is it? Well, I say that King Bratislav will not keep his word and all who leave now will be killed by his army.'

'How do you know this?'

'Why else does he demand we give up our weapons?'

Count Stephen's powerful stallion took a step forward and the elderly, grey-haired lord spoke out firmly. 'I agree with you. We stay.'

A ragged cheer, mostly from the *mutur*, caused many of those still shuffling in line to leave the town to look over at us.

'Stay! Join us! Join Count Stephen! Stay!' Even I participated in the cajoling cries, happier now that another nobleman was with me. A glance at Arnulf, however, showed that he was sulking and unenthusiastic: silent but eloquent in his frowns, his sagging moustache, and the tense posture of his thin frame.

Some of those we were crying out towards did come to us. Not many though.

Then came a time, around midday, when the town fell quiet. Everyone else had gone. Part of me wished I had left with them; here I was among strangers. And what would be the consequence of staying? Would we be attacked by King Bratislav? Had my desire to assert myself led me directly towards my death? I suddenly felt a flush of shame at the thought. For if so, I had also condemned Arnulf.

A group of riders cantered in, banners flying. It was Duke Shalk himself, in all his finery. 'What's going on here? Why aren't you marching with the army?'

'You march to be butchered.' Gerard stepped forward, arms crossed, voice steady. A murmur of agreement followed his words.

'You all saw that King Bratislav took his oath while holding the arm of Saint James.' Shalk's tone was reverent.

A snort of derision from Rainulf was all it took to set the *mutur* to heckling. Most of the shouting was coarse and ungodly and made reference to another body part of that holy saint. I was embarrassed to hear it.

'If you don't come now, you jeopardise the truce and the agreement. You give him excuse for attacking us all.'

'See this sword, Shalk?' Count Stephen rode forward, brandishing a beautiful, gold-hilted longsword above his head, turning to show it to everyone. 'This is *Lifestealer*, it was my grandfather's and my father's. It will be my son's. It does not leave my side.'

'Our weapons will be in carts within view of us at all times. And we will be parted from them no longer than it takes to cross the border into the pagan lands. Then they will be returned to us.'

'Do you not see that once given, you will never hold those weapons again? Our sack of Devinium will not so lightly be forgiven: the king wants his revenge. T'is but a ruse.' Again, Gerard called out. I admired his strength of manner almost as much as I disapproved of the lack of respect in his voice for a man who was by far his better. There was something in Gerard's posture too – a tough and determined stance, arms crossed, round head held high – that showed he was sure of himself.

'King Bratislav accepts that the citizens provoked us. And think about it, why punish us when he can send us against his enemies? Even if he hates us, he hates the pagans more...' From a shout, Shalk dropped his voice to a more normal level. 'Count Stephen, I'm sure I can get King Bratislav to agree to let you keep your sword. Come now, join us.'

'I do not trust this king as you do. I will not follow you any longer.'

A rowdy cheer from the footsoldiers and women among us lifted my spirits. But then Shalk's next words expressed my own fears exactly.

'What will you do? You can't stay here for long. If you go forward without his agreement, King Bratislav will destroy you. If you turn back – and abandon this holy mission – you are too few to survive the journey through the forest. By staying here now, you take a greater chance with your lives than by coming with me.'

'And yet, I stay.'

Again the cheers rang out. This time, with somewhat less warmth. Shalk had troubled us all.

'Then give the rest of us time to cross King Bratislav's lands.

Don't do anything to incur his anger. For his punishment might land heavily upon us.'

'Very well.'

'I have your word?'

'You do.'

'And what about you, young knight? Would Lord Rocadamour want you to betray me?'

Even the crows fell silent, seemingly as interested in my answer as everyone else. What should I say? He was probably right; my father would cuff me for a fool. But that choice I'd made when Gerard held my foot had set me on this path and in front of these men there was no turning back.

'I do not betray you. If your orders are folly and I refuse them, then that is my right.'

No one cheered. Perhaps it was because my voice would not ring out across the square in the same authoritative manner as that of Count Stephen and Gerard. The more effort that I put into shouting out my response, the more shrill I sounded.

'Very well. I'll report those words to Lord Rocadamour when our holy vows have been fulfilled.' With that Shalk turned and rode out, his men hurrying after him.

There were tears in my eyes and I had to keep my head averted from Arnulf. Had my foolishness and pride put us on the path to our deaths? Would there come a day when my brother and sister listened sorrowfully to Shalk, as he told them of my desertion and ignoble death on some distant forest path? A further realisation smote me like a blow: I was no longer on the way to Jerusalem. No longer could I dream of being first onto the walls of the holy city, with the army and perhaps even Christ looking on as my enemies fell back. Instead, I found myself facing a dangerous journey home, with no prospect at all of becoming a hero.

3

THE DEVIL'S OWN

Far below the town walls, on the opposite side of the wide wood-and-stone bridge, blocking our route back to the forest, was a solid-looking crowd of over a hundred of King Bratislav's footsoldiers.

'Well?' Rainulf Bluetooth cleared his throat, then leaned over the town walls to spit into the river below.

'I gave my word.' Count Stephen spoke as if that was the end of the matter. But I knew it wasn't.

'You weren't speaking for the *mutur.*'

Rainulf's lack of deference towards Count Stephen was distasteful to me. And I knew that as soon as this fierce man was finished fighting for God, he would be a criminal. Yet with a difficult journey back through a dark forest full of vagabonds ahead of me, I was glad of him all the same.

Having studied the bridge again, Rainulf looked up, caught me staring at him, and scowled. Then as I glanced away, embarrassed, he turned to Gerard. 'What do you think?'

'Shouldn't be a problem, if we go at it right.'

'What's the right way, then?'

'Archers until they come on, then our knights lead us in.'

'Our knights?' Rainulf flashed a humourless smile. 'All seventeen of them?'

'That's enough to make the difference.'

'If they'll fight.' The tattooed warrior looked meaningfully at Count Stephen.

Without his armour, Count Stephen looked slender, but tough. He had no beard or moustache, but an unshaven line of black and silver stubble on his cheeks emphasised a determined-looking jawline. He had a slight forward lean too, reminding me of the old yew tree outside of our church at Castle Rocadamour. 'We should negotiate, to see if we can talk or bribe our way past them.'

By way of reply, Rainulf coughed and spat again. This time the thug's contempt for our finest noble angered me. There was nothing wrong with Count Stephen's idea.

Seemingly aware of the offense that Rainulf was causing, Gerard smiled appeasingly and gestured with open palms. 'I doubt there's any point, but I don't see any harm in trying.'

'Very well.' The count turned to leave, but one of his men stepped into his path.

'Wait, sire. It is not safe for you down there.' The knight looked over at me. 'Send the boy.'

My heart leapt. Was I afraid? Or excited?

'Guibert is not going to ride within range of their bows,' announced Arnulf at once. Which promptly made up my mind.

'I want to go.'

All six men (and a dark-haired woman who stood companionably beside Gerard) looked at me and no one said a word. So I set off for the stairs, Arnulf hurrying after me hissing words that would have embarrassed me had they reached the ears of the men I was leaving behind. Why didn't I think of my father? What was to be gained from being so reckless? And then, when he saw I didn't falter, that I must secure my gorget before getting on my horse, that many a good man had died from an arrow hitting just above the hauberk at the neckline.

We rode onto the bridge together, Arnulf and I. My lance with the

Rocadamour colours tied to it was held in Arnulf's right hand, which he repeatedly waved towards King Bratislav's troops.

High up on the walls of the town, nearly all our men and women were looking out past the crenellations, watching me. I felt important and proud. I had never been an envoy before today.

On the other side of the bridge, one of King Bratislav's crossbowmen raised his bow and pointed the bolt tip at my face. In an instant a cold wave of fear took away my pride. Now I wondered whether in fact I was a fool. It had been easy up on the tower to say I would go and carry out the negotiations. I had felt brave in doing so. What vacuity. I was no braver than the men who remained behind in safety. Simply, I was more innocent of the all-too-real dangers of the situation than they. Gerard, Count Stephen and Rainulf weren't admiring me from up there, they were just glad it was me on the bridge and not them.

The thought struck me – simultaneously with the feeling that this might just be my last – that perhaps there was nothing to bravery, only ignorance of danger. All the songs I'd listened to about heroic deeds, all my daydreams about being the knight who stood alone against incredible odds, it was all childish nonsense. And, I realised with sadness, I would not live long enough to tell William of this revelation. To warn him.

On one of the gatehouse towers behind me, I could just make out Rainulf, with his long plaited black hair and shadowed skin, from Gerard, with his rounder, pale head. It was impossible to discern their expressions.

It took a long time for Arnulf and I to get any response from the hostile-looking men in front of us. Long enough that my fear of being killed subsided. I'd fired a crossbow many times, enough to know that at this distance King Bratislav's archers could hit me easily and their bolts would tear through my chainmail to my soft innards. The thought was frightening, but not one I could sustain from moment to moment while we waited.

So I was almost relaxed when a small nobleman, dressed in overly sumptuous purple silks, walked forward from the crowd on the far side of the bridge.

'Gentlemen?' He did not meet my eye.

'We want to leave.'

Unexpectedly, he smiled. It was a smile with even less warmth than Rainulf's. 'Do you want to join the others? There is still time.'

'No, we want to go back to France.'

His smile dropped. 'I'm afraid that's not possible.'

'Not even if we give you gold?' It suddenly occurred to me that I had no idea how much gold was available to pay this man. So my offer was a vague one.

'All the gold in the world won't do me any good if my head's on a spike above the entrance to the town.'

What else could I say to try to persuade King Bratislav's official to let us past? Arnulf's attention was on the crossbowmen lined up behind their captain; my sergeant wasn't even listening properly, so there was no point hoping for help from him.

'You'll have days to get away with the coins,' I pointed out.

'No. I won't. King Bratislav will be here tonight.'

Arnulf turned his courser about and muttered, 'Time to go.'

So we returned to the town. Just as I was about to go under the portcullis, I heard a cry from behind me.

'Young knight. You are all going to die.'

* * *

Back on top of the tower, I reported the whole conversation. When I got to the part about King Bratislav returning tonight, Gerard stopped me.

'Tonight?'

'That's what he said.'

Gerard rubbed his knuckles back and forth across the beginnings of a beard, thoughtful. Then he turned his blue eyes, full of concern, to Rainulf. An unspoken thought seemed to affect both of them, making their expressions grim. Next, Gerard turned to Count Stephen. 'Well?'

'Well what?'

'Do you still refuse to fight?'

'I gave my word.'

'How long would you say it takes to reach the Danube from here?'

'Four, maybe five days.'

'And wasn't King Bratislav supposed to escort Shalk there?'

'So I understand. But a king is a king and can change his mind. Perhaps when King Bratislav learned that we remained here, he chose to attend to us.'

'What's that?' Gerard's female companion was pointing eastwards and we all turned to see. Most of the sky above the treetops was blue, with only a few white clouds and those barely moving. So it was disturbing to see in the distance a dark smudge in motion, like smoke from a fire, but blacker.

'Rocadamour,' Gerard's voice was sharp, 'you've the eyes of a young man. What do you see?'

My pride flared in me, angry that a footsoldier should think to command me thus. Even so, I discovered within me a great desire to impress this man, so I stared long and hard. There was a trick I had been shown by Father, which was to close one eye, put the back of my hand up to the other, then open a tiny gap between my middle fingers to look through. I did that now.

'Birds,' I said at last, when I was sure, 'hundreds and hundreds of birds.'

'Well?' asked Gerard again, insistently.

Count Stephen straightened to his full height. 'Very well.'

At once, cries and orders began to ring out: Rainulf leaning over the inner wall to curse at his men below; Gerard, shouting down the stairwell for a man called Jacques; Count Stephen, more quietly, but looking equally as stern, consulting with five of his knights before leaving us.

'What's happening?' There was no one else left to ask but the sulky Arnulf.

'There has been a battle, or a massacre.' Instead of looking at me with the accusatory expression that I had anticipated, Arnulf was staring at me as though he were in church, looking up at an image of Christ. 'A cloud of birds like that means a lot of dead meat. And our bodies would be among them now, if you'd listened to me. How did you know?'

I looked again at the distant swirl of birds, imagining the feeding frenzy and the sharp beaks pecking at the soft bodies of those whom I had admired so much. Lying on the blood-soaked grass, staring up at the clouds, my life back at Rocadamour came to my mind. And I wanted to say to the shadowed man who loomed over me, 'Stop, just let me think about my father, mother, brother and sister. Let me have them in my thoughts as I die.' But I could not speak and in any case, there was no mercy in the man as he raised a huge hammer above me.

With a shudder, I found myself back on the walls of Devinium, where Arnulf repeated his question. 'How did you know?'

'If I am honest, I confess, I did not know. I ... was just aggrieved that you were once more ordering me about like a squire. And then, there's something about Gerard that makes me believe in him. Even though he's not a noble.'

'Yes. Even so.' Arnulf almost smiled and his moustache twitched as he clapped me on the shoulder. 'Come then. We'll line up with Count Stephen. Remember your training.'

As Arnulf led me to the stairs, a thin man with long, blonde hair (bound in a stiff pony-tail) arrived. He was aged about thirty, perhaps, and exchanged greetings of real warmth with Gerard, who then smiled at me.

'Lord Rocadamour, meet Jacques de Liles. In the entire army you will not have met a finer bow shot than Jacques.'

'Honoured,' I responded automatically.

Jacques gave Arnulf and I a nod, before looking to Gerard. 'What's afoot?'

Again, I had to quell a surge of resentment at being passed over by a mere archer, who had not deigned to reply to me.

'Are we not about to clear a way across the bridge and run for the forest as though the Devil were breathing on our necks? And he is too. King Bratislav is coming back for us and it wouldn't do to be caught here.'

'Christ, no.'

'Take a look below; can you hit their little commander?'

'The one in purple?'

'Himself.'

Jacques gave an appraising glance towards a flag that blew from a nearby tower; what wind there was came towards us from the bridge. Then he stared down at the figures below, his slender fingers stretching and clenching. 'No. Not unless the breeze drops or he takes ten paces forward.'

'Stay here then, can you? And when they cross, it would do our cause no harm should you kill him.'

With a thin grin, Jacques acknowledged the order. When the archer caught my eye I frowned. I refused to show any approval for such unchivalrous schemes. Yet – and I knew at the time that this was two-faced of me – my life was in the hands of these men and if this plan (rather than, say, meeting their captain in hand-to-hand combat as we ought) meant we would win a way through those soldiers and into to the forest, then I was not going to gainsay it.

That decided, Gerard turned to me and gestured towards the stairs, 'After you.'

Perhaps because I was one of the last to be ready, having no end of straps to attend to, both on Tenebrour's tack and in regard to my armour, it seemed only a short time before our small army was marshalled for battle. In front of me were two lines of archers (a mix of longbows and crossbows), then came the seventeen knights on horse, then a thick body of footsoldiers, and behind them, our elderly and the women and children.

This was my first battle. My first encounter with men who were intent on killing me and I them. What did I feel? Neither elation, nor fear. Strangely, it was Gerard who was in my mind. I wanted to prove his decision to leave the army of Duke Shalk correct and I wanted to earn his approval for my deeds. Indirectly, Father was present in my thoughts too. For I was already explaining to him why we had turned back, because otherwise we would have been slaughtered in a field. My first fight, I would tell him, was to scatter those of King Bratislav's troops who were trying to prevent us returning home.

'Now, Count Stephen, if you would!' This was from Gerard, whose stoutly armoured shoulders were recognizable, although his face was obscured by a heavy iron, cone-shaped helm. It was not natural that a man on foot should be in charge of the men on horseback. Yet despite his position among the footsoldiers, Gerard carried an authority that allowed him to direct our army. Two ranks of riders separated me from the man who by right of birth and title should be our captain, Count Stephen, and I kept my gaze upon the nobleman, ready to follow when he moved forward.

If Count Stephen resented being addressed in such a fashion, he did not show it. Pointing *Lifestealer* at the gate in front of us, the lord called out with a strong voice. 'Raise the portcullis!'

Slowly, with the shaking of chains and a drawn-out screech, the heavy, iron-covered inner gate was hauled upwards by footsoldiers assigned to the purpose. As soon they could duck beneath the sharp, metal tips at the base of the gate, our archers did so and they then pushed open the thick outer doors to run up to the first wooden planks of the bridge. Someone among them must have given a command, for with a rush of sound akin to a gust of wind in the treetops, the summer air ahead of me was flickering with swift-flying arrows.

A horn sounded urgently from the other side of the bridge; almost immediately, bolts streaked past us, some clanging ferociously off the portcullis or the stones of the gatehouse. Near me, a wounded man shrieked for help. I found that I had tipped my head down; I was looking at my saddle. With the protection of my heavy helm and my full chain suit, I could probably survive a bolt fired from such a distance. If I was unfortunate, however, a bolt might come through the eye-slot of my visor. My eyes were the most vulnerable part of my body and instinctively I leaned my head down to protect myself.

A shout from ahead, from the bridge, brought my head up with a snap. 'Here they come!'

Count Stephen raised *Lifestealer* high in the air. Then aimed the point of his sword in the direction of the enemy. With a whinny, Tenebrour leapt forward with the others, trotting at first, but we were at a canter by the time we thundered onto the bridge, three abreast.

I trusted my courser with my life: he and I had ridden together for years. So when a spear point was positioned in our path, our actions were thoroughly rehearsed. My steed dropped his head to the left, as he always did, while I slapped the shaft of the spear to the right with the flat of my sword. Now my stallion reared up, to bring both his heavily shod front hooves down on the man in front with a horrific crunch.

Agonised cries came from men and horses, the animals screaming with an intensity of distress that I'd never heard before. The noise made me dizzy. Even so, I kept my seat and pressed my knees to my stallion's flanks with all my strength. Urging him on, I dealt blows where I saw the chance, both with the sword in my left hand and with the sharpened bottom edge of the shield strapped to my right arm.

All of a sudden, I was over the bridge and the path ahead to the forest was clear. For a moment it crossed my mind that I could keep riding on, down into that tunnel of trees. Naturally, I would never betray my comrades in battle. And nor would I survive more than a few days on my own in that dark realm.

I signalled with my body that we must turn and Tenebrour obeyed with eagerness. As we came around, Arnulf cantered out of the howling press and down the far side of the bridge towards us. I flashed him a grin and waved my sword towards the fray.

'Wait!'

Surprisingly, he flung his sword down and began to pull hastily on his shield straps. His horse danced a little and as it turned, I felt my stomach lurch. The chainmail coating over Arnulf's right leg was torn, sliced open, hanging down towards the ground like a long shaving of apple-skin. And deep in the red raw flesh I could see the white of bone. Blood came from the wound in regular spurts.

'Tourniquet!'

Immediately, my own sword and shield was on the ground and I dismounted. Pulling at the buckles of my gauntlets, I threw them to the earth too. In my saddle-bag was the cord for the tourniquet, along with needle and thread and bandages. This too I had practised and seen done; but had never previously performed in a true emergency.

Blood made the work slippery and all the time his torn, heavy chainmail had to be hoisted over my shoulder so I could see the wound clearly.

'Tighter.' Arnulf was grimacing, speaking through clenched teeth, moustache trembling.

'Tight enough?'

'I can't see.'

'Ready for the needle?'

'Get on with it.'

I sewed the flaps of skin back together with six big, long loops of thread.

'O Christ!'

All my attention had been on the bloody wound. When I looked up, I was shocked to see how white Arnulf had become.

'Don't die. Arnulf. Please.'

'Just get the bandage on.'

He groaned again when I tied off the bandage as firmly as I could. Then I held him as he tipped off his horse, to lay him sitting with his back to a tree, wounded leg straight out in front.

'I must get back to the battle.'

'It's not a battle any more, it's butchery. And the *mutur* need no help with that.'

He was right. Those of King Bratislav's men who were still up were all running. With cries of triumph, our men were giving chase. It was like a grown-up version of my childhood games, but one that brought a bloody and terrible end for those who lost. Dozens of men sprinted past us with panic in their eyes, followed by dozens more with ferociously wicked expressions on their faces. My stallion snorted and edged sideways off the path, away from the running men.

A large warrior carrying a huge axe crested the bridge, his studded leather armour covered in blood. It was Rainulf, who saw us and stamped over.

'Is it bad?' he asked Arnulf.

'I'll live if it doesn't putrefy. My lord fixed me up well enough.'

'That's twice in a day that you owe him your life then.'

'I know it. Christ must be saving me for a purpose.'

Rainulf shook his helmeted head. 'Christ abandoned this army a long time ago. We're the Devil's own, if we are anything at all.'

4

IN THE NAME OF CHRIST

The bridge was slick with blood. Hands stained red, our peasants and elderly men and women were hurriedly searching bodies for coins and the unworthy thought occurred to me that they were like flies gathering on the dead.

'Aha!' Rainulf, still covered in gore, pulled a corpse clear. It was that of the purple-clad commander who had talked to me less than an hour ago. Likely the man's death was a result of Jacques having fulfilled his promise, the haft of an arrow protruded from the commander's ribs. If so, Jacques had my admiration for the shot, while the dead man had my commiseration for his ignoble end.

Having gathered the corpse's long brown hair in his left hand, Rainulf struck at its white neck with an axe held in his right fist. Three messy blows and the head came off.

'What the Devil are you about? Playing with that unfortunate man's body?' Gerard was splashed in blood around the waist and legs, but his balding head was freshly washed and glistened in the sun.

'This is going to hang over the gate.'

'Why?'

'What was it he said?' Rainulf looked up at me from his grisly trophy, 'something about having his head on the gate if he let us past?

Well, it turns out that was to be his fate either way.' He grimaced a kind of grin, showing the famous blue incisor that gave him the nickname 'Bluetooth'.

'Hurry your men. Let's get everyone across and burn this bridge.' Gerard was unsmiling.

The burly man straightened up slowly, as though his muscles ached from the battle. 'Since when do you command the *mutur*?'

'I do not. But you know as well as I that woe comes to the thief who sleeps in the house he has robbed.'

Rainulf did not reply, but went back towards the city, swinging the pallid head by its hair. One or two of the *mutur* shouted jests towards him. Back on the bridge, Gerard watched Rainulf for some time, with an expression on his face that was hard to read. Not quite anger, but something like it.

There were dozens of men and women hunting through the dead around me, taking whatever they found of value. Any of them would have done, I suppose, but I saw a girl about my age. She was pretty, with pale skin and long, curling raven hair that was almost as lustrous as that a noblewoman, although her clothes were coarse and patched.

'Hey girl.'

'Me?'

'Yes.' I waited while she pulled away a leather pouch from the body she was accosting. As she looked at me expectantly, I tried to imagine myself in her eyes (her deep brown, attentive eyes). A victorious knight on horse, one who had just fought valiantly in battle, I was, perhaps, someone right out of a *chanson*.

'Well?' she looked back at the bodies, no doubt impatient to get back to her search.

'I'll pay you to look after my sergeant. He's wounded and will need to be attended to on a cart while we travel.'

'Attended to?'

'Cleaned, fed.'

'Is that all? Not bedded?'

'Not bedded? What, do you think me a whoremaster? He is a brave man in need of care.'

'I know what you knights are like. You think you can take us whenever you want.'

'Look, that's him over there against the tree. Arnulf is his name. He could be dead in a week from that wound. He's not going to ravage anyone.'

'All right. Two pennies a day and you bring the meat for us all.'

'Granted.' I turned my horse away from her, disappointed. In truth, I had expected her to show more admiration for me and more pleasure in having been singled out to serve us. Without us, she would have no hope of returning home. Where was her gratitude? Such thoughts I quickly checked, they were vain and unworthy. Perhaps in her past were events that justified her assumptions about the lust of noblemen.

Two-hundred yards along the path that led to the forest were Count Stephen and his knights, watching as Gerard, with his characteristic lumbering gait, walked towards them. Beside the horsemen were two other figures: Gerard's woman and Jacques, the archer, whose long braids were currently loose and shone like gold in the sunlight.

'Lord Rocadamour,' Count Stephen waved to me to join him and I urged Tenebrour into a trot, arriving at the group just behind Gerard.

As I drew up, Count Stephen gave me a nod. 'You fought well lad.'

Perhaps I blushed. I acknowledged his compliment with what I hoped was a matter-of-fact gesture of my hand. Inside, I was aglow with the count's praise. His words rang true, too. Despite the disconcerting screams, the hatred in the faces, the sharp-edged weapons and the uncontrollable violence all around me, I had not been frightened. All my days, weeks, and years spent training had prepared me well.

'There's another bridge about five miles upstream.' The count pointed towards the earthen path that ran along the riverbank. 'We need some riders to go there and burn it.'

Where was my spirit of adventure? When the count looked at me enquiringly, I found that all I wanted to do just then was to lie down by Arnulf and rest. I felt cold too, though the day was warm enough.

Nevertheless. 'Very well.'

There was a hint of concern in the grey eyes of the woman standing beside Gerard.

'Jacques will come with you,' said Gerard, 'if he may ride your sergeant's courser?'

'He may.'

'And Robert will assist you also.' Count Stephen indicated one of his knights; a sharp-faced man, whose red hair was cut close to his head. Although Robert's smile was human enough, his ears stuck out wide and I couldn't help but think of a bat.

The woman with Gerard whispered in his ear, then delved in her satchel to produce a tinderbox.

'Take plenty of oil from the cart over there and this.' Gerard addressed Jacques. 'And hurry.'

* * *

Soon, we three riders were cantering along a path between river and forest, following two lines of brown earth tracks that carts had made in the grass and weeds. On our right the river flowed northwards with us, dark and cold. The thought of trying to swim that silent water was reassuringly intimidating. If King Bratislav wanted to catch us, it would not be easy for him once we had burned the other bridge.

Although Arnulf's steed was a fine breed, Jacques was making hard work of the journey and kept falling behind myself and Robert. Instead of moving to the rhythm of the horse's gait, he was sat heavily upon the saddle, being jerked about as though he were one of the straw men that we used for practice.

'You ride like a peasant,' I observed.

'That's because I am a peasant.' Jacques spoke without rancor and gave me a smile, as if to let me know that he wasn't insulted.

I said nothing, though I was somewhat shocked. I was not used to keeping the company of peasants and while Jacques clearly had worth as an archer, I was not sure of the proper rules governing our conduct.

'Sold the farm though. It wasn't viable after my parents died.'

'Get much for it?' asked Robert. Immediately (and I'm sorry for it now), the big-eared soldier fell in my estimation. No true-born knight would express an interest in the price of a farm. The warrior was probably a *stipendiarus*, a paid knight of Count Stephen's. That must be why the count and Gerard had put me in charge of this enterprise, even though Robert was some twenty years older than me.

'Not really.' Jacques's borrowed stallion gave a little dance, confused by its rider's signals. 'Enough to get me to Jerusalem I thought.'

'But it wasn't?' asked Robert.

'Didn't get me past Genoa.' Now caught up to us, on the far side of Robert, Jacques pulled a sour face. 'I was cheated out of my money. Luckily, I still had my bow. If you have the stomach for mercenary work, there's plenty of it in Italia. It's not necessarily that dangerous, either. In three years of campaigning, we never took the losing side. Not with Gerard as captain.'

'You didn't miss much,' said Robert quietly, looking into the distance.

'What?' asked Jacques.

'Jerusalem. Lots of people looking for your money, but not much sign of Christ.'

Robert's words surprised me. 'You were in Jerusalem then?' I asked him.

'Aye. With the first Count Stephen. About ten years ago.'

'Still, it takes the sin away, don't you think? To pray there. Where Christ was.' Despite Jacques's urgent efforts to keep up, his stallion kept dropping out of his canter and falling back, so that he had to shout at our backs.

'I don't think so.' Robert looked over his shoulder. 'Not since I've been there. It's just stones, same as stones anywhere else. Now, what you need, if you've a reason to make amends with God, is to find the right holy man out east. They've a lot of forgotten wisdom.'

Seeing that he had someone interested in what he was saying, Robert eased to a walk and I did likewise, so our three horses fell in with the same comfortable step.

'You met a holy man?' Jacques wanted to know.

'Oh yes. Three, I'd say, that really knew what they were talking about. None of them in a church. One lived in a cave near the desert; another was in a copse of trees by Ramelah and the third had a hut by the Jordan. Each living alone, except for the pilgrims who came to listen to their learning.'

'And what did you discover from them?' There was a surprising tone of respect in Jacques' voice. For some reason to do with his being a mercenary, I had not marked the archer as a devout man.

'Lots. And I wished I could have stayed longer to learn more. For a start, did you know the Bible doesn't have all that should be in it?'

'What do you mean?' I didn't understand Robert, whom I was now feeling wary of. His voice had in it the enthusiasm of men and women who carried obsessions in their hearts.

'There should be more in it. Lost words. Of disciples, like James, Christ's brother. And even older words, with prophecies.'

Neither Jacques nor I said anything to this. Me, because what Robert was telling us sounded heretical. How could Christ have a brother? Jacques, also, must have been pondering on the meaning of Robert's statement, because he had a question. 'But if they were disciples, why didn't their words go in the Bible?'

'Ahh, there you're asking the right question. Because Paul hated them.'

'What for?'

'For loving Mary more than he did.'

'But why should Paul love Mary any less?'

'Because he didn't know her. He didn't believe James's testimony about how by God's command she was born and how when Mary was twelve she was given to an elderly widower, Joseph.'

I shook my head at this nonsense and urged my stallion on to a canter, leaving them to it.

The sun was past midday and it was warm. Despite the need to shut my mouth as I rode through cloud after cloud of midges, the one-two drum of my stallion's hooves led me into daydreams. We were back on the bridge, Tenebrour and I. I'd done well enough in truth: ridden a man down, wounded two others. More importantly, maybe, the efforts of our knights, myself included, had broken the ranks of our enemies, causing their men to press back against one another trying to get out of our way. But now, I imagined that I had turned back to the fray and came charging a second time to rescue Gerard. Or Rainulf Bluetooth. Yes. Receiving a grateful wave from the tattooed warrior as I plunged on past, lashing out at his assailants with hard and deadly blows of my sword. On the other side of the bridge the poor people, with that raven-haired girl to the fore, cheered me on.

At the next turn of the river – eastwards, to my right – I saw a bridge and realised with a shock that there were men upon it, four footsoldiers, of the kind that served with King Bratislav. Of course they were all looking at me.

Turn back? That would look suspicious. I slowed to a walk while I frantically tried to decide the best course of action. Yet nothing came to mind. I stopped when I was close enough to hail the men. Three of them took steps towards me, grim faced, carrying spears with their points aimed at my chest; worse, the one at the back had bent over, to begin winding up a crossbow.

There were about twenty more yards to ride to the bridge. The three spearmen were on my side of the river, on a road that joined with the path I was on; their archer was plumb in the centre of the bridge. This was dangerous. Perhaps I should simply turn and ride back to my companions.

'May I cross?' I shouted.

'Why?' the accent was thick, even for such a simple word.

'To find my friends. I'm lost. I'm looking for Duke Shalk's army.'

When they heard that name, something evil passed over their faces like a cloud across the sun. One of them – a tough looking man, with a black beard shaven in sinister lines – glanced away, in the direction that the gathering of birds had been.

'Yah. Yah. Shalk. Here.' Pointing across the bridge.

All three smiled and edged away towards the forest, nodding, waving me through to the bridge. Those were ugly, hard-worn smiles. I could envisage my death if I rode past these men. That crossbow would be raised and fired as I came up to the archer. If there was any life in me after that, the others would gladly finish me off with their spears.

I undid the straps that bound my shield to my back and swung it on to my right arm, where I began to tighten it.

'Hey! Hey! No. Go that way.' A burly, red-faced spearman waved the point of his spear from side to side in the 'no' gesture.

The crossbow was ready and raised. I just hoped he didn't aim for my stallion.

'Haloo! Ah-hoo!' A voice echoed along the river from behind me and I glanced back for the briefest moment before returning my attention to my enemies. Robert was galloping along the path and it wasn't long before I heard the heavy, clumping sounds of his horse.

With his coif over his head, hiding his angular face and large ears, he looked positively noble. Perhaps that was my relieved mind, seeing Robert in a most welcoming light.

'What do we have here?' He raised his voice. 'Friends! Friends! *Freunder! Freunder!*' And Robert gave the soldiers the least convincing smile I had ever seen. Less convincing even than theirs.

They were worried now. Two knights, four footsoldiers. That was about even. Everything depended on their archer. And ours. I knew better than to look around for Jacques.

'Wait as long as you can boy,' hardly had Robert leaned over to patronise me than the bolt came from the crossbow. The twang of its release and a flicker of black at the edge of my vision was all the warning I had. I ducked and it struck my shield with a momentary scream, sending me reeling.

'Like that is it, you scum!' Robert drew his sword. 'Come on lad! For Christ!' And he was riding at the enemy.

It took me too long to regain my balance. By the time I did so, Robert was on the ground trying to fend off two jabbing spears. They got him, again and again.

The man with the dark lines of beard was not distracted by the fight with Robert, but was pointing his spear at me, waiting for me to move. And I did, turning away from him to my left, away from the river and towards the line of trees. My opponent should have thrust his spear into my stallion, but I counted on his greed and his desire to possess the horse and I rode around him and on up the path to help Robert.

The other two soldiers immediately backed off from a groaning Robert to face me, but I kept going, wide, to keep both on my shield side as I circled them. Jabs and feints from all three of the spearmen kept the whole battle turning and I was conscious that my unprotected side was now coming to face the bridge.

On my own, I would have broken off to ride down the crossbow man. But there was Robert, maybe dying, maybe not. A sweat ran down my body, instantly cold, and I shivered as I knocked away spear points. This was all going wrong.

Back home, I had often ridden an earthen practice ring while men tried to knock me off with wooden poles. The trick was to keep circling fast, out of range, and hope to slice the head off a spear.

A scream from my stallion and all my training counted for nothing, Tenebrour and I leapt madly on top of the spearmen, me barely hanging on to my sword. My horse's head came right up, frightening me with the wildness of his rolling, brown eyes. Still, he had lashed out with frenzied kicks and two of our enemies were down. The third? Where was the third?

On his knees clasping an arrow at his stomach.

My stallion was not obeying my signals; he was bucking and snorting. Then I saw the wound above his hind leg: dark blood was streaming from a bolt.

'Hurry!' The lithe, leather-armoured figure of Jacques came running from the trees, yellow pony-tail swinging wildly. 'Get the archer.'

'Come on!' I yelled at my stallion and squeezed as hard as I could with my legs. 'Come on!'

At last, Tenebrour turned and still with a strange kick to his gait, managed a canter that rattled the wooden bridge. The crossbowman ran, bow cord insufficiently wound for a new shot. Crashing through the bracken he made for the woods on his side of the river.

On our side, the west bank, the trees soon grew dense, with firs pressing close to one another. But on the east bank the woods were mostly maples, oaks and slender birches. There was plenty of riding room.

The archer could hear me coming and swerved to press his body to a wide, leafy yew tree. I rode past and turned, sword raised.

'Christ!' He held a small wooden cross towards me, one that he wore on his neck on a black leather cord. His look was pleading.

I doubt mine was.

I walked my stallion up to him.

The archer placed his two hands together prayerfully and babbled at me in his own language. Pale eyes searched mine for a sign of hope.

I poked him in the throat with the tip of my sword and blood, bright and red, shot into the air. Both of us were surprised and he immediately looked at me aggrieved, as if disappointed in me.

'You wounded my horse.' I explained to him.

His mouth worked, but poured forth blood. Then he fell over wriggling and coughing unpleasantly for what seemed a very long time.

I rode back across to our side of the bridge before dismounting to check the injury to my stallion.

'He'll live, God willing.' Jacques was tending to Robert.

The bolt had to come out and I had to put stiches in the wound. I led Tenebrour to where the grass was thick; then forced him around and around, pulling his head down until he settled flat, good side on the grass.

'Jacques. Come here and hold his head for me.'

'One moment.'

While I waited, I talked reassuringly to my steed. It was not so bad, I told him. Just a few little pricks of pain and then he'd be on the way to a full recovery. That's what I said, although my stomach clenched at the thought that this might not be true.

'All right.' Jacques knew what he was doing and lay right across the stallion's neck, caressing his mane and murmuring to him.

Quickly, and from the saddle side, well away from those lethal hooves, I yanked the bolt out. My stallion convulsed and snorted, but we kept him down while I put the stitches in.

'Ready, on three. One, two, three.'

We let him up again and both of us hurried back, jumping clear of possible kicks. But Tenebrour was tired and sore now, not angry. Then, with a disconsolate snort and his head low, the courser walked to where the riverbank was low and began to lap at the water.

Further down the path, Robert was lying on his back. He smiled when I peered down at him, evidently delighted to see I was well. In return, I found my heart warming to him.

'The archer missed you then?' he asked.

'Hit my horse.'

'Tut.' Robert shook his head in disgust. Then winced.

'How bad is it?' I asked him.

'Help me sit up and get me some water and I'll be all right.'

It took both of us and a lot of care to do that. The knight's ribs felt loose under his chainmail. When Robert was as comfortable as we could make him, Jacques looked anxiously at the bridge.

'Let's get this burned fast as we can eh? Wouldn't want to meet any more of the King of Hungary's men.'

Although I was supposed to be leader of this small undertaking, my thoughts were fluttering wildly and I had forgotten our purpose. Jacques was right to take charge. We gathered branches for kindling until he was satisfied (me avoiding the trees where the dead archer lay) and then soaked them in oil before starting the flames. There was just enough wind to assist the fire without threatening it, so the blaze spread quickly.

As the bonfire on the bridge grew fiercer, we tackled the ropes that bound the beams on our side. They were old and weathered, tougher than leather. It was hard work digging the point of a knife into them and working at the fibres until they came loose.

I sweated heavily, a different kind of sweat to the one that had come over me during the fight when I thought I might die here. Nevertheless, I worked as hard as I could; it was evident from glancing at Jacques and seeing anxiety in his watery, blue eyes that we must hurry. His gaze was upon the billowing grey smoke of the fire that was drifting upstream and rising as it did so. With the cloud spreading above the treetops, it would soon become a signal for any enemy troops in the vicinity.

Our side of the bridge was loose at last and we could prise up the planks and throw them on the fire.

'Good enough, I think,' said Jacques. 'Don't you?'

'Yes.' Most of the bridge had collapsed, leaving only a dozen stumps that emerged from the dark water.

'Let's try to get Robert up then and return to the others.'

5

THEY SHALL RETURN
AT EVENING

Walking, the midges were more of a problem than riding. Huge clouds of the tiny flies floated above the path in the afternoon sun and we learned to go single file to find a route between them if we could. Jacques and I were on foot leading our horses. Further back, poor Robert was hanging on tight to his saddle, white-faced. It would have suited his needs for us to move even more slowly, but we had to keep up a brisk walk, anxious that King Bratislav's army might return to Devinium and cut us off before we returned to our people.

'Jacques?'

'Hmmm?'

'Who's that woman always at the side of Gerard?'

'His wife, Brigid.'

'He has a wife with him? When he goes to war?' At home, I was used to seeing my father, Lord Rocadamour, departing for war. And never did any woman march out of the castle with our troops.

'A lot of the men do. We'd hardly see our women otherwise.'

'Oh, do you have a wife here too?'

'No. No, I've a woman and a boy in Genoa. Maybe.'

'Maybe?' From behind us, Robert snorted a kind of laugh, but then groaned.

Jacques turned. 'I mean, it's been two years. Who can be sure what has changed over two years?'

'Will you go to see them, when we get back?' I asked.

'If we get out of the forest alive, I'll look them up.' Jacques looked at me. It was a rueful expression.

From behind us, there was a sound, like Robert wanted to say something. Yet the effort was too much for him and he waved us on.

In France, on warm days like this I would ride for hours, sometimes hunting in the company of other young knights and squires, sometimes alone. I knew every field, copse and stream of Rocadamour and I wished I were there now. Back there, I was happy and enjoyed life without knowing what it felt like to kill a man. Until today, I hadn't realised how fresh blood smelled so much like a newly honed sword blade.

While I was making wishes, I wished too that I could pause to sleep, even just for an hour. The recent fighting had disordered my mind and I wanted to settle it. Killing that bowman, was that right? Unbidden, the dead man's last, indignant expression kept returning to my thoughts. Sleep would cure me, probably. Yet I could rest and ease my troubled soul later; for now we had to hurry as best we could with our wounded companion.

When at last we reached Devinium, Jacques and I paused, studying the walls of the town before we came within bowshot of them. The only sounds I could hear were the lapping of the fast-flowing river, the hum of bees, and the activity of birds (a magpie in a nearby tree was cawing loudly; from deeper in the forest came the rapid drum of a woodpecker).

A memory of my sister running through a grove of birches, laughing as I chased her, struck me so powerfully that I gasped aloud.

'See something?' asked Jacques anxiously.

'Sorry. It's just that I wish I were home. Away from the blood and the sad eyes of dying men.'

'Don't feel guilty,' Jacques gave me a sympathetic look. 'It was them or us.'

This was kind of him and I looked away quickly, feeling the presence of tears. It seemed as though the town were desolate. 'We could bear off through the forest, the road west must be over there somewhere.' I gestured.

'Not unless we have to.' In shaking his head, Jacques realised that some of his braids had come loose and with both arms raised he tied the dirty yellow strands back behind his head again. 'Quicker – and smoother for Robert – to use the path.'

I don't suppose any of us felt secure, yet if we were walking into an ambush, it was a subtle one. There was no sign of life behind the solemn, grey stones of the conquered and then abandoned town. Nevertheless, we walked as quietly as we could, no one speaking, all listening intently.

The bridge was utterly ruined. All the timber on the shore had been burned down to acrid-smelling, black charcoal, leaving four pillars of stone midstream around which the dark water flowed powerfully. Most of the bodies from the earlier battle – which seemed so long ago – were gone, thrown in the dark water perhaps. Thick clusters of bluebottles and other large flies were in constant motion on the patches of dried blood.

Above the gate of the city, a pallid head hung by its own hair, twisting somewhat from side to side in the light breeze. 'No', the official seemed to be saying. 'No. No. No.'

Soon, we were safely past the danger of being fired upon from the town walls but this did not make us more cheerful or talkative, for we walked into the forest as if we had stepped into Hades. Gone was the sun, all was shadow. Ahead the path was long and straight (an old Roman road) and marked with the recent passage of our army: ruts in the mud beside the stones; trodden ferns and grasses; discarded chicken bones; and dung from cows, horses, dogs and geese.

Having gone less than a mile into the forest, I stopped, suddenly aware there was a rider on the road ahead, half hidden in the dim and dappled light.

'Who's there?' I shouted.

'Adalbert, knight of Count Stephen,' came the response. 'You?'

'Lord Rocadamour and two men.'

'Is Robert with you?'

'Aye. But he can't call out. His ribs are broken.'

'Send him forward.' Adalbert sounded suspicious.

With his horse's hooves sounding out each step with a slow clap on the road, Robert went on ahead.

'My my. That is Robert all right. I recognise those ears.'

By way of reply, Robert gave Adalbert a vulgar gesture, but even that effort made him gasp in pain.

'You'll catch up with the army soon enough,' said Adalbert as we came up to him. 'They have a big chest of treasure on a cart, which is slow going.'

'You were waiting for our return?' I asked, glad that someone had remembered us.

'Not you alone. I must stay here as lookout until Count Stephen sends for me. Did you see any sign of King Bratislav's army returning to Devinium?'

'No,' replied Jacques.

'Well, perhaps we march without pursuit. Should it come, then I shall give warning.'

'Good luck then Adalbert,' said Jacques fervently.

'And to you.'

* * *

Despite Adalbert's prediction, it was not until the gloom of late afternoon that we reached our people. The rearguard included six of Count Stephen's knights, who were pleased to see Robert and solicitous of his wounds. A cart was found for him and so we made our farewells to one another.

As Jacques and I edged our way past the marchers, trying to avoid leading our horses into the ditch that ran between road and forest, it struck me how feeble and useless were most of the people who remained in the army. The news of an expedition traveling to the Holy Land had attracted peasants and burghers of all ages. Entire families of poor people had joined the enterprise: grandparents, parents, and infants. Some of these farmers and city dwellers bore arms, worthless rusty scythes or spears with flimsy points. Most didn't. Then too, we had monks and nuns of all ages marching with us.

One of the groups of monks was alongside us now. Their heads were bowed, their bare feet dirty and their lips moved in silent prayer.

When he had left Devinium to surrender to King Bratislav, Shalk had taken great crowds of these hangers-on with him. To their deaths, presumably. At the time the army had split, my heart had greeted with warmth every man or woman who had chosen to stay with Gerard. Yet now, I wasn't so pleased. They would all want feeding and they would slow us down in our race for safety.

Next, we made our way past dozens of carts and the biggest of these vehicles was a four-wheeler that filled the entire width of the road. Not only were two mares harnessed at the front of the cart, but half-a-dozen *mutur* were pushing from the rear. Inside the wagon were chests that clinked and rattled, around which were piled expensive silks. The plunder of Devinium. It too was moving slowly.

Of course, I was looking everywhere to see how fared Arnulf. By this stage he would have some idea if evil humours had entered the wound. If so, he would lose his leg and probably his life. And I found this thought unbearable. At last, I recognised my grey pony and beside her was my sergeant in a small, two-wheeled trap that was being pulled by a donkey.

'Arnulf!'

'Greetings lad. Did you burn your bridge?'

'Aye. How is the leg?'

The young woman I'd hired to look after Arnulf was leading the donkey, she turned and answered me. 'I got my friends to have a look. They say he'll live and he'll keep that leg. So long as he can rest and eat properly. Did you bring meat?'

I shook my head, feeling exhausted. Yet I realised I was obliged to go hunting before I could rest. I'd have to take Arnulf's courser.

'Arnulf, I killed a man.'

'More than one, I'd say. You fought well.'

'No. Up at the second bridge. An archer. He was trying to surrender, holding out a cross and saying "Christ". '

'Had he fired his bow?'

'At my head and at my horse.'

'Well, his life was forfeit then. Don't fret about it.'

I glanced at the girl, who stared back at me without expression; no doubt she was equally unconcerned about my troubled soul.

'I'd best tie Tenebrour to your cart here. He is wounded. He can walk with you.'

'Oh no.' With a wince, Arnulf lifted himself to look. 'Is it bad?'

'He took a bolt high up on the left-hand, rear quarter. It's crusted over with blood but no sign of puss.'

'Cateline! Hey my pretty Cat. Bring water for that poor horse.'

'We should report to Gerard,' beside me, Jacques spoke firmly. And he was right.

'I'll come back later Arnulf.'

'Bring some meat,' Cateline said.

Not until we had ridden right through the ranks of footsoldiers to the very front of the army did we see Gerard. He had gone ahead of the troops, a long way down road, with Rainulf Bluetooth beside him. It seemed to me that I was Orpheus, looking at them down a ghostly grey tunnel and with that thought came a premonition: these men were already in Hades and would never leave it.

Their voices, which had been argumentative, grew still when Jacques called out.

'Well met,' Gerard's care-worn face became youthful when he smiled with such fatherly warmth. 'What news have ye?'

Although Jacques made to speak, I answered quickly, for was not I the leader of our little enterprise? 'There were four of King Bratislav's men on the bridge, three spears, one crossbow. We killed them and burned it.'

Was that amusement in Rainulf's dark eyes? Why?

'And Robert?' asked Gerard.

This time Jacques waited for me.

'Knocked from his horse and struck a few times on the ground. Nothing that pierced his hauberk though. He should live.' I looked to Jacques for confirmation. He nodded.

'Any sign of King Bratislav on your return past Devinium?' Although he began by speaking to me, Rainulf's gaze shifted to Gerard.

'No.'

'Lord Rocadamour,' Gerard folded his arms, 'you're young, but you're no fool. What think ye? Will King Bratislav cross the river and will he come after us?'

'Yes, he will.'

'Why?' grunted Rainulf.

'Because he is king and wishes to demonstrate the strength of his authority. And because we are weak. And because we have the treasure of Devinium with us.'

'And if we leave our treasure wagon on the road? Will he stop then, when he has it?' asked Gerard.

'Possibly. But I doubt it.'

Both captains nodded, grimly.

Then Gerard sighed. 'So, what would you do?'

If I didn't have the feeling I was being used as a piece in a game of theirs, I would have been flattered that two such experienced warriors were attentive to my council.

'Get all those who can ride and go as fast as possible down the road.'

At this, Rainulf began to grin, a broad, blue-toothed grin. 'Abandon the priests and the nuns? The children? The wounded? Your sergeant, Arnulf? Gerard's Milan Company? The *mutur*? Aren't you knights of Christ supposed to defend the weak to the last drop of your blood?'

The light was probably too grey for my blush to be seen, but Rainulf stepped over and slapped my thigh all the same. 'Don't worry lad, I jest. I'd say the same if I were you: young and with a castle or two full of servants waiting for me. But I'm not.' His tone dropped, now deep and thrilling, like a voice from legend. 'I'm *mutur*. The vilest scum in Christendom. And I have my grip on a wagon full of coin. If anyone intends to take the treasure from me, they will have to prise it from my dead hands.'

They stared at each other then, Gerard and Rainulf, and neither was daunted by what they saw.

Jacques broke the spell. 'What are your thoughts, Gerard?'

'I want to leave the wagon and everything we carry that weighs too much for swift walking. Speed is everything here, so we must be fast and march all through the night and with the hope that King Bratislav has more urgent affairs to attend to than to chase us.'

This sounded wise, although my tired body and shattered mind recoiled from the notion of a night march.

'We could do that.' Jacques spoke softly. 'The Milan Company.'

'Leave the *mutur* behind you mean?' Rainulf spat. 'I should strike you down as a traitor.'

'We are but talking,' Gerard's words were appeasing, though his voice was firm. 'Thinking this through.'

'I know what you're thinking. You fleas on the dung piles of rotten dogs.'

'Do you now Rainulf? I very much doubt it. Because if you won't let go of your cart, then what I'm thinking is that we have to fight.'

'Fight?' I echoed, doubtfully.

'An ambush. We use the wagon as bait. Hope they drop their guard, then we hit them from the trees with our footsoldiers, while our knights come up the road.'

'An ambush?' Rainulf ran his hand over his beard. 'How many knights have we left?'

'Fourteen.'

'Archers?'

'About thirty.'

'Well, a score of scores of *mutur* and, what, a hundred of your band?'

Gerard nodded. 'And every man or woman who has a weapon hides deep in the woods too. To run in as soon as the trained men have engaged.'

'Any idea of the size of King Bratislav's army?' Rainulf sounded cheerful once more, convinced perhaps that Gerard was not intending to abandon him.

'Massive. But perhaps for the sake of speed, he'll just bring his cavalry.'

Rainulf smiled a bitter smile. 'Perhaps. That's the kind of wager I like though. Death or fortune.'

'Very well. Let's call a halt for the night and talk to Count Stephen.' Belatedly, Gerard looked at me. 'And you, Lord Rocadamour, do you agree that we should set an ambush?'

What should I answer? I was still embarrassed that earlier I had not expressed my duty to the poor and that Rainulf had caught me out. And I was tired too, very tired. So the appeal of making camp rather than marching all night was strong.

'I do.' I replied.

6

A DREAM THAT AFFRIGHTENS

'Where's the meat?' Cateline asked. Her tone was brisk, not hostile; she had a pot of stew cooking.

'Just this, sorry, I was too tired and it was too dark to hunt properly.' I tossed her the two squirrels I'd managed to hit using my hunting bow. Not worth the six arrows I'd lost.

Cateline shook her head. 'Arnulf needs better.' She threw back her long, black hair and gave me a stern look as if ready to argue with me, but then thought better of it. 'Well and well, just give me a silver shilling and I'll buy a hen.'

While she was gone I attended to our horses, unstrapping the tack and grooming them as best I could with the near toothless brush that remained to me. Of course, I stayed away from the matted hairs around the wound of my stallion. It was too dark to inspect the injury closely.

Near to Arnulf, who was asleep under his trap, was the pony with our supplies and I was pleased to find that as well as plenty of oats, we still had two sheaves of long straw. Although the warhorses had been given ample opportunity to graze upon lush grass on their walk back from the small bridge, they had also fought in two battles this day. So I cut open a sheaf and shared the straw between the two horses, keeping a little back for the pony. Then, I readied the oats into feeding bags.

The relief when I unbuckled my chainmail hauberk and let it slide to the ground was divine. I'd never ached so much. Taking my cloak from my saddlebag, I wrapped myself in it and sat by our fire and its bubbling pot. All along the road were small fires and the scents of cooking meat and vegetables: carrots and parsnips had been in good supply in the stores of Devinium. The evening air was filled, too, with the sounds of human voices, though other than the far-off chants of a group of praying men, the words around me were merely indiscernible mutterings.

It seemed easier to relax if I stretched out a bit. I put my head on my piled-up chainmail and then enjoyed the feeling of my leg muscles letting go some of the strain they had suffered over the long day.

My eyes closed and although I had no intention of falling asleep, I was soon dreaming.

In the solar – the great hall – at our castle, Father was receiving letters and petitions. I was bored and wanted to be outside in the sunshine, riding with my friends. Alas, Lord Rocadamour thought it a good education for William and I to witness the proceedings.

Then the sky beyond the windows changed to a silvery grey and I knew we were now in Hades. People still continued to enter the hall, however, and speak to my father.

Shaven-headed and gaunt, Duke Shalk walked up to the dais and I grew anxious at what he might say.

'Your son abandoned me, despite his oath. He said that it was not betrayal, for he had the right to refuse my orders if they were folly. What say you Lord Rocadamour?'

Father looked across at me, sternly. 'Well, Guibert?'

I could neither make a reply, nor move. My hands were locked to the frame of my chair, though not bound in any way. My feet likewise.

'Are you dead, Shalk?' Father returned his attention to the petitioner.

'I am.'

'And my son lives?' He pondered this, before announcing his judgment. 'My son was wrong to plead *diffidatio*. If every vassal did so each time he thought his lord was being foolish, there would be no order in the world. But I am glad he lives and thus his punishment will be light.'

'State it.' Duke Shalk insisted.

'He will be as a squire for a month and see to my warhorse.'

Shalk bowed and walked swiftly out, not hiding his displeasure. I felt relieved and grateful to Father. Not for long, however, for horror entered the room.

The archer I had killed today came in to the hall and every beat of his heart caused blood to spurt from the wound in his neck. With both hands, he held his cross and showed it to the people who lined the walls of the hall, crossing from this side to that to do so.

'Christ!' He exclaimed. 'Christ!'

When he came to my seat, I was fixed in place once more and terrified. His lip snarled. Blood leapt from him to splash on the floor and my boots.

'Hey. Your broth.' Cateline was pushing at my shoulder. There must have been an echo of my dream in my face as I woke up, because she was looking at me curiously.

'Fare you well, lad?' Arnulf was awake.

'Good, thanks. How is your leg?'

'Sore, but no pestilential humours have entered the wound it seems. Cateline here changed the bandages today and had a careful look for me.'

'Praise God.'

'Indeed, and your quick and steady hands.' Arnulf's hard-faced scowl of the past two months was gone, replaced today by a tender look of comradeship that I was still getting used to. 'Tell me more about the fighting at the other bridge can you?'

'I can.' I should have been proud of what happened there, shouldn't I? Yet for some reason I just felt tired. Also, I was aware that Cateline was sitting with us, eating and listening. 'Four of King Bratislav's men were there: three spears, one crossbow.'

'Oh yes?'

'Robert, Count Stephen's man, was unseated and nearly killed. I didn't know what to do. If I rode for the archer, they would have finished him.' My stomach tightened again, remembering that near-fatal moment of uncertainty. 'Then my stallion got hit by a bolt and jumped into the spearmen, lashing out and biting and accounting for two of them. He maybe even killed them, or else our archer must have, later.' Only now did I hear the groans of the broken men. They were still and silent by the time of my return across the bridge. 'Our archer got the third and I rode down the last.'

'How's Robert?'

'Broken ribs I think. He came back with us, in pain but spirited enough.'

Arnulf nodded and rubbed his unshaven chin with his long, dirty fingers. 'That was well done. Dangerous, a tight fray like that. Yes. Well done Guibert. You left your home still a boy. But you'll return to them a man. And a good one to have at your side in battle.'

A sense of pride brought a rush of warmth to my cheeks and I glanced at Cateline; she was blowing over her broth to cool it, her long, black hair tied back in a braid. If she were interested in our conversation and could appreciate how praise from a veteran such as Arnulf was well-earned, her expression gave no sign of it.

Two months ago, on leaving Castle Rocadamour, I'd wanted nothing more than to hear words like these from Arnulf, words spoken with earnest respect. Arnulf, to whom my father had given the task of guardian and who had taken to the duty as if his true vocation were that of schoolmaster not warrior. Arnulf, who used to think that unsupervised I would rush to a foolish and hasty death, with buckles undone, armour flapping, and saddle slipping. Did Achilles begin his famous career with a thin, nagging, middle-aged man holding his bridle? Did Roland? Yes, I had been determined to prove myself to Arnulf and Father. Now that the moment had come when I could hear approval in Arnulf's voice, I did not rejoice. I was glad to hear it, of course, but my daydreams had never included the sights, scents and screams of dying men.

'How about you Cateline? Where's your home?' Had Arnulf detected some unease in my silence? Was he deliberately shifting his attention from me? Probably not, he was a not a subtle man.

'Near Rouen,' she said.

'Came with Count Stephen's army?'

'Yes.'

'One of his servants?' I asked, interested in anything to do with Count Stephen.

'No. Of course not. My father sold the farm and we all came as pilgrims.'

This was a surprise. 'You're free?'

'What? Did you think me a serf?'

'Well. On the bridge, searching the bodies with the others...' I tailed off, uncertain. What was the difference between a peasant and a serf in circumstances like ours?

'If you troubled to talk to them, you'd find everyone here is free.' She waved towards the darkness. 'Even if they had to run away to become so.'

While I thought on this, unhappy at the thought of being in the company of runaway serfs, Arnulf spoke gently. 'Your family lass? Do they live still?'

'No. Mother was overcome by the red cough before we even left France. My sister went into the forest looking for mushrooms and never returned. And Father was on the east bank of the Reiber that time.'

No one spoke. The Reiber was a tough crossing; those who had swam over first to construct a platform for a bridge were slaughtered by king Slavniak's army while the rest of us hurried up and down river in desperate search of a ford.

Arnulf put his pot down. 'What will become of you?'

'When back at Rouen? I'll go on the next pilgrimage to Jerusalem.'

'I doubt there will be an expedition like this for a long time. Not after word of this disaster spreads.'

'Well then. I'll find work in the town until there is.'

'We might be able to help, heh? Guibert?' He gave me a searching look.

'For Christ's sake, Arnulf.' I stood up, suddenly angry and, if I'm truthful, afraid. Although I yearned to be home, I was sure that King Bratislav was right behind us. Although Gerard had spoken confidently of an ambush, we had too few fighters in our little army. 'Stop it. Both of you. Stop talking about home as if it were around the next bend! We're all going to die here in the forest, if we're not dead already. Don't you understand? King Bratislav's on his way and we can't outrun him.' My voice was shrill; I was embarrassing myself.

'Easy, lad.'

'And don't talk to me like a horse.' With that I left, walking up the road until I was past the campfires. There I paused, not wanting to explain myself to the guards further away in the darkness.

'O God.' I whispered. 'Bring me home again, to see Mother and Father and William and Alice.'

7

SPEECHES AND EXHORTATIONS

A more ideal place for an ambush we could not hope for. The road curved here, so that our knights could be mounted nearby but out of view of the treasure cart. Better still, on either side of the paved way the forest rose, so that our footsoldiers would be attacking downhill.

On top of the cart, Gerard was shouting in short, clear sentences. The whole of our small army was pressed close and the fact that the road was at the bottom of a dip meant that even those of us who were mounted and at the back could hear him clearly over all the heads.

Only the wind in the trees and the flutter of flags challenged Gerard's voice, for the crowd was still with eerie attentiveness.

'King Bratislav is coming. Haven't his men worked all night to rebuild the bridge? We have about one hour and they will be upon us. We cannot flee. We have to fight.

'This is good ground for us to fight upon. We will press them tight and the very size of King Bratislav's army will work against him. The *mutur* and everyone from Lotharingia will hide in the trees on the north side,' he gestured. 'And the Milan Company and everyone from Francia the south. Our knights will charge up the road on my signal.

'Everyone will fight: men; women; youths; monks and nuns. Borrow a weapon if you have none. Because unless we win today, everyone will die. Those of you who are not trained to fight in war, stay well back in the forest until the professionals are fully engaged.

Then come in roaring as loud as you can. Make it seem like our numbers are vast.

'This is going to be a hard, ugly battle. Make no mistake. And victory will go to the most vicious. That's us. Have no thought for your safety; you have none. Have no thought for retreat; there can be none. Have no thought of surrender; King Bratislav will kill you and it will not be an easy death. Have in your thoughts only this: how to harm and kill those who will otherwise kill you.

'Look around you. This is brotherhood, united in face of death. Fight for yourself, fight for your neighbour. Fight to revenge those cruelly deceived by King Bratislav.

'That is all.'

A great cheer, mostly from his own men, filled the space between the trees. It was loud and heartening.

With an impatient gesture, Rainulf had Gerard haul him up onto the cart. Gerard was a strong-looking man, whose muscular frame was emphasised by his thick leather shoulderpads and the curve of his body armour. Yet beside Rainulf, he looked small and aged. Equipped for battle, the leader of the *mutur* was imposing. Hair tied into four long, dark plaids, his tattoos were visible along his neck. Black leather and silver chainmail guarded his thick torso and powerful limbs. Rainulf carried a heavy, iron-studded mace as though it were a twig.

Tapping the lid of the treasure chest with his mace, Rainulf gave us all a grin, his discoloured tooth making him leer.

'I have just one thing to say and I say it to the *mutur*: we want this treasure.' He paused. 'So we have to fight for it!'

With cheers and cries from his own, Rainulf leapt back down to the road.

'About turn,' called Count Stephen and the knights with him led the whole army a few hundred yards up the road before halting.

Then the footsoldiers entered the woods on either side, to make their way back to the ambush spot. After them, the poor people took to the trees, with anxious faces and a tight grip on their pitiful weapons. With these peasants limped Arnulf. He could not ride, but, as he'd earlier observed, he could fire a crossbow well enough. One arm around Cateline's shoulders, he gave me a last wave and hobbled away through the trees. I doubted I would see him again and was surprised to find from the pain of this thought that I loved him. Was it possible to love a teacher who was all blows and reprimands? Evidently.

Soon enough, only those too wounded or feeble to fight were left on the road behind us knights. A handful of ancient, doddery monks and nuns were gathered in a circle, on their knees and praying. Among the invalids lying on our collection of carts was Robert, out of his armour, torso wrapped around and around in thick layers of bandages. He pulled himself up to a sitting position.

'This is bollocks.' The shaking gesture Robert was making with his head was emphasised by his large ears and sharp nose. 'Lying here, useless. Waiting to see if I'm to live or die.'

'You'll live,' said Count Stephen quietly. I stared at the elderly man, hoping that his words were not just fashioned for encouragement, that he really meant them. It was impossible to say. The count's deeply lined face was solemn, but it always seemed so.

'Well, gentlemen.' The count turned to his men and included me in the steady gaze of his grey eyes. 'The footsoldiers will fight well, no doubt. But their fate depends upon us. And we will save all our people, will we not?'

His men murmured their agreement.

With a strange, distant smile, Count Stephen turned his courser about and walked it to face the bend that led back to the ambush site. There was room for one horse each side of him, leaving me five riders back behind him in the final row. A pitiful fourteen knights in all.

I checked my tack, my armour straps, and my shield straps. Again.

Through the gaps in the tree branches above me I could see blue sky. Moss and ivy grew thick on the nearby trees. The floor of the forest was green with creeping honeysuckle and sorrel. It was a joy to be alive, to breathe, to listen to the chatter of the birds. To have all my limbs and live without pain.

Why had I been so eager to join the Holy Expedition? I had been so proud, riding out under the gates of Castle Rocadamour with Arnulf and our two poor squires. Above me, I had been aware of Alice's attempts to strew our path with rose petals; I was always the brave knight of song to her. William had waved from the walls too, enviously. How desperately jealous he had been of me, filling castle rooms with his shouts of frustration and his pleadings to be allowed to come with me. But our father would not budge and how right he had been. At least William would live to continue the dynasty.

What kind of preparation for battle was this? I could not think of home now, or the men around me would see my tears. Instead, I thought of Cateline. At least mine would be a quick death. Would hers?

Was there really a heaven? Would I see my family again there? How did the priests know?

At last, at long last, an arrow came whistling out of the trees to fly high above our heads.

Drawing *Lifestealer*, Count Stephen looked over his left shoulder, then his right. 'Forward!'

From a walk to a trot and then a canter as we came around the bend. My stallion – Arnulf's – was keen.

Then I saw King Bratislav's army and began to laugh aloud.

8

BESERKIR

The road ahead was thick with troops, filling the space between the trees as far back as I could see. King Bratislav had brought his whole army with him, not just a small, chasing body of knights. Our hopes were utterly, utterly gone. Strangely, I felt a weight lifting from me, as though my soul was ascending to heaven.

To the amazement of the knight alongside me, I laughed again, no longer afraid of being unlucky or that my lack of battle experience would bring me or my comrades to ruin. It didn't matter what I did. Nothing mattered but to die well, like a knight of legend.

Up ahead, as our small band of cantering knights came into their view, there was consternation and urgent cries from among our enemies. Whatever their marching formation had been, they were disorganised now. Soldiers were spilled all over the road and off to the side of it, while some dozen footsoldiers were dragging the treasure cart away. Most of King Bratislav's troops on our side of the cart were on horseback and were hurriedly attempting to form a line to face us.

'Gallop!' shouted Count Stephen.

Although I urged my mount to change his gait, I also let enough of a gap open up to the courser in front that I could safely lower my lance. We all did. These knights knew their business.

Let go the reins.

A thunderous pounding of iron on stone filled my ears and then an even louder sound: my own voice, as I screamed all my hate and rage at those who would kill me.

Leaning forward in the stirrups, I felt a huge shock as my lance struck a horseman in the chest. He went flying backwards off his steed, his body wrenching my weapon away. Sword drawn, shield high, my stallion carried me on.

Arm. Neck. Thigh. *Get down.* I slashed out repeatedly with my sword as I urged my courser onwards with my legs. It was surprisingly easy to kill these men. Their movements seemed slow and predictable. Cut through a wrist, to send a hand flying into the air. Stab into the teeth of an anguished face.

Now a terrible scream drowned out even the shrieks of metal on metal that were ringing out from all directions. It was my stallion, whose front left leg had been cut away at the knee.

My feet slipped my stirrups and I scrambled clear of his rolling body.

Take this for Shalk! And this for me!

I knew nothing of the battle but for what took place within a spear length of me. But in that small space, I felt invulnerable. Not that I was reckless. With cold calculation I ducked, blocked, parried and sometimes stepped inside the swing of mace and sword. I positioned myself so their own men shielded me from those further back and, as my balance allowed, I hewed and thrust through armour and flesh with raging blows of my sword.

Get down! And you!

The battle began to press tight around me now and it was cruel fighting, where you could see the clenched teeth and the pain in the expression of the man crushed against your shield. I could hardly swing my sword properly and was resorting to punches at mouths and eyes with the hilt.

All at once, a dangerous sense of my own mortality broke into the red battle craze that had possessed me. Here I was, in this confined space, Guibert, with a terrible ache in my left arm, wrist and shoulder. And this self-knowledge would have been fatal, I'm sure, but for the fact it was dispersed by the heavy crunch of a mace into the back of the head of one of my opponents.

'Come on!' Rainulf was a blood-drenched ogre, whose eyes were filled with insanity. He was screaming to his men behind him. 'Come on!'

Instantly revitalised, I struck out again and pushed, chopping away a mail-clad leg that I saw exposed below a shield.

'Come on the *mutur*!' I shouted again, laughing. 'Keep up!'

Hack. Step, care that my foot did not slide on the gore. Then stab. Heave.

It was getting easier again, the press loosened. And then, as the man to my right fell away, I saw Gerard. He was half crouched, a large axe in each hand and his shield worn on his back. I got a moment's acknowledgement from a gesture of one of his axes. Then he too was shouting.

'On! On! Follow Rocadamour!'

'Rocadamour!' his men took up the shout. Was it only yesterday that they had done the same?

'Come on then!' That was me, although it was an incoherent roar that no one would have understood. The footsoldier in front of me was white-faced and terrified. And dead before he knew it, head clean off.

The battle was a bloody competition and I was resolved upon staying ahead of Rainulf and Gerard. My sword and shield were light once more; my left arm had new strength. Again, I measured my blows, my defensive moves. Again, I found the responses of these soldiers predictable. It was almost a dance. Step. Block. Chop. Step. Duck. Stab. And onwards, always onward, through sprays of blood that turned the bright day dark and scarlet.

We were past the treasure cart and an extraordinary upsurge of screams and cries came from behind me. I took advantage of the cover of the vehicle on my left and the timidity of the soldier in front of me to snap a glance over my shoulder. The noise was our people: our wonderful monks and servants: our beautiful nuns and cooks. By God, they were raising a thunder of sound as they ran to battle.

King Bratislav's soldiers were hesitant.

'He flees! The king flees!' Jacques was on the cart above me, firing at a distant target.

Another great roar from our side, this time a cry of triumph and victory.

And on their side, they knew it too. For suddenly the fight went out of them and men were running for their lives through the trees.

'Come on!' I shouted again, leaping after the nearest figure.

Their army was disintegrating, but if King Bratislav regrouped further down the road, our enemies easily had the numbers to still win the day.

Every blow I landed was nothing now but a butcher's chop. Still, I dared not falter. Men scrambled and pushed at their fellows to try to escape. Men with panicked faces fell to the ground and tried to crawl out of the press. Others simply gave up and knelt and prayed. Or stretched out their arms in surrender. One or two, the dangerous ones, tried to rally their neighbours to fight.

Those spirited men fell with arrows in their chests and I admired Jacques as much as any knight for his skill in making war; he understood the need to keep the rout going and had an eye for where the tide might turn. Yet perhaps this type of fighting was peasant's work, for it felt like I was slaughtering cattle.

On my left were the *mutur*; on the right, Gerard and his men. And in all directions was blood, bone, intestine and brains; everywhere too, the strong scent of sweat and iron.

Again the press tightened, until the dead bodies of King Bratislav's footsoldiers protected the living. We pushed, grunting with effort, until the wall of dead began to give way and we were off again, climbing over the corpses to reach those who were desperate to get away from us, who were throwing aside weapons and armour, to sprint down the road or through the forest.

I was running now and at a great disadvantage in my heavy chainmail. Rivulets of sweat were running down my face and back. Blinking, I refused to let up. Not now. Not when it seemed my life had been returned to me. Let these men die, not me. They had come here intending to kill us all. I felt no kindness for them and spared none.

And then, at last, I knew we had won and that I had survived. Far down the road, riding fast through distant blocks of shadow and sunlight, were King Bratislav and his princes. His army would not rally this side of the bridge. Not with Gerard and Rainulf in pursuit.

Our commoners, too, had joined the chase. Unencumbered by armour, they caught up with our footsoldiers, stopping only to slit the throats of wounded enemies. Blood up to her knees, Cateline was among the crowd, stabbing soft flesh with a long dagger; getting revenge for her father and sister perhaps? Not one person paused to search the bodies for coins.

Standing there on the road, in the forest, exhausted, it occurred to me for the first time in my life that no man – or woman – was inherently better than another. A knight could be a fool and a servant a hero. Heroine.

After I had turned to walk slowly back up the road, the people running past gave me wide berth. A grey-haired monk stopped and crossed himself. A thick-set peasant woman pulled her boy close and wrapped her strong arms around him, while he stared at me, wide-eyed.

With my senses returning to order, I began to understand these reactions. From my boots to the very top of my coif, I was covered in gore. My sword and shield too. In a forest full of horrors, I was one of the very worst sights. And no doubt the expression on my face increased the fear of some that a devil walked among them.

Even Arnulf soon lost the smile of delight that had appeared beneath his moustache when he saw me.

'Are you wounded?'

'None of this blood is mine.'

He limped closer and clapped his hand on my shoulder. 'My God, you were magnificent.' I nearly fell at his touch. My strength was entirely spent.

'Magnificent?' I found it hard to swallow. 'You never told me. No one told me. Is it always like that?'

'War?' His wise, pale eyes were sad. 'Sometimes.'

'Rocadamour!' Count Stephen came over, unaccompanied. 'I salute you. Or I would if I could.' He tipped his head apologetically towards his right arm, which was splinted and bandaged across his chest. 'The youngest of us all and the bravest. Well done, sir. If you were one of my men, I'd give you a castle for your deeds today.'

Those words should have lifted me into the world of my daydreams. Yet I could barely manage a faint smile to acknowledge his compliment with politeness. There was no glory in cutting open other men, hearing them scream, seeing them die. War was savagery and no more noble than the actions of the wolf or the lion.

'Come on, let's get this armour off you and get you bathed.' Arnulf, who could barely hobble himself, offered me his arm.

'Wait.' I walked on past Count Stephen, who stood aside to let me step over the dead, searching.

Lying across the road, trembling in his entire body, was Arnulf's bay courser. As I came close, the stallion focused a dark and frightened eye upon me.

'I'm sorry.'

Hurriedly, Arnulf caught up. 'O Christ! The bravest horse I ever knew.'

I hadn't the strength even to put down the warhorse. Fortunately, having seen my intention, Arnulf reached out. 'Let me.'

There was a tear in his eye as he wound up his crossbow. His face, normally as firm as a schoolmaster's, was soft and lost, moustache sad.

I didn't stay. Though I couldn't help hearing the unpleasant impact of the bolt striking flesh and bone.

Half way back to the carts, I came across Robert. He was lying in the middle of the road, looking up at the trees and sky.

When I leaned over, anxious, he smiled. 'Thank you Guibert, for my life. I didn't want those sods to have the pleasure of killing me.'

'What are you doing?'

'I couldn't just wait on the cart, not knowing. But once I seen the buggers run, my strength seemed to go out of me.'

Not until Arnulf arrived to help could I raise Robert, but then the three of us made our way on, ever so slowly.

Robert made an effort to speak. 'When we rode out from Rouen, by Christ we were a fine sight.' He winced as we struggled to lift him back on his cart. 'Nearly thirty knights in a column of two. Burnished armour, glistening in the sun. Count Stephen at our head: no truer lord. We were going to fight the infidel at Jerusalem and we were proud to be so Godly.'

Robert's head dropped ruefully. 'After today, I don't think but five of us will return. Assuming, that is, any one at all escapes the black forest.'

'Aye,' Arnulf muttered, as much to himself as in response. 'It was some sight, that impossible charge. Brave men, every one of them. And I thought it hopeless. That with so few knights against so many, none could live. But I was wrong in that at least.'

'I just wish I could have ridden with them,' Robert sighed disconsolately. 'I'd be a proud man if I could say I'd charged into that fray alongside Guibert of Rocadamour.'

9

THY SLEEP SHALL BE SWEET

Later, when the shadows of the trees were enveloping us and inviting us to rest and forget, we heard a crowd approaching. From beyond the bend of the road came first a murmur, like that from the seashore on a calm day. Then, as the sounds grew louder they also grew more distinctly human. From the surging roars came individual voices and shouts. There was a pattern forming, a song almost.

'Who are the *mutur*?

'We are the *mutur*!

'And who ran from battle?

'King Brat ran from battle!

'Who are the *mutur*?

'We are the *mutur*!'

When the mass of men came into sight they gave a roar and from their front rank came Rainulf at a run. How he had the energy to do so astonished me. I had barely the strength to pull myself up from the cart, where I had been lying beside Arnulf.

With huge lumbering strides and a fixed blue-toothed grimace, Rainulf ran to our cart and effortlessly flung me up onto his shoulders. To retain my seat there, I had to grab at his tightly bound plaids. It didn't seem to trouble him.

'*Beserkir*!' He grinned up at me. 'Our young *Beserkir*.'

'Ro-cad-a-mour!'

'Ro-cad-a-mour!'

From disparate voices at first, then taken up as one.

'Ro-cad-a-mour!'

My name filled the forest.

Around me were the most cruel and bloody-minded men I had ever known. Their savagery at the fall of Devinium had disgusted me, especially the rapine. Yet they and I had fought this battle as one and now that they claimed me as a brother of theirs, I went willingly. Though I did notice that Arnulf was watching this scene from the cart, face sombre and longer than ever.

On Rainulf's shoulders I was carried to the baggage carts of the *mutur*, one member of the troop after another pushing through their ranks to call out praise to me, or simply to grin and nod at me. Soon, flagons of beer were being passed from hand to hand. And then bottles of mead. With surprising gentleness, Rainulf set me on my feet and began to strip his battle gear.

'Stitches!' he shouted, looking down at his muscular body. Blood was oozing from fresh wounds to his already heavily scarred torso. While he was being sewn up and bandaged, Rainulf studied me from beneath his dark eyebrows. Although he had the physique of an ox, his stare was driven by a calculating intelligence. It was how I imagined Satan might scrutinise a potential recruit.

'You, son, are more of a devil than you look.'

'You, however, are quite the devil you look.'

He liked that.

'Drink?'

I shook my head at the offer of a dirty bottle of amber liquid.

'We have wine somewhere. A fine wine for our lord!'

'No. Water though, would be welcome.'

Someone passed me a leather skin and I drank deep.

With a groan of delight and pain in equal measure, Rainulf lay back against the pale trunk of a birch tree. I sat too. For a while he said nothing and I had nothing to say. We listened to the boisterous shouts of men who were glad to be alive.

'I was your age when I fought in my first battle.'

'Yes?'

'Hainville Bridge. Heard of it?'

'You knew Sitric Longsword?'

'That's it. I carried a spear for him.'

'What was he like?'

'A true hero. The right hand of the gods. We won't see his kind again. After the battle we were all on our knees, arms tied behind our backs. King Philip was walking up and down the rows of prisoners, looking at us. There was no mercy in his eyes and none of us asked for it. We just stared right back at him.

'Eventually, Philip says something like, he has heard much of Sitric's courage and he intends to test it. "Well and good", says Sitric, "give me any weapon you please and put me against three of your best men."

' "Oh no", says Philip, "I'm not going to risk losing any more of my men. No, what I'm going to do is have my executioner swing his axe into your face while I watch to see if you flinch."

' "Be it so", says Sitric, "I'll not flinch. But by your Christ, will you allow me one request?" "Perhaps", says Philip, "name it." "Long ago", says Sitric, "I took a vow that I would not cut my hair so long as Harald Sveinson lives. Would you have one of your men hold my hair out of the way of the blow, so that my vow is kept?"

' "Very well", says Philip and gives the nod to a knight beside him. So they set up: Sitric on his knees, the executioner before him and the knight at his side, hands full of hair. Sitric's was longer than mine even. Here comes the axe blow,' Rainulf motioned with his two hands, 'and at the last moment Sitric yanks his head to the side, pulling the knight's arms down. Neat as you like, the axe goes through the knight's wrists and he's looking at stumps that are gushing blood.'

Rainulf began chuckling and winced as one of his wounds caught him.

'Then what happened?'

'That's the story told. There's nothing more. They beat us senseless because we wouldn't stop laughing at Philip. When I came around most of my comrades had gone. Heads off. Sitric too. The executioner was worn out by the time I returned to myself. Me and a couple of other lads.

'Then the next day Harald Sveinson – who was a blood brother of Sitric's – sent a messenger asking to ransom any of us still alive. So I went and fought with him for a couple of years.'

I'd never heard Rainulf speak like this and I wanted to learn more of his life. How had he come to lead this band? But he was silent. I waited, until I realised he had fallen asleep.

As I got up, Rainulf opened his eyes. 'The *mutur* believe that one day they will have a king. The legend says that a lord will give up his castles, silks, wines and gold to live with the *mutur*, owning nothing but his arms. King Mutur will lead the men to an island where food and women are plentiful and this will be their kingdom for ever more.'

'Do you believe this? Is it what you hope for?'

'Until today. No.'

And before I was twenty steps away, he called out once more. 'Think on it.'

There was quite a crowd gathered at our cart, much to my dismay, for I just wanted to sleep.

'Here he is. Three cheers for Lord Rocadamour!'

'Hurraah! Hurraah! Hurrah!'

From out of the mass of people stepped Gerard, face flushed. He was holding the reins of a tall black destrier in his left hand. With his right, he thumped me on the shoulder.

'We are fortunate to have such a hero among us.'

Those who could hear Gerard's words cheered.

'Aye!'

'That's right!'

'My company want to gift you this stallion. Here.' He lifted my hands and put the reins in them.

'Thank you,' I muttered. And I was grateful. If this magnificent horse were well trained, it would be far more valuable than any horse I had previously ridden.

Gerard and Rainulf had this in common, they knew how to read a man. After taking regard of me, Gerard's affable enthusiasm changed to a look of sympathy.

'Well done. Very well done. You won us that battle. But we'll talk more on it tomorrow. If you wish.' With that, he turned away. 'There's still work to be done before we eat,' he shouted, then began issuing orders to his officers, Jacques among them. The archer and I shared a nod. I liked him. He was my comrade.

With several more cries of my name, the crowd began to disperse, until I was left facing Cateline.

Saying nothing, she took my hand. I tied my new stallion to the cart and went with her through the trees.

'Are you wounded?' she whispered.

'No. Just bruises.'

'Here.' Having thrown down her cape, with gentle tugs and pushes, she laid me out on it. Then she sat across me and leant forward, so that her black hair made a canopy around my head.

There was a look in her dark brown eyes that was terrible in meaning, yet I could not understand it.

My arms clasped her waist and I pulled her down and close, so the softness of her bosom was pressed to my chest.

Then shivers came, powerful irresistible shivers that had me trembling from head to toe like I was subject to divine possession. 'O God!' I started to sob. 'O dear God.'

Cateline raised her head, her own eyes moist.

'Hush. It's done. It's all done. We live.' She slid her cool hands around my neck and held me tight in her arms.

Melting, a part of me was falling. It was as though I had been walking in darkness alone on the walls of a castle, while carrying unbearably heavy chains. Cateline had only to touch me gently and those chains fell away.

My shivers continued, my tears continued, but I didn't fight them. They were cleansing me. And would continue to do so as long as Cateline lay upon me.

At long last, I lay still in the dark forest. And now a new feeling ran through my body: an urgent fever that brought strength back to my soul.

Still reeling from the revelation that no one was better than anyone else, it seemed to me that Cateline was a princess. Or rather, she was herself – a farmer's daughter with clothes of coarse wool and hair that smelled of camp fires – but that I did not care to lie with any other woman, be she a princess or no.

A lady who had never experienced the certainty of her own death, never witnessed a battle, nor carried a knife to slit the throats of wounded enemies, such a lady could never understand and comfort me like this.

Beneath her dress, Cateline's soft skin was on fire too.

When our bodies came together, she regarded me without shame.

'This is a gift I will never forget,' I whispered.

'Foolish knight.' She shook her head. 'This is not a romance.'

'What is it then?'

'A reward.'

After a long look into her feverish eyes (uncannily like the battle-fury-filled eyes of Rainulf) I gave up trying to understand her.

And we kissed.

10

BRING FORTH THE PRISONER

Four of us were looking at a kneeling prisoner, standing in a circle around him: Rainulf, Gerard, Count Stephen and I. Our captive was battered and bedraggled, yet beneath the mud and dried blood his garb was the same purple silk that all of King Bratislav's nobles seemed to wear.

'Speak again: the tale you told to me,' urged Gerard.

'About what?' The prisoner responded tiredly. He was elderly, with grey hair, although his carefully shaped moustache and chin beard were black.

'Shalk.'

With a slow look, assessing his audience, the man licked at dry lips and spoke. 'We escorted your army to a certain place, a pasture; at boundary was a wood filled with rough men, including those who had escaped Devinium.

'It was closed trap. On three sides, the wood; behind Duke Shalk, our army. Some of your people, they guessed; they were shouting. But what to do? All weapons in carts behind us. Once all your people were in pasture, a bugle by the king gives the order. And then they die.

'Everyone die. Man, woman, child. Except Shalk. King Bratislav wants Shalk to watch.'

Rainulf folded his powerful arms and his dark look did not auger well for our prisoner.

'But why?' murmured Count Stephen, with a shake of his head. He appeared frail this morning, without his armour, like a grey-haired monk not a warrior. The lines across his forehead were deeper than ever.

A look of alertness flickered over the nobleman's face. 'I say, it not good. I say, we march your people to the lands of the Magyars. But King Bratislav say, we must revenge for Devinium. And we must show next army of Franks coming to Jerusalem to honour us.'

'What happened to Shalk?' I asked.

'In chimney for king's kitchen. They lower him in from top. In chains.'

'By Christ! What on earth for!' Count Stephen leaned over as though to strike the man, though with one arm in a sling it would not have been easy.

'We have tradition. Take the air from those... evil must go from him who cannot breathe. And King Bratislav thinks man who uses name of Christ but permits Devinium must be man with the Devil inside.'

All four of us responded, shocked, but it was my question the prisoner fastened on, turning his head to look at me with sharp grey eyes.

'Alive? Yes. Probably. The king has not eaten at castle yet.'

'And are you worth something to King Bratislav?'

'Me?' He gave a shrug, which caused him to wince. 'Maybe.'

'Wait now. We've no time for dealings with that false king.' Rainulf looked angrily at me. 'We've time only to fill this man's lungs with smoke and leave him dangling from a tree. And that's all.'

'What's your name?' I looked away from Rainulf, back to our prisoner.

'Duke Carisbald.'

'A duke indeed?' Count Stephen raised his eyebrows. 'Are you related to the king?'

'I'm cousin.'

If this man were lying, he was a most accomplished dissembler. There was no desperation in his voice, if anything, a laconic drone, as if to suggest he was resigned to his death and had no hope.

'Then perhaps we can still save the prince.' Count Stephen allowed himself a smile.

'Sod Shalk for a fool and sod this liar. The *mutur* are marching west and we will march swiftly.' With that announcement, Rainulf took several strides away from us, although my next words caused him to pause.

'Rainulf's right.' I spoke loudly. 'Go west. All of you. Yet let me have Duke Carisbald and I'll ride back as far as the bridge to see if we can save Shalk.'

Gerard, whose wide, round face was normally open and affable, looked pensive. 'There's a many a slip takes place with those kinds of exchanges, even if what we've heard is the truth.'

'I'll take no risks. And I'll catch up fast, either way.'

'Shalk's not worth it. Not worth losing you for.' Gerard shook his head.

But I persisted. 'Imagine it was you in that chimney. Wouldn't you want us to try and rescue you?'

'That would be different. Did I ever tell my people to give up their weapons? Did I lead them to die unarmed amid the screams and blood of all my officers without hope of fighting back? I did not.'

With a snort of approval for these words, Rainulf continued his march back to the army.

'I say let the boy try. After all, think of the reward that Shalk's family will bestow upon those who obtained his ransom.' Wiser in the ways of mercenaries, Count Stephen's words brought a thoughtful expression to Gerard's face. The captain of the Milan Company turned his worried, blue eyes to me.

'If you say so, count, then I'll not oppose you. But will you let Jacques go with Lord Rocadamour? Should *Duke* Carisbald prove false, he'll not live to enjoy the success of his ruse.'

If our prisoner had any thoughts on this subject, he very wisely did not reveal them.

* * *

Eastwards down the road once more. Was it only two days since I had ridden this aisle between the trees in the company of Duke Shalk and thousands of people who were now food for birds? There was something wicked about this forest, compared to the light and cheerful woods around Rocadamour say. Perhaps it was the dense press of trees. Also, too, tales of demon residents played upon my thoughts to the extent that it seemed that only a few yards from the road and I would be in dark bushes and thick undergrowth that would swallow me up, never to let me go.

When our army first entered the forest proper, after crossing the river Kee, a priest – Duke Shalk's chaplain – had gone ahead to walk under the branches. As he did he made the sign of the cross, spoke verses in Latin and splashed holy water on the ancient paving of the road. It was explained to me by a fervent nun that demons still lived in the old forest, posing as ancient gods and demanding sacrifice from those who used the road. Christ, however, would protect our army.

Perhaps because of the sins of the *mutur* on the women of Devinium, or perhaps because of our own sins, I no longer felt protected by Christ. And it did seem to me that riding back through this stretch of forest once more was no longer safe. A demon could indeed be lurking in the shadows. Or simply our human enemies.

Beside me rode Jacques and I was glad of it. A rope connected Jacques' bridle to Duke Carisbald, who was up ahead of us riding my small pony, the other end of the rope tight around his slender chest.

All along the road were signs of the panicked rout of King Bratislav's army: abandoned spears and shields; helmets; satchels; crossbows, quivers and bolts; and even royal banners. This was the debris left after our people had helped themselves to the better equipment they had found. Underfoot too were unburied, fly-covered corpses. Wide swathes of blood were splashed across the paving. It cannot have been a cheerful sight for Duke Carisbald, but he held his head up as he rode along this route of defeat. Nor was it a cheerful sight for me, though it marked our victory. If there was any place on the earth that was liable to attract demons, then it was this stretch of road, with its hellish look and its stench of rotting bodies.

It was not even midday when we reached Devinium, to see a new bridge of bright yellow, freshly cut planks resting on the stone ruins of the old. There were soldiers on the bridge as well as on the walls of the town, all of whom began shouting to one another as soon as we came into view.

'Hold up there.' Jacques called ahead to our prisoner, who reined in his pony and turned to us expectantly. 'All right, you can go ahead, slowly, and stop before that single beech on the right.'

While Jacques and I remained in the shade created by the edge of the forest, Duke Carisbald was out in the sun. His pony stood still, taking mouthfuls of the wild grasses that filled the space between forest edge and riverbank.

'Be ready to flee,' Jacques muttered, eyes busy, then he raised his voice. 'Just one of them to come over, any more and I shoot you and we ride away.'

The duke turned in his saddle and nodded, face pale.

Walking onto the bridge, a soldier in dark leather armour, bearing a large axe, shouted something in their language above the sound of the river's rushing water. Our prisoner shouted back and the authoritative tone was clear, even if the precise meaning of his words was not. The soldier turned back.

Jacques was holding his loaded crossbow across his saddle. He glanced at me and shook his head. 'I don't like this. I wish I knew what they were saying.'

'Not much. Probably just that only one man is to come over and talk.'

'Perhaps.'

We waited. What should have been a summer afternoon to relish, with its warmth and soft breeze, was instead a time of growing anxiety for both of us. The scene, with its shimmer of heat in the air above the road, the motionless figure of Duke Carisbald, and the empty sky, seemed portentous rather than somnolent. Like an indrawn breath the moment before a shout.

Every sound from the forest drew Jacque's searching gaze. The faint rustle of an animal, or the branch that shook with the arrival of a bird, caused him to swing his bow towards the noise.

'What's taking so long? I say we shoot him and go now.'

'Already?'

'There's been time enough to row a dozen archers across the river.'

So there had. I now heard the stealthy movement of approaching soldiers with every clap of a dove's wings, every rustle of leaves.

'Should I go through the forest and take a look along the river beyond the town walls?'

'No,' Jacques shook his head. 'Let's stand or fall together.'

Our tense wait continued. Just at the point where I decided that some action on our part was necessary (although I could not bring myself to order Jacques to kill our prisoner), another man crossed the bridge, waving his hands high to show that he was not armed with a bow.

The newcomer was an unarmoured, dark-haired man, with a closely shaven black beard in the overly elaborate style of their people. Once he had our attention and had observed that we made no move to stop him, he walked briskly to stand just in front of our prisoner's pony, where an animated conversation began. Their words were no louder than the drone of a wasps' nest and in any case would have held no meaning for me. While I watched the expressions in the negotiator's face as they alternated between humour and anger, Jacques continued to stare into the forest, first on one side of the road, then the other.

'By Christ! This does not feel right. I will be glad when we are away from here.'

We let the two men talk a while, but then I was overcome by the belief that the conversation by the solitary tree was entirely a ruse designed to distract us while encircling soldiers drew ever closer through the forest. 'Pull the rope, let's have him back,' I ordered.

When he felt the tug, Duke Carisbald turned and waved to me. With a nod of goodbye to his companion, who retreated to the bridge with a sombre look on his face, the duke rode back to where Jacques and I were waiting. From his steady gaze there was no telling if Carisbald planned treachery.

'Well?' I asked.

'Commander sends a message to the king by bird. Maybe king sends Shalk here; probably he won't.'

This candid admission appealed to me. Perhaps that was deliberate on the duke's part? Did he have my measure?

'This is no good. We hadn't thought this through properly.' There was a kind of appeal in Jacques' voice, which had risen while he was speaking.

'I agree. We can't wait here for that long. It could take days.'

If Duke Carisbald was troubled by our words, he didn't show it. His expression as he looked from one of us to the other was as dull as always.

'What about all three of us leaving now and we arrange to return here in two days?' I suggested.

'And ride straight into a company of their archers? No thanks.'

'Well, what do you propose?'

Jacques' reply was a murmur in Occitan, the language of my home town: 'You know what I think.'

'Duke Carisbald, we can't wait. We don't want to take you away and come back. Have you any thoughts on how this exchange can happen?'

Before our prisoner could reply the flapping of a bird's wings drew our attention to the other side of the bridge. There, a pigeon was scrambling up through the air and commencing the first of several circuits above the gate towers of Devinium.

'North?' Jacques glanced at me, then Duke Carisbald. The pigeon had disappeared from view in an upstream direction.

'North. To the king.' Duke Carisbald shrugged, apparently without concern. The reason for Jacques' question, however, was that all of King Bratislav's castles and towns lay to the east.

Whatever the king was doing, he was away from his favoured residence, where Shalk was chained.

Jacques let out a heavy breath. 'Come on, let's go. We are never going to see Shalk.'

'You are probably right, but still.' I turned to Duke Carisbald and stared at his calm grey eyes. 'Duke, I am going to let you walk free across that bridge, if you will swear by the cross that you will do all you can to release Shalk.'

'All I can do?' He frowned. 'I not defy King Bratislav and lift Shalk out. But I swear this: I will say to king, Rocadamour is noble and honorable knight, who set me free. I will ask king to match your action. Maybe he agrees.' He paused and for the first time lifted the mask of placidity that normally disguised his emotions. It was to give me a rueful smile. 'Probably he won't.'

'On the cross.' I repeated.

Solemn again, Duke Carisbald held the small wooden cross that hung from his neck. 'I swear to this.'

'Off you go then,' said Jacques.

The duke dismounted and took several steps towards the bridge. Then paused and looked back, right at me.

'Come with me, young Rocadamour, and legends will be sung of you. You are hero. Go back in that forest and die. I say this, though I should not: King Bratislav has sent riders to Prince Slavniak telling that you travel with all treasure of Devinium. King Bratislav grants that treasure and forty mares too if prince destroys you all. And even if the prince does not, there is much evil in that forest.

'Be my knight for a year and day; then I give you all you need to go to Jerusalem: horses, tent, gold.'

It seemed to me that these words were entirely free of deceit. This was not a trap but a real prospect. And I had not rid myself of the sensation that the shadows of the forest were those of Hades and we were all dead, that perhaps we had died in the field with the rest of Shalk's army, it was just that we did not know it. If I refused the offer, I would succumb to the spell; if I went with the duke, I would break it.

'Thank you for the honour, Duke Carisbald. You make me a generous and noble offer. Yet I cannot take it; I must ride with my comrades.'

'I thought so. But I had to speak.' Having made his offer, the duke turned and walked slowly towards the bridge.

With a query on his face, Jacques raised his crossbow. I shook my head and he lowered it again.

'Let's hurry then.'

I took the reins of the pony and followed my companion, who was already cantering down the dark forest tunnel.

11

AMONG MY PEOPLE ARE FOUND WICKED MEN

Judging by the darkening shadows of the forest, it was late in the afternoon when Jacques and I regained our small army; they had not made much by way of progress. Defending the rear were the *mutur* and these ranks of crudely armoured ruffians greeted my return with heartwarming cheers and shouts, which, while ribald and coarse, were meant well. Were these rough men so bad? Certainly, my feelings of contempt and disgust towards them had gone entirely. Perhaps they looked upon me as a candidate for King Mutur? Let me be truthful here: I relished the thought that I had the approval of these fierce warriors. While I delayed to exchange greetings with the *mutur*, Jacques bid me farewell and – in his clumsy fashion – urged his horse onwards.

After the organised ranks of the spears and axes of the *mutur* came the treasure cart. It was a large rectangle of planks (with sides) on an axle that connected two enormous wheels. These were solid wooden discs as tall as a woman, with a thin layer of iron around the rim, around the rim of the left wheel at least, that on the right had been worn away through usage. Ahead of the cart, four workhorses were harnessed to its long central tug, but not very efficiently. The cart had been designed for two horses and although someone had extended the tug with a mast of new wood, the improvised tack that joined the front two horses to it pulled cruelly on their necks.

The entire vehicle creaked and swayed alarmingly as it jolted over the paving and I could see why a dozen *mutur* soldiers had been assigned to keep to the cart, pressing strong hands against the planks of its back and sides as though staunching a wound.

Once past the cart, the road was clearer. Stretched along the route as far as I could see were the poor and wounded of our army, with their donkeys, cows, pigs, geese and dogs. Among them, somewhere, were Arnulf and Cateline and indeed, after some careful riding through lines of brown-cowled monks and peasant families with their children, I came to my friends.

'Guibert. A welcome sight!' Arnulf was hobbling beside our small transport, using a crutch to keep the weight from his wounded leg. Even at his clumsy pace, he was still moving faster than the treasure cart. Holding the bridle of a donkey, Cateline gave me a smile and my heart beat faster for it. I'm sure I smiled in return, despite the fact that I was uncertain how I should act. Had she been a servant girl, we would pretend nothing had happened. Yet this was different. This time, I was proud of the fact that Cateline was… what? My lover? My betrothed? It was a new situation for me.

In his pale blue tunic, arms and neck exposed, Arnulf looked relaxed despite his efforts with the crutch. 'Well? What happened?'

'Nothing.' I tossed the reins of the pony to Cateline who caught them and tied them to our cart.

'You are your own man these days and I've no sway over you any more. Yet I could have told you it was a waste of effort. And a dangerous enterprise too.'

'I don't regret making the attempt.'

'Count Stephen has been seeking you,' said Cateline.

'He is up ahead?'

'With five knights he forms the vanguard,' Arnulf shook his head, 'no doubt they will want you to ride with them too.'

'Just five? Robert was right then.'

'Aye, there are other knights of Count Stephen's among the wounded who will ride again one day, God willing. But not many.'

'I'll go on up, so.' This was in any case my aim, since I felt it urgent to report Duke Carisbald's warning.

'Guibert.' Cateline called out. 'Whatever tasks they have for you, remember you need time to hunt too.'

'Indeed, well said. Can you pass me my bow and quiver?'

My hunting bow was small and light, little use against a man in armour of course, yet much more effective for deploying quickly on either side of the saddle than a war bow. Face screened by her black tresses, I searched in vain for another smile from Cateline. We did momentarily touch fingers as she passed me the bow. Was there meaning in that? I hoped so. Then I straightened in the saddle.

Passing through the rest of the army, I was greeted with many waves and shouts of appreciation from the poor and injured. Naturally, this made me ride a little more proudly. If I could show my family these scenes, I would have accomplished all that I had daydreamed about the morning I departed Castle Rocadamour. At the same time, however, the pleasure I should have enjoyed from my new-found status as a hero of the army was significantly diminished by my memories of the battle. No matter how I tried to keep them from my thoughts, awful memories assailed me.

A long way down the road past the wounded – far too distant given the danger of an attack from out of the trees – were Gerard's troops, the Milan Free Company as they were sometimes called. These men marched in proper ranks at a good even pace, equipped in readiness for battle. It was a heartening sight.

Huddled off the road in the relatively wide spaces between the tall maple trees that were common in this part of the forest were a group of around a dozen people. Among them were Gerard, his wife, Jacques, and several other men whom I had seen before as Gerard's close companions.

'Lord Rocadamour, please join us!' Gerard's smile was genuine, his bright blue eyes shone with pleasure at seeing me.

With a twitch of the reins, I turned to the group and dismounted, as much to give my destrier some rest as to be able to approach the gathering more closely. My new stallion immediately began to nose for green grass among the honeysuckle and vines of the forest floor.

'You got something of value for your hostage then,' Gerard said.

'I did?'

'The information your captive told us concerning Prince Slavniak is important.'

The thought that I had done some good by riding east with our hostage – and not simply revealed how inexperienced I was in such affairs – cheered me. It was strange that despite his humble background, Gerard had an effect upon me like that of my father, in that I very much wanted his approval.

Gerard's wife smiled at me. Hers was diplomatic, not warm. It was a prelude to her speaking and she must have anticipated the prickle of hauteur that rose in me as she did so.

'Lord Rocadamour, you carry respect among the *mutur*, would you not agree?'

At once it seemed as though the eyes of everyone here were upon me, ready to judge me, to measure my response at being questioned by a peasant woman. Remembering the lesson about worthiness I had learned only yesterday, remembering also Cateline and the women who fought for us in the ambush, I quelled the part of me that wanted to snub her.

'I agree.'

'Then perhaps you would be so kind as to talk to them. They stubbornly refuse to abandon the treasure cart, but it will be the death of us all. Soon it seems, Prince Slavniak's people will be at our heels and their attacks will be far worse than when we travelled east along this road.' She had been careful to be mannerly in her speech at first, but now as she warmed up, her words came in a strong northern accent. 'Imagine our enemies in the forest, coming at us every day, two or three or four times a day. They'll pick off our wounded, our elderly, our children. Then as we march closer together, arrows will fly from the darkness and find their targets. If we charge into the woods, they will run, only to return again when our soldiers rejoin the road.

'Just twenty archers could do us great harm if we are moving as slowly as that sodding cart. Because while our soldiers chase them away, the army will make such little progress that we will all be dead long before we leave the forest.'

'Melinde is the veteran of as many campaigns as I,' said Gerard, 'is she not speaking the truth?'

'She is. Yet for all that, Rainulf is not going to leave the treasure behind.'

'Nor need he.' Melinde was eager to answer me. 'We should distribute the coin now, so everyone carries their share in their pouches. The heavier gold and silver ornaments can be dispersed among the faster carts.'

With hardly a pause, Gerard took over, 'And that way too, crossing the Reiber will be manageable.'

Now they waited, allowing me to see the reason in what they were saying.

'That seems sensible,' I replied.

'Then try and make Rainulf see this sense, please Lord Rocamadour; come with us, for he listens to the Milan Company with nothing but suspicion.' Again Melinde took up the point, brown eyes fixed firmly upon me. They were used to each other, Gerard and Melinde, and I wondered if Cateline and I would ever be like this, able to advance our thoughts as a pair.

'I will, but first I must find Count Stephen and give my report.'

'He patrols the road ahead.' This from a young-looking man with brown skin and hair thick with black curls.

'And he agrees with us,' added Gerard. 'It's just the sodding *mutur* who can't understand the issue. Or don't want to.'

With something of a heavy heart, I remounted my destrier. If it were up to me, I'd give up the cart and the treasure for the sake of a chance of getting home. Not least because the money had been plundered in terrible scenes following the fall of Devinium. On hearing a rumour that some of the citizens had swallowed gems and small silver and gold coins to hide them, the *mutur* had slaughtered the prisoners – both men and women – to search through their guts for hidden wealth.

As far as I was concerned, the treasure on the *mutur's* cart was the unlawful plunder of fellow Christians; yet I also understood that my thinking was shaped by the fact that I owned a pouch of silver and most of the other survivors of the expedition had nothing.

After riding past the efficient-looking vanguard formed by Gerard's company, I had to continue nearly a mile before I saw six knights in the distance, their horses at a walk under the dark green canopy.

'Well met Lord Rocadamour,' Count Stephen raised a palm in greeting and I showed mine. 'How fared your mission?'

'Not too favourably, in all truth. I chose to let Duke Carisbald go with just a promise to assist Duke Shalk. Yet,' I hurried on, 'I did learn this from him: that King Bratislav has sent riders to Prince Slavniak granting the prince all the treasure we carry and forty mares if he destroys us.'

'Has he indeed?' From under his coif, Count Stephen looked tired and unhappy.

'My … servant. She said you were looking for me?'

'I was. To invite you to ride with us. Seven knights is few enough, but six even fewer.'

'My thanks for the honour. It did occur to me though, as I made my way through the army, that perhaps my station should be at the rear, with the *mutur*.'

'How so?'

'Before long, there may be work for a knight on horse there, chasing away those enemies who try to steal upon us through the trees.' This was true, though I was also thinking of Rainulf's tale of King Mutur.

'That's probably how it will be.' The count looked downcast and shook his head. 'I should spare you a knight from the van as a companion, for all that we are barely a force worth reckoning here.'

'That would be welcome. First, though, we must persuade the *mutur* to give up the cart and share the treasure among all. Already, they are some four miles behind you.'

'You have been talking to Gerard already, I see. Very well, let us call a council of march this night at my fire.'

* * *

That evening, Arnulf, Cateline and I ate a stew with the meat from a brace of hare (brought down by my bow), filled out with parsley and dandelion leaves. And we also passed around a hedgehog that had been spotted by Cateline while she led the donkey. It was not the custom in the regions around Rocadamour to eat hedgehog, although Arnulf claimed expertise in its preparation. The trick, he said, was to bake the spines in clay, whence they were held while the meat could be peeled away. Our meal was not a success and as Cateline and I cursed the vicious pricks to our fingers, Arnulf blamed the poor quality of the clay to hand.

Afterwards, having wended my way through praying nuns and past hearths surrounded by tired and sleeping children, I found the council. Count Stephen's camp was a circle of hammocks, strung between a dozen sturdy beeches. His servants had a lively fire burning at the centre. Already present were Gerard, Melinde, Jacques and the other officer of the Milan Company, the lithe, curly-haired soldier. Soon after my arrival came Rainulf and three of his men: large-chested, long-haired villains.

'Well?' Rainulf planted his feet firmly and folded his arms.

No one spoke and it took me a moment to realise that Count Stephen was waiting for me to address the council.

'You've heard that Prince Slavniak has been offered our treasure and forty mares if he destroys us?' I asked the brutish warrior

'What of it?'

'We need to march more swiftly.'

'Fast or slow, there's a reckoning coming with Prince Slavniak and I intend to piss on his decapitated head.' The firelight in Rainulf's dark eyes glittered with diabolical confidence.

Uncomfortable with such vulgarity and uncertain as to my loyalties, I felt lost, like the child that I had been only last summer. There was something admirable and manly in Rainulf's defiant behaviour. Yet with it was a kind of burning insanity, one potentially ruinous to us all.

Perhaps sensing my difficulty, Gerard took a step towards the *mutur*. First checking with Count Stephen, who gestured assent with his left hand, Gerard then turned to Rainulf.

'Look, we've had our difficulties, you and I. Still, we have common ground here. Our companies will only leave this forest if we assist each other and if we move as swiftly as we possibly can.'

By way of response, Rainulf gave a slow smile, showing his dark fang.

Undeterred, Gerard pressed on, waving his hands to emphasise his words. 'It's the cart. You took nearly an hour to come up to us after we had camped. And that with us treading soft all day. Get rid of that cart. Keep the treasure. Of course keep the treasure. But you don't need it in a huge and unwieldy pile. Spread it out; give every man and woman something to carry.'

'And then we outrun Prince Slavniak? With our wounded and our poor? What difference does your suggestion make, other than to take command of the treasure from me?'

Surprisingly, Count Stephen drew his sword. An action that immediately made him the centre of attention.

'This is *Lifestealer*. When my father's father held the ridge at Gilsedge, it drank the blood of twenty men. When my father turned back the King of France and filled the river at Bouillon with bodies, it tasted twenty more. I have carried it without shame and so will my son.

'It is not the destiny of *Lifestealer* to fall from my hand in this Godforsaken forest. Though your folly attempts to make it so. Do not hold us back tomorrow.'

Rainulf spat contemptuously in the direction of the count. 'Your son will inherit forty castles or more. My bastards will have nothing. This talk of swords is nothing but vanity you have learned from songmakers.'

Insulted, Count Stephen nevertheless was in complete control of his voice. It deepened and became as thrilling as though he were taking a vow before a church full of witnesses. 'I know what manner of man you are, Rainulf. Don't give me a reason to kill you. For I will not hesitate to do so.'

'Old man. You are far from your home and you have but five knights remaining to you. We *mutur* are near sixty. Here, your title means nothing. This is not the place for you to be making threats.' Rainulf's three companions adjusted their stance, bringing their weapons to readiness.

'Calm, gentlemen, calm.' Jacques looked anxiously from one to the other.

For my part, I admired the strength in Count Stephen. It was a different kind of strength to that of Rainulf, the kind of patient, enduring strength of a rocky outcrop. Even so, it seemed unlikely to me that if they came to blows the slender, elderly man had any hope of besting the thunderous strength of the captain of the *mutur*.

'Are you all finished?' No one answered Rainulf, who glanced to his companions with sinister amusement. 'Then I have a solution to your concerns. March ahead, without us.'

'Come on Rainulf, what little hope we have depends on our fighting as one.' Thus spoke Gerard.

'Not true, my friend. Think on it. Who will Prince Slavniak attack? Those with nothing? Or those with the treasure? While we defend our wealth, you can hurry on to the Reiber.'

'There is a comradeship between us, Rainulf, like it or no.' Gerard's pale head was glistening in the firelight, making it seem as though he were sweating with worry. Perhaps he was. 'We would not leave the *mutur* to die alone in this forest.'

'The *mutur* can look after ourselves. And your love of us extends only to the treasure we gathered up from Devinium and have pushed inch by inch along this road. March on. March on the morrow and leave us.'

At this response, Gerard's expression grew severe and he looked at every one of us as if making an appeal.

With a clap from his large hands, Rainulf startled me, along with a blackbird from its perch in the tree behind me. 'No one has anything else to say? Is it agreed: we march with the cart; you march as you please?'

'I've something to say. With Count Stephen's permission.' This was Gerard's officer, the one with the dark complexion and darker curls. After receiving a nod from the count, the small man turned to Rainulf. 'You seek all the treasure for yourself by this plan, no matter the risk to the lives of all. Other than the *mutur*, who shares in the gold by your reckoning?'

'No one, Andreas.' Once more, Rainulf grinned his sinister grin. 'After all, it was the *mutur* who were first onto the walls of Devinium. And while everyone here twisted their hands with false remorse, it was the *mutur* who emptied the buildings of wealth. And it is the *mutur* who have pushed that cart over every bump of the road.'

'Not that you'd let anyone else near it,' muttered Jacques, but dropping his head when Rainulf glared back at him.

Faces given an orange tint by the flames of the central fire, Melinde and Gerard had been huddled together to exchange whispers. Now Gerard strolled over to Rainulf; so focused was he on the leader of the *mutur* that Gerard seemed to forget that Count Stephen was the head of our council and without looking for permission, the captain of the Milan Company addressed Rainulf with some bitterness.

'Do you not recognise anybody else's claim to that treasure then?'

'I do not.'

'Not those who fought side by side with you yesterday?'

'That was yesterday.'

'Not those who outnumber you, two to one?'

'So, now you come to the real argument.'

'The only one that you will listen to.'

'And yet...' Rainulf gave Gerard a long, appraising stare. 'And yet. You won't fight the *mutur*. Not when it means there will be too few survivors for anyone to escape the forest.'

'You're right. I'm going to get my company out of here.'

'As will I.'

'Your unbending greed will destroy you.'

'Perhaps, but perhaps not.' With that Rainulf turned and his guards followed him into the darkness.

12

AN EMPTY ROAD

Dawn in the forest was sudden and violent. Not in regard to the coming of light, for that was a subtle and slow change through many hues of grey. The heralds of the new sun were the birds of the trees. And when they gave voice, they did so as one and it was as though their numbers were greater than the grains of sand upon a beach. Above, to the sides, up and down the road, they whistled, screeched, cawed and shouted their existence.

Only those of our army who had died during the night failed to wake to such a gale of sound. I opened my eyes to see Cateline looking at me. Her face was wan with fatigue.

'I wish I could sleep for days at a time,' she said tiredly.

'Well you shall. When we reach Rocadamour, we shall spend entire days in bed.'

Her smile was sad. 'I do not think it likely we shall escape this grim forest, but if we do, I cannot envisage myself in a bed of fine linen with you, living like a lady.'

'I'll insist upon it, no matter what Father says.'

'You misunderstand. It is me for whom such a scene is not appealing, whether your father would agree to it or no. I have not been brought up for courtly life and ...'

'And?'

'I lay with you because you deserved it, for what you did for us. And also because I think we will all be dead soon. Why not enjoy a little sweetness while we can? But I'm not some farmer's daughter with designs upon a local knight.'

'No. I never thought that.'

'You are brave, Guibert. You fight and you ride like a man. But in every other respect you are still a boy.' Already, she had buttoned up her tunic and had risen from our bed of fern. She turned from me, to concentrate upon blowing the fire into wakefulness. Flushed and dismayed by her words, I did not respond, but watched as Cateline took a clay pot from our cart and left the road in the direction of the stream the army had camped by. What did she mean? That I was too childish to be her lover? My heart beat wildly with anger and hurt.

From underneath the cart, Arnulf gave a groan then came into view. 'Cateline is a fine young woman.'

'You listened?' I responded, aggrieved.

'How can I not? You are right beside me.'

'Well. Cough or make some noise, so as not to eavesdrop.'

'In any case, I have spent the last two days in her company and she is quite remarkable.'

Despite my embarrassment that Arnulf had been witness to an exchange that had stirred up hot waves of shame in me, I was curious. 'How so?'

'There are people in this world so filled with dark humours that they can never be happy, regardless of their advantages. Then there are people like Cateline, who despite cruel blows from fate, enjoy what opportunities for joy life gives them. And she is brave and wise in many practical ways.'

'She would make a good lady wife?'

'I believe she would… If you can win her.'

'Would you say that to Father?'

'I would.' Arnulf rubbed at his greying moustache, somewhat ruefully. 'But the strongest argument for allowing Cateline to be your lady I dare not raise with Lord Rocadamour.'

'Which is?'

'Which is that his own mother was a miller's daughter, bedded by the first Guibert.'

'Oh.' I sat up. 'I remember her, a little. She was buried with great ceremony in our church. All the nobles of our province were there.'

'Exactly.' He lowered his voice as Cateline neared, 'But I say no more on it.'

While Cateline busied herself making our porridge, I pretended Arnulf and I had been discussing other matters, by asking a question of real concern to me.

'Arnulf. You speak of humours. What manner of person am I?'

While looking from me to Cateline, Arnulf's expression had been cheerful. Now it dropped, bringing back the dark equine look to him that I had been accustomed to these last months.

'In all honesty, I cannot say. Bravery, yes. But what else runs in your blood, I no longer know. I've seen men change with too much warfare and become dark, cruel. The kind of person who enjoys the act of ending a life. Your father is not such a person and nor, I hope, will you be.'

This hint that something about my soul disturbed Arnulf, I found satisfying, although perhaps I should not have. Three days ago, my sergeant would have been completely sure of me. Hadn't he taught me all he knew, both of manners and of warfare? Now, I was pleased with his uncertainty. Whoever I was becoming in this forest, I was no longer being shaped by any other person. I made my choices according to my own tastes, not theirs. And one important choice ahead of me was whether to become King Mutur.

* * *

Later, after we had eaten the porridge, Jacques came over to us, riding on a pony. His hair was tied back in a bright yellow bunch and his features were sharp in the morning light, like those of an inquisitive mouse.

'Gerard says we are leaving soon, whether the *mutur* march with us or no. You and I are to cover the rear.'

'Just the two of you?' exclaimed Arnulf.

'No, with us will be half of the Milan Company, some fifty men, but Guibert and I are to patrol on horse further back still to watch for Prince Slavniak.'

'Have you earned this assignment because of your riding skills?' I grinned at Jacques, whose thin face also broke into a smile, revealing his crooked front teeth.

'That must be it.'

'What says Count Stephen? Are these his orders?'

'Gerard has led our company on many a dangerous march and commands the largest army here. He may not be a count, but really, it is he who leads the army now. Of course, Count Stephen gives his assent to Gerard's orders, but has he any choice?'

'I follow no man but Count Stephen. If he is satisfied with the arrangement, then so am I.' I spoke without rancour, for I did not resent the fact that Gerard, a footsoldier, gave the orders for our army. Unnatural as it was by the standards I was used to at home, we were a long way from Rocadamour. Not only did Gerard have right of command from the large number of soldiers who followed him, but I trusted in Gerard's experience. If anyone could bring us to safety, it was he. Nor had I forgotten that my crow-eaten body would be lying in a field right now if not for the captain of the Milan Company grabbing my foot two days ago.

Pulling himself up by the boards of the cart and reaching awkwardly for his crutch, Arnulf limped towards my destrier. With an equally serious expression, Cateline lifted my chainmail hauberk from the cart and staggered.

'My God, how do you fight in this?'

I hurried across to help her. 'It's not so heavy once it's on.'

With Cateline's help, I armed myself and – still smarting over her earlier words about my boyishness – pulled away when she went to kiss me on the cheek.

It was a foolish gesture and at first Cateline looked amused, then she held my gaze with a more sombre expression. 'Don't suffer over what I said. I'll be praying for you.'

Turning away without responding to her, I knew Arnulf would expect me to double-check all the fastenings and buckles of my tack and I did, gaining his gruff nod of approval. Then, with his help, I was up in the saddle once more.

He passed me my lance.

All along the road, the people of the army were busy stowing their goods. Pushing through them towards the rear were a body of Gerard's men, most protected by armour made of thick slabs of dark leather. Those who also wore a layer of riveted pieces of metal over the leather appeared to be covered in bristles, like walking hedgehogs. Leading these men was the brown-faced commander I had often seen with Gerard. He marched without helm and his black beard was visible, as curly as his hair.

'Andreas.' Jacques gave him a gesture, half wave, half salute.

'Jacques. Lord Rocadamour.' He tipped his head to me. 'Go ahead, please.'

With a last glance at Arnulf, who looked concerned, and at Cateline, who was busy packing the cart (which was unfortunate, as I wanted to turn away disdainfully while she looked at me), I urged my stallion to a walk.

There was a clear space of several hundred yards between the last members of the army – our night guards – and the camp of the *mutur*. It seemed that the thuggish host were determined to see the rest of us go on ahead of them, for most of their men were still lying down and there was very little sign of activity among them.

Once Andreas had formed his soldiers up on the road, in a column five wide, ten deep, we all waited patiently for the army ahead to begin moving. A light breeze swayed the tree tops and carried to us the scent of bluebells from a thick carpet of the flowers to our right. It took perhaps an hour before Andreas gave the order to march.

Jacques and I watched the rearguard move away down the tunnel of trees, walking away with a steady professional tread, until they were nearly out of view. Then we too set off, urging our horses to a walk. The *mutur*, however, were still gathered around their campfires.

'What do you suppose they are thinking?' Jacques had seen me looking over my shoulder.

I shook my head. 'They may be good fighters, but staying back like that is dangerous. Dangerous for us all,' I muttered.

'Exactly. It gives Prince Slavniak two small battles instead of one hard one.'

'Nevertheless, perhaps they are right to trust in their strength. Perhaps they will save the rest of us from having to fight?'

'Perhaps,' echoed Jacques, but skeptically.

The forest seemed innocent that morning. Shafts of sunlight found their way through the branches of birch, oak, and beech, even through thick hazel groves. The road was like a quilt of light and dark patches. Sometimes a huge stretch of the road was lit by the sun and there one could look up at the blue sky. The same cheerful, light blue that would greet the members of my family as they rose for the day. Yet for all this natural calm, I was anxious. Were there soldiers gathering deeper in the forest, behind the tree trunks?

I was not comfortable walking our horses down the road, not with a fear that from out of the shadows a swift arrow might strike my back. After suffering from these thoughts for an hour, I decided it was better to wait without moving: watching, listening, rarely speaking. Then canter up the road until we had caught up with the rearguard again.

These pauses among the trees were silent, even our horses seemed to be listening for something. And they grew longer. After one particularly long wait on a stretch of road that gave a fine view back under a canopy of elm branches, I fully expected that I would soon see the *mutur* approaching us. Yet nothing stirred, other than the flies and wasps that appeared and disappeared as they meandered in and out of channels of sunlight. There was something disproportionate about the elms, with their trunks dividing low to the ground, to allow huge sinuous branches to stretch up high and entwine with their neighbours, creating a cathedral vault of brown and green.

I could bear it no longer.

'I must see how far back they are, or what has happened to them.'

'The *mutur* you mean?'

'Aye.'

Jacques looked troubled. 'We are already a good ride from the army. What if our enemy comes between us and them and there is no one to give the warning?'

'I hear you. But where are the *mutur*? I must find them.'

'Must you? It is their choice to march so slowly.'

'If I ride hard for five miles and do not see them, then I'll turn back.'

'Very well,' I was getting to know Jacques a little and from the tightness around his mouth, I knew he was troubled. 'I'll come with you.'

'You don't have to.'

'No, but it's better we stick together. If you didn't come back, I'd have to go look for you anyway.'

We exchanged a look: it was one of comradeship and it reminded me that I no longer cared if a man be a peasant or a knight. Anyone could be my friend.

At a canter, we returned over the ground that we had already travelled. Our horses watched out for uneven parts of the road unassisted, for Jacques and I were constantly looking into the forest.

Five miles or more passed under the rhythmic beating of our horses' hooves and I began to admit to myself that it was time to turn about. Yet there was always just one more corner or one more gentle hill to crest, surely we would then find the *mutur*? Yet we did not.

Instead, with a gasp from me, we found their cart.

At first I assumed the worst. But there was no sign of a battle. No spent arrows, broken weapons. No bodies, nor blood.

Leaping from his pony, Jacques ran back and forth.

'They went this way,' he pointed to the trees on the south of the road. 'Into the forest.' Then he was in the saddle again. 'Hurry, we must tell Gerard.'

'What does it mean?' I asked him as his knees banged urgently against the flanks of the pony. 'What's happening?'

'I'm not sure, but we know this for certain: they no longer stand between us and Prince Slavniak.'

13

LYING LIPS PUT TO SILENCE

Our ride through the warm afternoon was swift and by the time we regained our army the sweat of my destrier had formed long foaming lines of pungent lather on his flanks. The gait of the stallion, which was so smooth at a trot, was uneven at a gallop and for most of our urgent journey I had been concentrating on my balance. Even so, my thoughts moved back and forth in wonder at the mystery. Why would the *mutur* leave the road for the forest? This made no more sense to me than to jump from the decks of a ship into the sea.

The forest was vast and ancient and dangerous. The Romans had forced their way through, to be sure. But since then no lord or king had gained any land from the forest. From time to time, not more than once every ten miles, an earthen path would join the road, testimony to the existence of human communities deep within the forest. Such communities of lawless, demon-worshipers would be no friends to the *mutur*, and in any case, these paths were always to be found to the north of the road.

To the south, eventually, were unclimbable mountains. Or so I had been told by Arnulf. And even if there was a way through those peaks, you would then find yourself among the cruel bandits who lived on the north-eastern borders of Burgundy. Perhaps, there were allies of the *mutur* among those outlaws?

'What news?' called out Andreas as we slowed to a trot to pass the rearguard.

Jacques, who must have been sore from his jolting, uneasy ride, simply said, 'The *mutur* have gone.'

'No sign of enemies,' I added.

Again, we had to pick our way through the confusion that was the journey of our poor, the wounded and those hauling our baggage (with a wave to Arnulf as I passed our cart and a hurt glance at Cateline). Then at last Jacques and I were with the van and Gerard.

Dismounting, Jacques gave his report on foot, while I stayed on my destrier, though I did call for water for him.

'The sodding devil!' exclaimed Gerard. 'He's racing us to the Reiber.'

'What do you mean?' I asked.

'I mean, he has run through the forest and is back on the road ahead of us.'

'But why?'

'To put us between him and Prince Slavniak.' Gerard was pacing swiftly now, turning back and forth.

'He is not making for Burgundy then?'

With a disconsolate sigh, the sturdy captain of the Milan Company shook his head. 'Too far, too dangerous.'

'More dangerous than facing Prince Slavniak?'

'Yes, more dangerous.' Gerard snapped. 'Have we not considered that route?' He shared a look with the ever-present Melinde. 'Think back to last night, to Rainulf's words. Do they not make sense now? He was provoking us to march on, so that he gained the room to leave the road unobserved.'

This was hard to deny. But the argument that Gerard had just presented disturbed me much more than the idea of Rainulf and his men trying to find an escape route through the wilder reaches of the forest. If the *mutur* were on the road to the west of us, then Rainulf was more treacherous than I wanted to believe and his words to me about King Mutur only lies.

'If you have a fresh horse for me, I'll ride on and look.'

'Very well.'

As I dismounted and waited for a horse, Gerard began calling men to him and giving them orders. Without shouting, despite the passion that was visible in his flushed cheeks and perspiring, bald forehead, his words soon had men and women running back to relay his commands to our people. As soon as I could do so I left the army, to ride past an astonished Count Stephen and his five knights and rush on down a road tinged orange by the setting sun.

Gerard's men had given me a bay courser to ride; this horse was resistant to my anxiety, again and again dropping from gallop to canter and even to trot. After an hour or more of this, my legs were aching severely. At last, I saw in the fading sunlight a glint of metal and my mount and I made one final effort.

I crested a rise and I found the *mutur*. The selfish, double-dealing, lying *mutur*.

Not a cart remained with them, though some men led donkeys and ponies by the halter. They were walking swiftly, perhaps at twice the speed of our army.

There were no smiles and jests for me now. Only scowls.

When the news of my presence had been passed along, Rainulf came back down the road at a lumbering run, his dark plaids bouncing against his heavy armour, his eyes cold.

'Well, Rocadamour, what are you doing here?'

'Gerard guessed your intent. I had to see for myself was it true.' I swallowed. 'Why Rainulf? Why abandon us?'

'What do I owe you? Or Gerard? Or the helpless? I act for the *mutur* alone. If we are to see Lotharingia again with our treasure, then we cannot wait on those who are too slow.'

'And King Mutur, what about him?'

From beneath his bushy eyebrows, Rainulf's stare was scornful. 'You must have been dreaming, little lord. There is no such person. And if there were, he would be a man, not a boy.'

I wheeled about and rode back east into the deep shadows of the forest, before he could see the tears that had come unbidden to my eyes. Twice this day I had been called a boy.

Why should I care to prove myself to a farmer's daughter? Because she knew my worth as a lover. Why should I care to prove myself before a criminal mercenary? Because he was the most savage warrior I have known. Because when he reached my side in the ambush near Devinium I loved him for it and thought that he loved me. Brothers in bloodshed. Was I a hero? Or an immature foolish boy? No matter how much I reassured myself, it was agony to think that these two people, whom before this day had begun, I had thought admired me, in fact thought so badly of me.

Deep in twilight, with the pounding sound of my courser's hoofbeats matching the pounding of my thoughts, the appearance of our knights came as a shock. Suddenly, I was cantering up to Count Stephen, whose eyes were pools of grim darkness.

'Well?'

'Yes, they are ahead of us. And moving fast.' I assumed he had spoken to Gerard about my mission.

'Fast for those on foot, but not for us.' He straightened in his saddle; tall and fierce. 'If we were on my lands, I'd hang them all for desertion.'

'But we are not on your lands. We're in this Godforsaken forest. And even the devil doesn't want us!' I really did feel abandoned by Christ.

'Calm yourself, sir. Report to Gerard and inform him that I am intent upon riding ahead to see if Rainulf can be brought to his duty.'

I did as Count Stephen instructed. But after I had spoken (in control of myself once more), Gerard consulted with Melinde, then turned to me and shook his head.

'That encounter would end badly, so it would. I must dissuade the count and urge him to stay with the army. We will press on through the night and see if they do the same. Whether or not we catch Rainulf, speed is our only hope.' Gerard looked over to one of his officers and raised his voice. 'We will rest for an hour and eat. Then march on by torchlight. You especially, Lord Rocadamour, make the most of this pause. You've ridden hard today.'

It was true. I almost yelled out with pain as I dismounted into the upraised arms of Gerard's men. Then, unsteady on my feet, I gratefully exchanged the willful courser for my intelligent destrier.

14

HE SOWETH DISCORD

Up the road, a surprisingly long way up the road, all was schism and strife. Gerard and Count Stephen had caught up with the *mutur* at the east bank of the Reiber. There, the ferryman had delayed Rainulf's men by cutting loose his ferry rather than surrender it. Pretending to be bringing the flat-bottomed craft across the river in response to the cries of the *mutur,* the man had stopped half way and hacked through the connecting ropes while the *mutur* howled and attempted to kill him with arrows. Soon enough the ferry had been plucked from its guide ropes by the river's powerful current and borne away, twisting and rocking on the dark river. The ferryman, so I learned, had then escaped both the *mutur* and the river by clinging to the guide ropes and pulling himself to the west bank.

Hampered by a lack of proper tools, the *mutur* had spent most of the night working to build a raft strong enough to carry their horses. And before the new ferry was complete, the vanguard of our army had ridden up to them in the form of Count Stephen and his five knights. Not long afterwards, Gerard and his men arrived at the river crossing, in disciplined formation.

Thus, the scene when Jacques and I drew up. Beside the river, standing with weapons in hand in front of the partly constructed raft, were the *mutur*. Their scowling faces were lit by the torches they had erected and by those held by people in the half circle of men and women who faced them. On the road nearest the *mutur* were Count Stephen and his knights on horseback. The forest at this crossing had been cleared back in years past, to some twenty yards distance from the water and this gave room for Gerard's men to fan out on either side of Stephen, their lines curving to reach the river bank and contain the *mutur*.

Then, there were our crowds of elderly people, women, children, monks and nuns. These people were rightly furious with the *mutur* and they held once more the improvised weapons with which they had fought King Bratislav. They stood behind Gerard's men, filling out the ranks of footsoldiers and in contrast to the sombre silence of the professional warriors, these angry people were shouting rebukes and jeering at the *mutur* for their plight.

It seemed to me that soon there would be fighting and that I had arrived just in time to assist Gerard and Count Stephen.

As I walked the stallion towards the front of the army, the people beneath me fell silent and moved to give me room. In their eyes was expectation.

'Rocadamour, you are most welcome sir!' Count Stephen exclaimed as I halted among his men. He gestured towards Rainulf. 'As you can see, we have found the *mutur*. And the advantage is ours.' Count Stephen's wrinkled face formed a grin of stern satisfaction. 'They cannot cross the river until they complete the raft. And that is not possible for them now.'

'We all need to cross and soon, for no doubt Prince Slavniak is marching close behind us.' I found myself looking back down the road into the blackness of the forest, as though even now I might even see our enemies arriving.

'True, young Rocadamour. But the question is, will we take that raft and complete it with the agreement of the *mutur* or will we have to cut them down first?'

I looked at the front ranks of the *mutur,* all hard men, all holding great axes or two-handed hammers. Count Stephen had immense confidence in the capabilities of his knights if he thought besting the *mutur* would be a simple matter.

Pushing through the crowds towards us were Gerard, Melinde and Andreas. A large group of interested onlookers gathered around our group.

Melinde was the first to speak. 'This is no place to tarry. We must be across that river before Prince Slavniak finds us and we have many carts and animals. Think on this. If we manage five crossings and back an hour, we will be doing well. That's mayhap twenty crossings before dawn.'

Twenty. I wasn't the only person to look back towards the torchlit baggage train of our army and I doubt I was the only person thinking that it would be well into the following day before all were safely across.

'So then,' Count Stephen's stallion stepped sideways, causing the people near him to press backwards to keep clear. 'Gerard, prepare your archers and let's get on with our task.'

'Bloody and deceitful men shall live out half their days!' cried a priest.

'Amen,' came the response, along with a ripple of motion among the gathering.

'Wait! Let me talk to Rainulf.' Angry as I was with the *mutur,* as we all were, I did not want to fight them.

'Very well,' Gerard gave me a calm nod, 'do not forget so, that time is pressing.'

Melinde stepped towards me and stroked the neck of my stallion before lifting her wide and care-worn face to meet my eyes with an intense scrutiny. 'You can promise that no harm will come to them, so long as we get the raft and can cross our people first. They just need to leave the raft and wait their turn.'

Turning my stallion to face the river, I walked towards the *mutur*, with Count Stephen's knights making room for me to ride on down. Grim faced, Rainulf's men also parted their ranks, so that I could walk my stallion to the partially completed raft, on which lounged their leader, cracking walnuts in his fists and throwing their meat into his mouth. Rainulf chewed for a while, the muscles of his jaw rippling beneath his dark beard. I waited patiently, wanting him to speak first so that I could measure his humour.

'Go on then,' he said at last. 'What do you want?'

'I want to save everyone from a battle with Prince Slavniak.'

He smiled, an unexpected and wicked expression. 'I thought you were developing a taste for blood.'

This was a jest, but it brought to mind Arnulf's words that morning, of men who came to enjoy harming and killing others. Was I becoming such a man?

'No.'

'Well,' Rainulf tossed aside some broken shells and picked up two more walnuts, 'Gerard is trapped between me and the prince. What's he going to do?'

'Attack you.'

Rainulf nodded. 'It will mean his death and that of Count Stephen.'

'And yours.'

'Probably.' The casing of the nuts broke with a large crack.

'Rainulf?'

'Aye.'

'What is it you want from life?'

Surprised, he sat up and stared at me with dark eyes in which were reflected orange flames.

'Not much. To live freely, to have coin enough for food and

women.'

'Why then talk about killing Gerard and Count Stephen, instead of how everyone can cross this river? How we can all escape this forest and survive to live as we wish?'

'Because Gerard scorns me, though he is the same manner of man as me; for all that he refuses to admit it. Because Count Stephen thinks me the scum of the earth.'

'Aren't you?'

He chuckled. 'Do I need to witness the contempt of a man whose refined ways are paid for by the toil of a thousand serfs? I do not.'

'Do you feel loyalty to your men?'

'Sod you Rocadamour. And tell me, if it came to fighting, which side would you take?'

'Gerard's of course.'

'Why? Because you think him more noble than me? His company has killed woman and children too, you know.'

'You betrayed me, Rainulf.'

'Are you thinking of what I said about King Mutur?' He regarded me with intense concentration. 'Your meaning is that if you were made King Mutur, you would fight with us?'

I did not answer.

'It is not fully in my power to make such a grant. But I can promise you that I will advocate for you.'

'No, Rainulf. I've learned something about promises this last day. Men make me promises when they are weak. Yet as soon as they are strong again, they break their word.'

'You only learned that now?' Rainulf laughed aloud, at me, at himself. 'Come then Rocadamour, what's Gerard's offer?'

'Move away. Let them cross first. Then you cross afterwards.'

'Is that all?' he scowled, suspicious. 'What about the treasure?'

'He didn't say. But if you move, they will rush to the raft and not stop to ask for the silver and gold you carry. For their lives depend on crossing that river and soon.'

'And ours too. What guarantee do we have that Gerard will let us cross afterwards? That he won't leave us stranded here to face Prince Slavniak's men?'

'How about this, that you have *my* promise.' My own words made me smile and for a long time he just stared back angrily. But suddenly he grinned, a row of white teeth and one black one on show.

'Go now, Rocadamour, I need to talk to my men.'

On my return to Gerard's army, I did not answer the many questions shouted up to me by voices from the crowd. Instead, I turned my stallion to face the river and looked over at Rainulf, who no longer seemed filled with indolence, rather he was gesturing vigorously as he spoke to a small circle of his officers.

'Well?' Melinde was at my horse's flank, her brown eyes questioning me.

'I don't know. He gave no indication.'

'But he heard you out?'

'He did.' Even as I spoke, the group around Rainulf broke up and the *mutur* began to march northwards along the river bank, away from the crossing-point. They formed up again on the mound that we had built to cover those who died the last time we crossed the Reiber. Cheers of a somewhat mocking nature broke out among our people. Several of the *mutur* made lewd gestures in response. Still, the raft was ours and without bloodshed.

'Well done, Lord Rocadamour.' Melinde squeezed my calf through the chain mail with surprising strength. 'Very well done. Now go rest and rest your stallion.'

It was true that I was tired, terribly tired. And so I forgave her forwardness. While Arnulf attended to the destrier, describing to me as he did so a past battle over a contested river crossing that he had once experienced, I stretched out on our cart. And fell asleep.

* * *

When I awoke, it was to the shrieks of the forest birds. Another dawn was near. Today, I could see the sky properly and it was a relief to be able to do so after so long in the tunnel of the forest. The moon was still up and a few late stars were visible too. As soon as my memories had returned to their proper order, I looked over the edge of the cart at the river. There were dozens of torches over the far side. And on this side, not half of our carts and beasts remained.

'Good, you're awake.' Cateline was looking at me with a kindly expression. 'It will be our turn soon. Arnulf and I can manage the cart, the pony, the donkey and the wounded stallion in one crossing. But not the destrier.'

'That's all right. I'll take him. Where's my armour?'

'Here. I washed the blood out of it.'

The metal was cold, wet, heavy and went on with difficulty. 'It needs to be rubbed dry,' I said gruffly, 'or it will rust.'

For a moment, shadows of anger formed upon her face, then Cateline shrugged and picked up a cloth. 'Hold still then.'

Cateline went at the task for what felt like a long time. No doubt it would have been quicker had we talked to one another throughout. But my tongue was still. I could barely explain to myself my feeling of shame that I was not man enough for her, let alone speak aloud such a thought. And when she was done, I wanted to thank her, to smile and perhaps to see a smile in return. But equally, I wanted her to understand how much her words the previous dawn had stung me. In the end, I said nothing but farewell.

Away from our camp, up on the road, I saw Jacques on his pony leading a dozen soldiers with a variety of mounts and armour. What united them was that each one carried either a crossbow or a longbow.

'Good day, Jacques. What new adventure is this?'

Jacques frowned. 'Another dance with death. We go to slow down the advance of Prince Slavniak's men.'

'Fortune smile upon you.'

'Amen.' With a whip of his reins and several kicks to his pony's flanks, Jacques and his fellow archers were on their way back into the dark canopy of the forest.

As I watched the small column of riders follow the road, leaving my view once behind tree trunks and foliage, I realised that I had grown attached to Jacques. He was unselfish and dependable. Heartfelt prayers formed in my mind that he would return to us unharmed.

A tree stump gave me a seat and I let my new destrier graze upon the lush grass nearby, while I admired his powerful form. This was a great gift that the people had given me.

From the crowds gathered near the river beneath orange torches, two shadows detached themselves and walked over to me: Gerard and Melinde. Her left hand was holding his inner arm, her right lifting her skirt above a section of ground churned muddy by the passage of the army's carts.

'You can cross the river on the next trip if you like,' said Gerard.

'That's kind, but I'll wait until all the poor people are over.'

Melinde smiled. 'You are honourable.'

'I suppose so.' I looked at my hands, the roughened hands of a warrior, or a peasant. 'If such be the criteria for honour, then you are honourable too.'

'This is the most dangerous time for those of us on the east bank,' said Gerard.

'Dawn?'

'No. I mean that with more than half my company across the river, the rest of us have no hope should Prince Slavniak arrive.'

'I'm not sure Prince Slavniak is coming.'

'You think not?' Melinde sounded curious as well as hopeful.

'I think that many men are liars. And that Duke Carisbald could have been one of them. Maybe he was trying to trick me into giving up on our army so that I would come away with him. And to bring this fine destrier with me.'

'You might be right.' Melinde knelt close to me and touched my knee. 'What is the matter, Lord Rocadamour? Why do you look so coldly upon us this morning?'

Without meeting her eyes, I asked, 'Is it true that Gerard has killed women and children?'

'I'll tell no lie. It is true.' The strength in Gerard's voice brought my gaze up to meet his. Such clear blue eyes. 'When a man is paid to wield a sword, he loses the right to follow his own wishes.'

'Then don't take the money.'

'I tried being a farmer. It didn't suit.'

'We go to Jerusalem to lift our sins. Isn't that enough?' Melinde stood up and proclaimed her words, as if addressing everyone nearby and not just me.

I did not reply, tempted as I was to point out that our backs were now to Jerusalem.

'Who was it spoke of me in this way?' asked Gerard, 'Rainulf Bluetooth?'

'Two months ago, when I left home, I thought it a simple matter to judge men: the greedy, the cowardly, the honourable, the weak. Now, it seems to me impossible to know any man,' I looked at Melinde and then briefly over at Cateline, 'or woman.'

'If I could live my life over again,' Gerard crouched down in front of me, so we were face to face, 'I would make sure I was a long way from those places.'

'But you were there and there was nothing else you could do.' Melinde's expression was hard and the knuckles on her hand as she gripped Gerard's shoulder were white.

'What manner of a man are you Gerard?'

'He's the finest man you'll ever meet, Lord Rocadamour, though he is no noble. There have been moments I'm a witness to that you would not believe. And I'm not talking of bravery, though he is as brave as any. The real magnificence of this man is that in a crisis he can see through the confusion to what needs to be done. Where others deceive themselves, he looks the at the truth, no matter how unwelcome.'

Gerard sighed and looked downcast. 'I'm just a man like any other.' He shrugged off his wife's hand and stood up. 'Not good. Not bad. If you want to judge me, judge by my deeds and not anyone else's words about me, especially Rainulf's.'

With that, they went back to the busy crossing point, while I stayed to watch colour come to the sky and to the foxgloves, wood lilies, and parsley that grew among the grasses that filled the ground between the edge of the forest and the river. Yet again I missed Rocadamour and my brother and more still my sister. Perhaps I would see them in due course; the army was nearly across the river.

15

HE THAT PROVOKETH A KING TO ANGER...

By the time my destrier and I were ready to be hauled across the river, the sun had risen over the treeline, to set the ripples on the surface of the Reiber sparkling. Not that the sight was a cheerful one. I was only too aware of the dark, black depths into which I would plunge and drown should the creaking and waterlogged raft give way beneath me.

Even after reaching the west bank of the Reiber safely and even with the return of Jacques, unharmed, with all of the archers, I could not join in the merriment of the people around me. For them, having escaped the oncoming army, hope soared, along with their appetite. Cooking fires filled the air with a sharp, fruity scent that came from a kind of leek that grew in thick clusters in the moist soil near the river and which the poor were frying in fistfulls.

Wine flagons were being passed to and fro and were drunk from undiluted (I declined those that came my way). Cheerful songs (such as that concerning the foolish mule from Montreuil, which made me homesick again) could be heard on all sides.

Yet I was filled with dread. Because the *mutur* were on the wrong side of the river and Jacques had returned with the news that there was only an hour or two before Prince Slavniak's army was upon them. There was therefore no pleasure to be taken from the sight of sunlight upon verdant forest and shimmering river, only foreboding and a sense that Fate was mocking me. How sweet it was to draw breath on a summer's day, but would those on the other bank be able to do so this evening? If the *mutur* did not cross soon, they would be slaughtered to a man, in a repetition of the massacre that had taken Cateline's father from her.

The *mutur* were standing on the far shore, cursing us with shouts and gestures, while before them the raft, laden with empty boxes and bags, was unmoving.

'You made an oath, Gerard, that you would bring us across the river.' From beside the landing place, Rainulf cupped his hands to shout and his words were clear.

'And so we shall. First, however, you must pay the price of the ferrymen.' A big cheer came up from the crowd at Gerard's response and another when he added, 'Hand over the treasure Rainulf!' It seemed as though everyone had stayed to see whether the *mutur* would be massacred or not and unlike me, they seemed to treat the matter like an ancient Roman spectacle. Happy to be safely across the river, the plight of the *mutur* was merely entertainment for the rowdy farmers and their wives. With dismay, I saw that Cateline was among those who were mocking the *mutur*. Her face was animated with a merry, wild-eyed energy.

'This isn't right,' I said to Jacques, whom I had earlier sought out in order to find out the details of his latest adventure.

'Perhaps not. But there is justice here.'

'How so?' I said, bitterly.

'If Rainulf had not been unfortunate, then he would have crossed with all the treasure and – I would guess – then wrecked the ferry to ensure that we were caught and thus delayed Prince Slavniak.'

'I do not think he would have done that. Yet even if he is the murderous traitor you say he is, what about *render not evil for evil*. Were you never taught that?'

For a moment Jacques' searching glance met mine, but then he looked away and rubbed his fingers across his chin, where a thin blonde stubble was growing. 'No. My schooling was of a different sort to yours.'

Angry, I pushed through the jeering people, until I was near the wooden post on top of which Gerard had climbed so as to call over the river to the *mutur*.

'Gerard! Let them cross Gerard. Prince Slavniak's army will be upon them any moment.'

From all around, men and women, commoners of all ages, turned hostile faces towards me. 'No! Make them pay!'

'There is a pattern here Lord Rocadamour,' Gerard turned to look down at me over the heads of the peasants. 'We only do what Rainulf would do in our place. And he knows it.'

'That's right!'

'Hear him! Hear him!'

Across the water, the *mutur* were moving. They drew up in three lines facing the eastern forest, backs towards us, and my heart sank. It was insanity to think they could hope to win the coming battle on their own.

'It's Rainulf,' I shouted up to Gerard, 'he is too stubborn. He will not back down. You must.'

Even as I proclaimed this I was proven mistaken, the nearest rank of the *mutur* broke from their formation and began to gather the bags and boxes from the raft. Rainulf began to do so also, before suddenly screaming with rage and smashing a chest to pieces with ferocious blows of his two-handed axe. That done, he fell to his knees and it was several minutes before he stood up.

'Very well Gerard! You win!' Rainulf cried across the river, his fury visible even from here, in his furrowed brow and clenched, flawed teeth.

'Hurray!' A really mighty cheer went up from the people around me. And the crowd now began to enjoy themselves further with a cheer each time a bag of coins or chest of silver ornaments was thrown onto the raft.

'What are you doing, mocking the *mutur*? Can you not understand that they will never forgive you for playing with their lives?' I called out to those around me. 'There will be retribution for this.'

The only face that showed any sign of disapproval for what was happening was that of Melinde. She was well back from the bank, up on a grassy rise beside a copse of silver birch. Framed by her short greying fringe, her expression was severe. Her gaze was at a point beyond my right shoulder, at Gerard, and she was shaking her head, slowly.

'No, Lord Rocadamour, I think not.' Gerard was smiling, oblivious to the disapproval of his wife. 'Rainulf is like a March storm, all fury and violence at first, then calm. And we will give them their fair share of the treasure in due course. That will take the edge off their anger.'

Again, good-natured cheers from the crowd greeted Gerard's words. He leaned down towards me and in a quiet voice added, 'There is a risk that this insistence upon his handing over the treasure provokes Rainulf to some wild act in the future, but given the choice of making enemies of my own company or enemies of the *mutur*, it was an easy one.'

Once the *mutur* had stopped loading the raft with bags of coin and silver ornaments, eager hands pulled the ferry back to the west bank with such speed that despite the fast-flowing current, a strong wake formed in the water on either side of the vessel.

'Do we think this is the lot?' asked Gerard loudly as his men lined up to quickly move the silver to the shore, passing the treasure from hand to hand.

'No!' roared his company.

And a cry grew up among the commoners nearby, 'We want more! We want more!'

'More Rainulf,' Gerard shouted across the river. 'Let's have the rest!'

With a groan that was audible to us across the lapping sounds of the river, Rainulf stamped up and down on the earth. 'Come on! Come on! Let us cross!'

'The rest.'

'Sod you, Gerard. All right.'

Again, the triumphant, mocking cries of the crowd surged up all around.

In complete contrast to the mood all around me, I was in agony as the ferry was hauled slowly back and forth over the river.

Was that an unusual number of birds visible above the forest top to the east? Did they presage the arrival of Prince Slavniak's army? And I had other worries too. Once the *mutur* began to board, they packed so many men on to the raft for the first crossing that I was alarmed by how low it was in the water: would they sink it in their desperation to cross?

With rather less enthusiasm than they had demonstrated in hauling the treasure across the Reiber, Gerard's company pulled the *mutur* through the water. As they did so, the crowds began to disperse and the mocking shouts noticeably diminished. It was one matter to shout provocative remarks against the *mutur* when there was a river between the wag and his target but another when the grim-faced thugs were on their way over.

As soon as they could leap off the edge of the raft and make the riverbank, the first group of *mutur* took charge of the ferry rope.

'Come on,' said Gerard as he jumped to the ground. But I stayed to watch the empty raft scurry urgently across the river to the east bank. Again, men hurried aboard the ferry until the wooden base was barely visible in the water. Distressingly, there were still more than half the *mutur* left to face the menace of the eastern forest.

When the next raft-load of warriors was ready, their comrades pulled them to safety with powerful and rhythmic heaves upon the wet rope. In contrast to the ebullient chatter that had existed among the commoners when I had arrived, now hardly a soul spoke. More and more of the people drifted away towards the place – some thirty yards away – where the road entered the forest to the west. If the men of the *mutur* drew the conclusion that none among the other people of our army had any concern for their survival, who would blame them?

It was another three journeys to and fro before Rainulf, the last of the *mutur*, stepped on to the ferry. I could relax at long last. Or, nearly so, for before they began to cross the river, Rainulf struck at the guide ropes with his axe, cutting them on either side and causing the tailing ends of the long snakes of rope to drift downstream, as did the raft of course.

Rainulf and his men disembarked when the raft hit the riverbank some fifty yards north of us. They then cut the raft lose entirely and pushed it back out into the river, so that the current swept it onwards and swiftly out of view.

'What should we do with the ropes?' asked a young member of Rainulf's company when their commander reached us.

'Throw them into the forest, deep enough they'll never be found.'

It took three strong men to carry each of the waterlogged ropes.

'Well, Rocadamour?' Rainulf's face was flushed, whether from heat or anger it was terrible to glance upon. His mouth kept twitching, showing all his teeth; his eyes were sunken but intensely bright; and strange muscles rippled under his cheeks.

I felt that if I misspoke, my life would be lost to the frenzied assault of an insane man and so my mouth – suddenly dry – would not move, nor my eyes look upon him.

'Ware arrows!' One of Rainulf's men shouted.

We all turned, to see horsemen riding into the clearing of the eastern side of the river. Some were already dismounting and drawing bows.

'Ware arrows!' The cry spread and those of the commoners still remaining in the clearing ran for the forest. All of us did. And if Prince Slavniak's men failed to take a life, their arrival at this moment might well have saved one.

16

THE SONG OF COUNT STEPHEN

That night Cateline, Arnulf and I ate black carrots and rabbit, cooked with fistfuls of rosemary in the animal's fat. We should have been happy; after all, the army was across the Reiber with no losses. And if Cateline and Arnulf were cheerful enough, I was not. The *mutur* were camped at the rear of the army once more, about a hundred yards away. And some of their anger was within me.

'What if it had been your father there on the east bank, while Gerard demanded the treasure?'

For a long moment Cateline looked at me with cold eyes. Then she spoke severely, 'How dare you speak of my father.'

'I just want you to see that what happened today was wrong. Arnulf? Don't you agree?'

My sergeant, who had been scratching the bandages on his leg, pulled a backpack close to him, so he could lean on it and sit up straighter.

'My philosophy is that if it ends for the best, it was the right thing to do.'

'But that's absurd.'

'Not as absurd as it might sound, young Rocadamour. And this philosophy allows me to rest easy at night.' He pursed his lips thoughtfully, moustache exaggerating the expression. 'There's nothing more troubling to sleep than an uneasy conscience.'

'Do you think the *mutur* will sleep easy tonight?' I found I was nearly shouting. The inchoate background chatter from the fireplaces either side of us ceased. I dropped my voice, 'Do you think *they* would agree that everything has ended for the best?'

Arnulf shrugged; head down, Cateline concentrated on scooping the last of her meal out of her bowl. Perhaps she was aware of my gaze, for she stopped and looked up at me.

'The *mutur* tried to run away with the treasure and leave us to the wolves. Why do you care for them?'

'Why did you not care if they were killed today? Have you forgotten so soon their courage when they fought at the ambush?' I tried to put as much disappointment into my next words as I could. 'You're not the woman I thought you were.'

'Of course I'm not. You don't know me at all!'

'Now, now. Let us not spoil this fine bit of rabbit.' Arnulf waved his arms with genial understanding, but the gesture was wasted on Cateline; her head was tipped forward, black tresses screening her from us both. 'If I've learned anything from having lived twice as long as you youngsters, it is that harsh words are easily spoken but not so easily forgotten. Sad, isn't it, that people are not the opposite way around?'

I thought about this. 'Let me apologise, Cateline, about your father. I didn't mean any harshness.'

At that moment, two shadows came up to the fire.

'Is that Lord Rocadamour's camp?'

I looked up at an angular face, large ears and twinkling eyes. 'Robert! Welcome, find a place.' I moved sideways for him.

And he was welcome, doubly so. For further to the pleasure of seeing the knight at my fire, I was pleased with an excuse to stop the argument. It was clear that Cateline did not care that the events of this day would have stirred the *mutur* to the bottom of their murderous souls.

'This is Tourpin.'

In contrast to Robert's long nose and clean-shaven cheeks, Tourpin was a fleshy, bearded man, who although not as old as Arnulf had streaks of grey in his wavy black hair.

'Welcome Tourpin. Alas, we have eaten already. But we might have some mead left. Have we?' I asked.

'A mouthful each, maybe.' Arnulf sounded rueful. 'It's in the cart, in the green satchel.'

Without saying a word, Cateline got up to fetch the drink. Robert, as he sat down with great care, let out a groan. Body still thick with layers of bandages, Robert's head looked small in proportion, although his expression was lively enough and he turned to me with a smile.

'Tourpin is a poet.'

'Indeed!' Arnulf's face immediately shone with anticipation. 'What songs do you know?'

'Oh, I've learned one or two. But that's not why I've come.'

'No?' I was curious. Cateline had returned with our stoppered clay jug, which she held out to me across the fire. I gave it first to our poet guest.

'Thank you.' He drank from the jug – a modest sip only – and passed it to Arnulf who was on his left; then Cateline (to my surprise) took a drink; then Robert and lastly the jug returned to me. Arnulf was right, there was hardly enough left to fill my mouth, but I savoured what sweetness there was.

'Tourpin has been writing a new song,' explained Robert. 'For Count Stephen.'

'Aha,' Arnulf settled back.

'And …'

'I'm in it,' I realised.

'Exactly.' Robert's grin, exposing his crooked teeth, was uplifting and although I felt a little trepidation at what I might hear, I found myself smiling in response.

All of us were silent, indeed, the people nearby were silent too. A branch in our fire cracked. Tourpin spoke, in a low, deep voice, made melodious by its northern accents.

King Bratislav looks upon the ruins of Devinium.
He calls his dukes and counsellors before him:
"See, O lords, our misfortune!
"Shalk of famed France has done this to us.
"But we shall have our revenge.
"Advise me now, wise counsellors.
"Save me from shame; speak well."
But none dares to reply, only Duke Carisbald,
The cunning fox…

Robert coughed. 'Skip along there, Tourpin. To Guibert.'

After showing a moment's displeasure, Tourpin rallied himself, then began to recite again. As he did so, other men and women crept a little closer to our fire, forming a second circle around it.

Count Stephen draws Lifestealer *and raises the famous blade.*
"Good sirs, there are but nine of us.
"Ahead, a thousand riders in bright hauberks.
"Beyond them, ten thousand men on foot.
"With sharp spears and hard hearts.
"It is certain that we have seen our last dawn.
"But let us not mourn. Death comes to all.
"While breath remains, we raise our swords and strike.
"To mete out bloody vengeance in this fight!"

Young Lord Rocadamour now gives voice.
"It may be, sir, that this day is our last.

"But out of greed our enemies have opened their ranks.
"Let us fall like raptors upon them and learn our fate.
"For though so few have never yet so many best.
"Ours is the right and our cause be blessed."

They thunder down the road, three abreast.
"This young knight," Count Stephen tells himself,
"Is as brave and noble as a Hector, born again.
"Perhaps he will accomplish great deeds today."
At breakneck gallop the count rides to give the first blow.
With spur to brave Gallifon, he lets go the reins.
Then lashes Lifestealer *through helm and brain.*

The fight is on and though at first dismayed,
King Bratislav shouts to all his men.
"It is just nine knights, hold your ground!
"Not even fair France can produce such a knight
"As can prevail against our numbers.
"So remember Devinium and hold fast.
"See! Already two lay on the ground.
"But wait, what mighty roar is that! Now another,
"From the trees on either hand. Coming fast,
"Are the men of most infamous bands.
"The Milan Company and even worse. Those
"Who do not shun to eat the dead: the defilers:
"The ungodly: the cruel: the mutur.
"But hold your ground! They are but four score.
"And from this day on, will exist no more."

Count Stephen is hard pressed by his enemies,
And proud Gallifon is pierced to his lungs by a spear.
Flesh and entrails are spilled upon the road, the count

Must leap or be trapped by his falling steed.
A hammer crashes and his shield is a ruin of splinters,
Now with broken arm he has no defence.
He strikes true with Lifestealer *on all sides.*
The eastern men are closing in, with eager looks,
And triumphant smiles. The battle is theirs.
But a horse screams fierce and from above.
Like a fish on a hook a man is plucked to writhe
Upon a lance. And Count Stephen is in the clear.
Lord Rocadamour calls out, "Fare thou well?"
"Charge on!" cries Count Stephen, "fear for me not!
"Go to where the press is thick and the fighting hot."

Throwing man and lance to the ground,
Young Rocadamour draws his sword and strikes
Through iron and flesh with every blow.
And even when his steed is on the ground,
He's quickly up and those who dare stand before him
Soon learn that he cannot be denied.
Mars himself strides down the road this day.
Where a trail of bodies marks his passage.
Red from fist to face, from helm to foot
His enemies fear his every step.
Trembling, a man looks on with dread.
Then his body falls, having lost its head.

King Bratislav cannot believe the battle is not won.
"Who is that devil? Has he been stopped?
"No, my ranks part once more and on he comes.
"With the Milan Company to his right.
"And the mutur *to his left.*
"We have no easy task, to halt these men.

"But there, at last, their charge is spent.
"Duke Carisbald will push them back and more.
"He will throw their bodies to the floor.

Count Stephen and his last three knights
Have found each other in the fray.
And back to back guard each other well.
Though the count knows that soon enough
Jabbing spear and slicing axe will take another
Of his knights. But even as his thoughts grow dark
A monstrous roar comes from the trees.
Another army has appeared where none should be.
It is the cook, the nurse, the old and the sick.
The smith, the washerwoman, the former serf.
In their hands are tools not weapons of war.
The world has turned upside down.
To the monks, the nuns, adolescents and wives.
Count Stephen and his knights owe their lives.

Achilles they say was young at Troy.
And Alexander had cut the Gordian knot
Before his beard had grown upon his jaw.
Now rages our prodigy, Lord Rocadamour.

"Follow the youth!" comes the shout from all.
Rocadamour laughs and cries, "Let those who can keep
Up. For I am thunder and lightning. I am
Storm and wrath. I plunge my blade through iron
And bone. Unquenchable heat burns through me,
Like a forest fire." The eastern men cannot halt
This bloody blaze, this flood of ichor.
They panic and flee, an army no more.

King Bratislav flinches at the sight.
"By my right hand, this battle is lost.
"Even Duke Carisbald falls from his saddle
"My troops turn from the fight, faces white,
"While terrible screams come from beyond the crush.
"My counts, we must be gone, already the first
"Arrows and bolts seek our lives."
In shame and sorrow, the king rides away.
His men left to live or die as they may.

'And there you have it!' declared Robert.

The poet closed his mouth with a frown, though applause rang out from around our fire. I was surprised at how many people had gathered close.

'Well done, Tourpin, well done indeed. You must come to Castle Rocadamour', said Arnulf earnestly. 'Lord Rocadamour will reward you well for such a splendid work. *I am thunder and lightning.* Well said, well said.' He struggled to his feet and leaned into the darkness of our cart.

'I knew you'd like it', said Robert and turned to me. 'What about you, Rocadamour? What did you think?'

I could imagine our hall: my parents, William and Alice and all our knights, listening to this song. The image of the scene was at the same time a wonder, a daydream come true, and source of sadness to me. For if I were to be suddenly granted a wish, it would be to leave this awful forest and to find myself back among my family and friends.

'I liked it of course. What knight doesn't wish to be the hero of legend?

From the cart, Arnulf tossed several silver coins into Tourpin's lap.

'But?' asked the poet, looking at me before he turned his attention to the coins.

'I didn't rescue Count Stephen, nor speak to him.'

'Oh, is that all?' Tourpin chuckled, a deep warm laugh, one that found an echo among men, women and children in all directions. 'Tis art. The song requires it. If you want history, speak of your deeds to a scribe. If you want fame, then have me leave the verse as it stands.'

'Very well.' I found myself hoping that Cateline had been impressed by the song, but her pale face was impassive. 'If Count Stephen minds it not.'

'Oh, he enjoys the song,' Robert waved his left hand through the air. 'Don't be concerned for his sake.'

'Again! Tourpin, sing it again!' An elderly woman called out from our cart, where she had taken a seat.

'Aye, especially the line about the cook.'

'Says Cookie!'

The good cheer of the crowd could not help but lift my spirits too. The poet stood up, bowed, and drew breath. And as Tourpin's melodious voice rang out once more, I settled back, knowing that I had a broad smile on my face.

This time, Tourpin could sing the whole of his song without interruption, Robert biding himself patiently until my name was mentioned in the verses, whereupon he nudged me and grinned with complicity.

Again, warm applause greeted the conclusion of Tourpin's performance. Applause from a surprising number of people.

'Thank you, thank you. If you haven't a penny, an apple will do nicely.'

A moment later an apple hit the poet on his large chest and fell to the ground near me.

'Too kind.' He picked it up and gave me a wink, before rubbing the apple on his arm and taking a bite.

Someone had a drum, which began to beat. Another had a whistle, which began to play a melody that I recognised. Nor was I the only one, soon a dozen voices were singing *Apples and Pears;* then followed *Jack's-A-Sleeping.* By the fourth song, a skin of wine had been passed to me (which, though its scent and taste was rank, I drew from so as not to be considered rude) and I was amused to hear the gusto with which Arnulf and Robert were singing; even Cateline had allowed good humour to fill her. Her face was relaxed and she gave me a smile that set my heart beating swiftly.

Yet how did this revelry sound to the men sitting quietly in the darkness to our east?

17

FOREST BEASTS

On Gerard's instruction, the army waited a day, just out of view of the river crossing, ready to attack any advanced party that dared cross. After that day had passed, with no sign that Prince Slavniak's army were even gathering at the Reiber, let alone attempting to cross the river, we took the decision to hurry westwards once more. And although I retained a certain anxiety that we would suddenly be assaulted from the east, three days passed with no cry of alarm from our scouts; the feeling grew in the army that Prince Slavniak had ceased his pursuit of us.

A sense of foreboding nevertheless seeped into my heart. In part it arose from the sustained hostility of the *mutur* towards the rest of the army. No good could come from the way they kept themselves apart from the rest of us. Those – like me – who tried to talk to the *mutur* were greeted with silence and angry looks. Would they even fight alongside everyone else, should we find ourselves in battle again?

The forest too, played a role in forming my anxiety. Here, thick clusters of spikewoods lined the road, their twisted branches reaching towards us like straining arms. Knots in the squat trunks of these trees gave them faces with angry expressions. The road, also, became less friendly, losing its easy-going solidity. For long stretches – miles at a time – it was broken up, with the invasive roots of those same spikewoods forcing up the old Roman slabs and even splitting the thick stones.

This was the wildest part of the forest. No lord governed here, despite the claims of the Duke of Saxony to all the lands up to the banks of the Reiber. There were bears, wolves and ferocious boars here aplenty. But the beasts living in the shelter of the dark trees were not the main danger to our army. Of far greater concern were the communities of outlaws that lived in the depths of the forest. Last month, when we had marched eastwards, even though our army was vast compared to the tiny force that were returning, we had suffered from the forest pagans. Those of our poor people unfortunate enough to fall behind the army through sickness or accident never caught up with us again. Our scouts would report the discovery of bodies on the road, decapitated, possessions taken: boots, belts, cloaks and sometimes even shirts and trousers. No doubt, these robbers and murderers were lurking again at the rear of our army even now, waiting for someone to fall so far behind that our rearguard (the *mutur*) were out of sight.

Gerard, however, seemed to be in excellent humour. 'A grand day, Lord Rocadamour, and another day closer to home.' He was marching some fifty yards ahead of his troops, more or less half the distance to Count Stephen's knights. Walking with him was Jacques and, of course, Melinde.

From my vantage in my saddle, I looked down at Gerard's balding, close-shaven head. 'I care not for these woods and will be glad when we reach the lands of Bishop Wernher, though he be no friend of ours.'

'Bishop Wernher,' Gerard repeated, no longer sounding so cheerful. 'Aye, he could be a problem. We'll cross that bridge when we come to it.'

'Did you try talking to Rainulf?' asked Melinde, looking past Gerard's shoulder to meet my eye.

'I did. But he told me to leave.'

'And with a colourful expression, I'm sure.' Gerard shared a grin with Jacques.

Melinde frowned. 'Do you think he'll join our ranks in battle, should the need arise?'

'Of course he will. He's not going to bring ruin and death to his own people out of petulance.' Gerard lifted his arm to Melinde's shoulders, to pull her to him affectionately, but she fended him off impatiently, the better to see me.

'I'm not so sure.' I adjusted my seat. 'There's something … unpredictable … Rainulf is a hard, dangerous man.'

'He is dangerous,' agreed Jacques. 'But if he wants his share of the treasure – and he does – he'll play his part in getting us through to France again.'

Shouts came from behind us, interrupting our conversation. There was motion too, but it was confused, soldiers running back down the road, pushing past women and children who were hurrying the opposite way.

Immediately, I turned my destrier and rode east towards the trouble. I had not waited to see if Gerard and the others were following me, but when I was forced to slow to a walk because of the crush, I heard Gerard shouting out from nearby.

'What's the alarm? What's amiss?'

'Pagans!'

'Over here!'

By the time we arrived at the point where soldiers from the Milan Company were formed up and facing the northern line of trees, it was far too late.

When I saw Arnulf looking around wildly, sword in hand and his leg bandages soaked red, my stomach lurched.

'What happened?' I called across to him.

'Guibert. They've taken her. Cateline. And Tenebrour.'

'Who?'

'Seven men, two of them with antlers on their helms.'

In response to the urgent command of my body, the destrier pushed his way through the press, men staggering as they were forced out of my way by the thrust of his powerful legs.

'That way?'

'Yes.'

And I was off into the spikewoods, ducking branches and searching for the widest spaces. Head down near that of my horse, whispering encouragement to him, we made good progress despite the thorns which seemed to deliberately hold us back. After perhaps ten minutes of riding like this, however, I began to feel as though a cape of despair had settled on my back. Unhappiness sank into my body and I signalled the destrier to halt. There was no sign that any man had ever been in this part of the ancient forest, much less a horse. My dash to find the raiders had been useless, worse it had wasted valuable time. I had to go back and look for the trail.

There was a large crowd gathered at the spot where I had entered the forest, including Rainulf and the *mutur*, who had come up to the rest of the army.

'No good.' I called out. 'We'll have to find their trail, who will come with me?'

No one answered.

I looked at Jacques, but he just shook his head.

'We have to keep marching for France.' This from an apologetic Andreas.

'I'll give ten silver shillings to the man who comes with me.'

Still no response.

'Go on then!' I shouted at them all in a fury. 'Take to the road once more. But I'm riding after her.' Whatever fate she faced now, it would be a grim one and one that most probably would end with her death. I could not abandon her to that darkness, even though it seemed like the rest of the army could.

Unexpectedly, Gerard spoke up for me. 'Sing out. Three volunteers for Lord Rocadamour, for God's sake. Have you all forgotten what we owe him?'

Heartened, I rose in the saddle. Yet I saw no willing faces, only dour, anxious ones.

'For shame. All right Rocadamour, I'm with you.' Gerard took an axe from the man next to him. 'Anyone else?'

'You know, none of those who chased the pagans into the forest were ever seen again.' Melinde spoke softly, but there was a murmur of agreement from all around. She placed a hand on Gerard's arm. 'Don't go.'

'Fear not. We'll return. Keep the army moving.' Gerard shrugged off her hand and raised his voice. 'Let Andreas be your commander.'

Despite the evident pain that was shown by repeated violent twinges of his moustache, Arnulf limped to me with a satchel and a nosebag of fodder from the cart.

'Here, take these.'

'Which way, exactly?' Gerard asked him.

'See the three aspens in a row? Between them.'

'Grand so. Ready then?'

'Thank you Gerard.'

'I'll lead. For the trail.'

And without farewells, he entered the forest. As my destrier walked after him I looked around. There were plenty of grim faces and, in Melinde's case, a tearful one. Arnulf too looked as though tears were near, though that was probably the agony of his wound.

From his position on the road further back, Rainulf raised his hammer in salute to me. Surprised, I nodded in return.

'Wait!' I was just entering the forest when Jacques ran up. 'God knows what it is about you. This is the worse one yet and I fear my luck is all spent. But I'll come.'

'Good man,' said Gerard from up ahead.

'Thank you Jacques.' With such a fine archer at our side, the prospect of our being victors if we met these seven men was much improved. Some of my despair lifted. As Jacques passed me to assist Gerard in locating the trail, I found myself smiling at his back. The round-about appeal to fate with which Jacques greeted every risk was clearly a superstitious ritual. And perhaps he was not always so resigned to imminent death as he made out. Encouraged by this thought, I did not let the obvious anxiety of Arnulf and Melinde affect my courage.

There was no talk as we made our way deeper into the forest. What was there to say?

After an hour we came to a wide, shallow stream, something of a river even, with a bed of flat rounded stones, red in colour.

'They made their way along here,' Gerard pointed north, downstream. 'It's the east bank I'll walk upon; Jacques take the west, will you now, and Rocadamour, you should ride in the water looking at the bed. Let's move slowly and make sure we don't miss the place where they got out.'

My destrier was willing enough to enter the stream and took his time drinking from it. He was reluctant, however, to step downstream along the stones. I decided to dismount and follow Gerard.

When he saw this, he said only, 'Keep an eye on the bed of the stream for signs that your captured stallion walked there.'

An hour of attentive walking. Then another. Nothing. Had we missed their turn? Had the raiders really taken to the stream for so long, afraid of pursuit? Gerard must have been sharing my concerns for he stopped and called Jacques over.

'What thoughts, friends?'

'I don't know.' Jacques shook his head. 'I think we might have missed it. There were a few rocky places where a horse might have left the water without much of a sign.'

'Aye. Anything on the stream bed?'

'Not this last hour,' I said.

Gerard sighed and looked around. Here, the forest was old and thick. The fallen trunks that lay in the dark of the afternoon shadows were covered in moss, mushrooms and toadstools.

I was discouraged.

'It seems to me,' said Gerard, 'we may as well continue. But then towards evening, make for higher ground to see if they betray themselves with a fire.'

'Very well.' Jacques crossed over to the west bank. And we had not gone a hundred yards when he called out.

'Here!'

My heart leapt.

When we reached him, Jacques opened his hand. A thin leather cord, only two inches long, was resting on his palm. 'It was just there, by that orange fern.'

'You've the eyes of a hawk!' Gerard exclaimed. He got down on his hands and knees and parted long grasses. 'Aye, they tried to hide their trail by stepping on these, because they bend and spring back rather than break. But the hooves of your stolen horse have left their mark underneath.'

'I wonder was it Cateline?' I picked the leather cord from Jacques and held it close. 'She uses ties like these.'

'Is she cunning?' asked Jacques.

'I suppose so. Why?'

'Because if I were a prisoner and my group were using a stream to hide our trail, I would prepare something that I could drop: something that might be found without being too obvious to my captors. Then I'd wait until we left the stream to leave it for those who were coming after me.'

'Yes, that was Cateline.'

'Good,' Gerard stood up, 'so she believes you are coming for her. And that means she'll try to stay alive. No matter what that entails.'

18

I WILL TRACK THEM DOWN

When the shadows of the forest floor became too dark to see the trail, Gerard chose our camp. Above the orange-tinged trunks of alder, oak and beech was a sky that was still light, with just the earliest stars visible. Our enemies would be making progress towards wherever it was they were going, for another hour at least. But we could no longer be sure of their path.

As I dismounted, perhaps my concerns showed in my face, for Gerard patted my arm consolingly.

'The weather is dry, thank God. Their spore should still be clear enough in the morning.'

I didn't reply, but began to unstrap the tack from my destrier.

'Is this our camp?' asked Jacques.

'Aye.'

'Don't you think it might be a water course?'

'Could be.'

'Well. Aren't we risking a damp night?'

'It will not rain tonight.'

'I'm not so sure. Let's go up that slope a little, to the bluebells.'

'Very well so,' said Gerard, after a pause and a glance towards me.

After I'd brushed down my horse and given him some oats, I led him up to the two men and undid my own armour, which slid heavily to the ground. Then I spread out the chainmail and sat upon it, Gerard on my right and beyond him, Jacques.

'What have we got to eat?' asked Gerard, 'I'm starving.'

I looked in the satchel that Arnulf had given me. 'Peas. Strips of dried pork. This cheese.'

Gerard's hopeful look faded. 'We can't risk a fire to cook the peas.'

'I've boiled eggs.' Jacques tossed an egg over to me, then handed another to Gerard. 'I've some apples too, but think to save them for the morning.'

'Is there water?' Gerard asked, after quickly eating his egg. I got up and brought back my water skin and my wine skin.

'Good man. Boiled eggs always make my mouth dry. I'd have another all the same though, Jacques, if you had more.'

'One more each.'

The cheese was old and hard. It took me a while to cut the block into three, taking care not to slice my hand. After we'd eaten that, we shared the pork strips.

'Not bad,' said Jacques. 'I've had worse suppers.'

Gerard smiled. 'Many's the night we had nothing at all.'

I was still hungry, but he was right about the peas. I had my hunting bow with me though. 'Once we've rescued Cateline, I can hunt.'

'And there is plenty of food in the forest this time of year if we're no longer in a hurry,' observed Jacques with a wave of his hand. 'Nuts and fungi and nettles and the like.'

'Ah well.' Gerard took a long drink of water. 'So here we are.'

'Twixt somewhere and nowhere.' Jacques lay back on his cloak.

'Well,' I said, 'not nowhere. They must be living somewhere.'

'True,' allowed Jacques, 'some runaway village.'

'How do you mean, runaway village?' I asked, wondering at cottages that could move.

'You seen them I'm sure, a cluster of wooden homes made by escaped serfs, or outlaws.'

'Oh. Not really. Sometimes a serf runs. But they hardly ever get far. One time, though, Count Theobald sent one of ours all the way back from Troyes. Runaways would never manage to set up a home or a village of their own kind.'

'No, not in France maybe,' said Gerard somberly, 'but I've seen such villages in Burgundy and Lotharingia, some of them towns nearly. And it's probably something like that we are going to find here. This land hasn't been farmed since the Flood. It's wild and out of the grasp of any lord. I'd come here myself, were I an outlaw.' He paused. 'And a pagan.'

Jacques shook his head. 'Not I. I'd miss the comforts of life. I'd go east. To Byzantium. I'm told they pay well for good soldiers.'

'With your wife and child?' I asked.

'If they wanted to.'

'What about you, Guibert?' Gerard had drawn out a whetstone and was putting a new edge on one of his knives with slow, careful motions.

'What about me?'

'If you had to run as an outlaw, where would you go?'

'There's no man who could make me an outlaw.'

'Not even the king?'

'Well, possibly. But he doesn't trouble us much at Rocadamour.'

'So, where would you go?'

'A long way away I suppose. Ireland maybe?'

Gerard gave a start. 'Now there's a fine choice.'

'Would you ever go back?' asked Jacques.

'Are you from Ireland?' I spoke at the same time.

'I am,' Gerard replied. 'And I would go back. Melinde and I thought we'd end our days at Jerusalem. But that's done with and so it's to Ireland we'll travel. God willing, we survive this damned forest.'

'What's it like, Ireland?' I wondered aloud.

'Like?' He paused in his work. 'It is a great land for a youth. A land of sports, storytelling, feasting and boasting. And it is a great land for a monk. But I wouldn't recommend it to a knight or to an outsider.'

'Why not?'

'There are a hundred kings in Ireland, each with a dozen princes, each with a dozen lords and each of them has at least a dozen followers. But every one of these men reckons a descent from the high-kings and that he would make a great and famous king himself one day. So fortunes rise and fall there faster than anywhere else in the world.

'In Italia, I've lived there long enough that I can usually pick the winning side. Right Jacques?'

'That is why I love you.'

'But in Ireland. Well, the man you back can rise one day and be out the next, blinded or killed and you with him. Melinde and I are nearly old and will be happy to live out our last years on a farm near Clonmacnoise, where I grew up. But would you be happy as a farmer?'

'No.'

'You would not. An outlaw in Ireland, you would ride and fight for a lord and you would pay the consequence when that lord falls, as he will.'

'Very well. Ireland is out then.' I spoke with a smile and Gerard smiled in return, before returning to the care of his weapons.

'Jacques?' I leaned forward to see him better, past Gerard.

'Hmm?'

'When did you meet Gerard?'

'I can tell you that exactly. It was the feast day of Saint Acestes, on the Piazza del Campo of Siena, shortly before the horse races they have there. Remember?' He looked at Gerard.

'Of course.'

'There was an archery contest. The final round had the prize, a pouch of silver, on a cord against a board on one side of the square. My opponent picked the token that let him go first, but was six inches out. I cut the cord, first shot.'

'Not a man in the square failed to cheer,' added Gerard, 'it was the most beautiful sight, a bolt traveling so far and hitting so slender a target.'

'After the noise and the pushing had died down, Gerard came up to me and said he wanted me in his army.'

'Well, it was John Crescenti's army, I was his captain.'

'Indeed. But I said "no". '

'He had a bag of silver. What need of being a mercenary? But I'm glad I asked.'

'As am I. Because that silver didn't last the night. Too many thieves had their eyes on it and there's no authority can control the crowds of that town on race day. I was lucky to escape Siena unwounded. After that, Gerard's offer seemed a more attractive one.'

'And here you are,' Gerard waved his arm like a generous host, 'in a dark and Godforsaken forest, hungry and a long way from the comforts you enjoy so much. Aren't you glad you came along?'

I'd noticed before that Jacques laughed easily, with a kind of snigger, and he did so now, while Gerard's lively eyes turned to me to check that I too was amused. His smile grew broader.

Later, in the dark, Gerard asked quietly, were we both awake.

We were.

'In that case, Guibert, would you run up a tree now and see if our raiders have been foolish enough to light a fire?'

'Very well.'

It was very, very dark, just a little starlight to see the tops of the trees by. So picking a good, climbable, tall one was not easy. A nearby oak seemed the best prospect and the two men lifted me up until I could reach the lowest branch and pull myself up. Climbing trees was another pastime of my youth and I had no fear, not even at night. After all, there was always a branch in reach of my hands and under my feet. In fact, it was easier, with no sight of the ground. Up and up

I went, higher and higher, until the whole treetop began to sway with my weight.

The night sky was clear and full of stars, with only a few constellations masked by clouds. The *Via Lactae* was brighter and milkier than I'd ever seen it before. To the south, there was something in the blackness: a very faint hint of colour that I couldn't fix upon but which was definitely present at the edge of my vision. It could well be light from the campfires of our army, which lay in that direction.

To the north, however, there was nothing but complete and utter blackness. I stared and stared into that dark, wide-eyed and attentive, for a long time. Then, just before descending, I had a feeling that the sky was not quite as it should be. For a while I just waited; then my mind found the mystery. It was Venus. She was flickering like a star, not a planet, and sometimes disappearing altogether. I climbed down.

At the bottom of the tree, Jacques and Gerard greeted me and held my lower legs as I hung from the bottom branch.

'Well?' asked Gerard.

'No fire, but I think perhaps their smoke was rising through Venus. She was sometimes invisible.'

Gerard gave me a pat. 'Good eyes, Lord Rocadamour, you have very good eyes.'

'Which direction is that?' asked Jacques.

Drawing my foot back and forth through the leaves and twigs and acorn-cups that lay thick around the oak tree, I made a line, which pointed between north and northwest.

19

VENGEANCE RENDERED

Not much dew fell in the forest, but in the morning (heralded by a huge roar of birdsong) I rubbed down my destrier vigorously for a good while all the same before putting on his tack. Jacques and Gerard waited patiently until I mounted – with aching, cold legs – and then they set off.

'Do you still have the trail?' I called out to them.

'We do,' answered Gerard.

And that was the last word spoken by anyone until we reached a spacious copse in which a large willow stood out among the birch.

From over his shoulder Jacques drew his bow and began to wind it.

'What's amiss?' I spoke quietly.

Returning to me with a look of lively excitement, Gerard took the destrier's bit and walked me further into the copse. Once past the nearest arms of the willow, I could see the rest of the tree and the heavy scars it bore. Someone had cut through a dozen branches with a saw.

'They live near here, I'd stake my arm on it. There's a path of sorts now too.' He pointed to the ground to the north, where a line of flattened grass ran through the trees.

'Ready,' said Jacques, with a steady, unconcerned voice. My heart, by contrast, was jumping with excitement. Though none of us had spoken as if finding our enemies was anything but a certainty, the greater part of my recent thoughts had dwelt upon the fear that we would lose the trail and that I would never find Cateline again.

'Hold back twenty yards, will you.' It seemed so natural that Gerard would take charge that I no longer had the slightest resistance to the idea that a footsoldier should command a knight. Such social distinctions no longer appeared as absolute as I had been brought up to believe.

Up ahead, Jacques led the way with cradled crossbow; Gerard was close behind him. The signs of human activity increased: more trees with sawn-off branches, some entirely chopped down to the stump; a wider, more frequently trodden path; swathes of grass and flowers chewed down to the ground by animals (goats or pigs?); old and dried out dog droppings.

Then, strangely, Gerard staggered.

Immediately, I urged my mount to hurry forward, fearful that he had been struck by an arrow. As we drew near to where he was kneeling, gasping, my destrier suddenly stiffened, front hooves planted firmly and unmoving; I nearly fell forward over his neck. This too was alarming. A warhorse was trained to keep moving onwards, even into murderous battle with its lethal blades and deafening screams. What could possibly have brought my horse to a halt?

Then it reached me, a stench of decay and death so powerful I felt my stomach convulse and I vomited onto the ferns below. That act brought me some relief from the smell and I regained some control over myself despite recurrent spasms of my stomach.

'What is it?' I called out.

White-faced, Gerard straightened up, shaking his head. It was Jacques who replied, removing his face from the crook of his elbow to do so.

'Come and see.'

Despite a growing revulsion at the putrescent smell, I got off my trembling horse and walked up to where Jacques and Gerard were standing appalled.

The grove beyond them was a bowl shape, like an old Roman amphitheatre, one made from earth, grass and bushes. In the centre of the grove was a huge, ancient yew tree, whose long arms reached in all directions to the sides of the glade. The lower branches were stripped of leaves, instead they bore corpses of animals. Hanging upside-down, feet tied to the yew tree, were dozens of creatures, large and small, a badger, dog and rabbit among the latter, a horse, deer and bear the former. All of them were missing their heads.

On a second look, what I thought were rocks around the base of the tree were skulls, mostly old and entirely stripped of flesh. Some, however, were still in a state of decay. Among them were human faces. Unable to turn away, I looked again at the decaying bodies and especially those in the green shadows of the far side of the yew tree. As I feared, there was a headless human corpse dangling from cords around its feet; to my relief it was male.

Then, to the north of the horrific pagan temple, a dog began barking, loud and in earnest.

All three of us reacted as though being awoken from slumber. Running back to my horse, I mounted, with difficulty, then I drew my shield around from my back and hurriedly tightened its straps over my right arm. Sword out in my left hand, I turned the destrier to our left, leading the horse on a circuitous path through the woods towards the far side of the grove, towards the barking. Because he had run in a straight line, Gerard was ahead of me, while Jacques remained by the grove, preparing his crossbow.

Distant voices. The dog silent now.

If we stopped to try to learn more about our enemies, they would have the advantage. They knew this forest and would creep about until able to ambush us, perhaps from behind. It may have been that I was going to my death, but at least I wasn't waiting for it like a fool.

As I rode past him, I looked over my shield to Gerard, his worried eyes glanced up from a pale face. But he didn't say anything and all at once my fears flowed away from me as though I had emerged from a cold river into warm sunshine. To Gerard's evident amazement, I laughed aloud as I approached the edge of the tree-line and beyond it, a man-made clearing.

Ten strides more and my destrier brought me into bright sunshine, causing me to blink to adjust my vision. On my left, a narrow stream formed a silver boundary. On my right were two cabins and behind them, pens with pigs inside. Ahead, a kind of earthen plaza, about forty yards square, with three more cabins marking the far side of it. One, I noticed – with the kind of heightened powers of observation that come in a crisis – had a pair of chickens on the roof. There was a post in the square, to which Tenebrour was hobbled (how glad I was to see him again). Here was the barking dog: a savage, throaty mongrel three feet high. Here too were four men and a youth, hurriedly arming themselves; three bore spears, two longbows, and they were spread out without formation. That left at least two more men from their raiding party somewhere, perhaps indoors or perhaps in the trees beyond the stream? Plus other men and women might live in this vile, pagan village.

'Give me back my horse and the girl and I'll leave you unharmed.'

'Nei!' The man who shouted at me was the eldest, about Gerard's age with a thick black and white beard. Then he added something like, 'ziy cough get horse zu uns!' Staring at me in hate, the elder made the action of a dagger being drawn across his throat. The other men took heart from his confidence and raised their weapons.

Not wanting to give any others – especially any archers – more time to get into position, I attacked.

Screaming as loudly as I could, I rode as if intent on reaching their leader. Instead, however, I swerved to ride for the far corner of the square, the one away from the stream. This split my enemies, three on my left, two on my right. An arrow embedded itself on my shield, another smacked against my ribs on my left side, turning my war cry into a gasp. But the chain links of my armour held and the arrow deflected on past. A spear that jabbed at me from my left was fast but easy to anticipate and I slashed away its head. On my right the youth stumbled and didn't even get a blow in.

I had no intention of staying to fight and letting the pagans surround me; I kept going, riding up to the farthest of the three cabins, planning to circle behind it and re-enter the square from by the stream. By then Gerard and Jacques would be ready to help. And if the raiders chased me, I might stop to fight if I could isolate one or two of them. As I rode around the back of the wooden cabin, however, I was surprised to see that instead of a clear route, there were pig pens. Despite having slowed for the turn, I trusted in the training of my warhorse and urged him to take the nearest fence with a jump. He cleared it with ease – God love him – and now I was riding through the filth, scattering the terrified pigs.

Only the dog came after me, ducking under the bottom rung of the fence to leap yelping at my horse's flanks. Caught by a lashing hoof, the dog's raging howls were cut off, changed to an agonised howl. My steed now having lost his gait, we couldn't jump again as I had planned. But the next fence was flimsy enough and the destrier crashed through it without our losing any speed. As I rounded the side of the last cabin and returned to the open space, I ducked a flickering arrow and another stuck in my saddle by my thigh, penetrating deep enough to draw a whiney from my destrier.

One of the pagans was down! Jacques, faithful Jacques, must have arrived because their bearded spokesman lay in a pool of blood, bolt in his chest. From what I knew of my friend and his crossbow, Jacques (ducked back behind a tree somewhere?) would need another minute to prepare his second shot.

I rode at the nearest man – an archer – this time in earnest. Next to the man who was my target, the youth made a better effort with his spear, it was an obvious lunge, however, and easily deflected with my shield.

Fear made my archer miss his nock and my sword collapsed his bow and cut his arm off near the elbow. In the meantime, the man whose spear I had emasculated on my last pass straightened up from where he had just picked up the spear of his fallen leader. Since I was off balance, his thrust could have been dangerous. But to the loud twang of Jacques's bow, a bright spurt of blood jetted from his neck. The bolt had passed right through the man's throat.

My destrier slowed to a canter then a trot around the square. Although we were no longer moving in haste, my thoughts were racing. So, two pagan spearmen and one archer were out of the fight; the other archer now dropped his bow and leaping over the stream ran into the forest. Only the youth remained on his feet and I stared at him over my shield. The point of his spear was wavering.

'If I run, you leave me?' he asked.

'If you stay for two more minutes, you'll be killed by a crossbow bolt.'

He backed away, towards the cover of the cabins.

'Run!' I shouted. 'And don't come back.'

Instead, he surprised me by dropping his spear. 'My father. Let him me help.' The lad pointed to where the wounded archer sat holding his stump, blood pouring from it.

At the word 'father', the scarlet glow that filled me dissipated and I was myself again. I pitied him and, after all, he was nearly my age.

'Go ahead.'

The boy ran to wind a tourniquet around the stricken limb.

From the trees on the far side of the stream came Gerard, bright red blood on his waist.

'You all right?' I called out.

'Unhurt. I killed one, the other ran.'

'Hey boy. Where's the girl?'

'Over there.'

Patting my destrier on the neck and whispering nonsense to calm him, I walked him to the indicated cabin and dismounted. It took a moment for my eyes to adjust from the bright day to the dark interior but there she was: naked, gagged, face down on a pile of deerskins, tied with arms and legs stretched out in an X. Cateline's head could turn enough to see me.

In order to draw a dagger, I dropped my sword to the earthen ground and hurried to kneel beside her, cutting through the gag easily enough, though the ropes took more effort.

'Thank you, Guibert.' Though said with a choked, dry voice the heartfelt gratitude in her words was as intense a sentiment as I'd ever heard. The thought of what she must have endured brought tears to my eyes.

Sitting beside her, while she rubbed her wrists and ankles, I was lost for words. I wanted to say how sorry I was for her suffering. Yet I knew that she would grow fierce if she detected pity in my voice. So I took off my gauntlets and rested a hand on her – cold – back.

'I'm so glad we found you.'

'As am I. I trusted that you'd try: trusted in your honour. But I was afraid that even with the horse leaving prints, you'd lose the trail.'

'Did you drop a cord at the first stream?'

'I did.'

'That was well done.'

I was looking around the room and had recognised her clothes, when she looked up sharply at the sound of voices. Gerard was talking to the men outside.

'How did you know our army was on the road?'

'We not know.' It was the boy speaking, nervously. 'We wait the road sometimes, maybe someone comes.'

Before this morning, I had frequently sensed Cateline remove herself from me, to withdraw to a world of her own thoughts. But never was this so evident as it was now. With dead eyes and a frozen face, she stood up, naked, white. Like a soul returning from Hades, she walked out into the sunshine from the dark cabin, not before picking up my sword in her right hand.

'Cateline!'

I reached the door in time to see her stab and hack at the boy, until she was drenched in red blood and he had stopped moving. Horror filled the face of the father, with the agonised lines of his face all the more taut as he turned his eyes from the body of his child to the spectre whose sword flashed in the air above him. He didn't flinch as it came down.

'Christ!' murmured Jacques, aghast.

Dropping the sword, Cateline walked slowly (as if in a dream) to the flowing water and began to wash the gore from her arms.

'It was her right.' With a face that displayed equal shock, Gerard nevertheless defended her actions.

'I agree.' I picked up my sword and went towards the stream.

'She's another Judith,' Gerard added, as if to convince himself.

'No,' Jacque's voice dropped to a fearful, reverential whisper. 'It's like we're in the presence of one of the Erinyes, come again from the ancient past.' And he crossed himself.

Cateline was shivering. Hurriedly, I went back for her clothes. Having rubbed her dry, I left the empty-eyed Cateline to dress herself while I examined Tenebrour.

As I talked to him, my stallion was delighted to see me, skipping too and fro and bumping my chest with his wise-looking head. Encouragingly, his wound was dry and healing well. It was still too soon for him to carry a rider, except perhaps in emergency. But he could carry some of our equipment.

'Shall we butcher a pig?' asked Jacques.

'We shall not. There are bound to be more of these villages around here and we don't have time. What's more, I am in no hurry to see any more blood, even that of the pig.' For a veteran of so many battles, Gerard looked surprisingly shaken.

'I'll take a couple of chickens though. We'll be glad of them tonight.'

'Very well, so.'

With Jacques first, next Gerard, then Cateline leading Tenebrour, lastly me on the destrier, we walked steadily through the forest towards the road. It should have been a triumphant, happy journey, another success against the odds, another heroic act of chivalry. I felt nothing like this, only weariness.

20

FLY AWAY, BLACKBIRDS

It troubled me that Cateline did not speak as we travelled. And what could I say to her? To talk of anything but her experiences seemed false; to talk of them, cruel. What's more, I was haunted by the thought that pagan warriors were hurrying after us and that there was a real danger my decapitated body would end up swinging by the heels from an old yew tree, my head beside the trunk. It was in grim silence then that we tramped southwards through the spikewoods.

Eventually, there was not enough light to see the ground that we walked upon and Gerard called a halt. While I tended the horses, the others cleared brambles from a patch of undergrowth that was nearly completely screened by a dense thicket of waxy holly leaves. There we sat, barely able to see one another despite the fact our feet almost met at the centre of our little clearing.

'Could you understand what they were saying, Cateline, your captors?' asked Gerard.

'No.'

'The boy said they were not expecting us on the road, but that they were just waiting for anyone who might fall to their ambush. Do you think that's true?'

'I've no idea.'

'Did you see more of them than the seven who took you?'

'No.'

'Do you think there are more settlements nearby? That we are in danger still?'

There was no answer to this from Cateline.

'I think there are plenty more,' said Jacques after a while. 'Those sacrifices we saw looked like they served a great many more people than seven.'

'They must have women somewhere too,' mused Gerard.

The thought that we were being pursued troubled me and for a while we discussed our plans for dawn, deciding that to continue back to the road remained the wisest course of action.

I put my arms around Cateline, intending to draw her to me, so she could lie her head upon my chest, but she resisted with surprising strength and determination. Instead, she remained sitting, arms clasped around her knees.

Laying on my side, worried at the harm that had befallen Cateline and listening to the birds and animals that rustled the branches of a now black forest, I fully expected to be awake for hours. A langour, however, crept over me and with it came dreams of home: again and again I discovered the hiding places of William and Alice as we played in the woods.

* * *

If we were subdued making our way back through the forest, we became rather more cheerful upon reaching the road with no sound of pursuit having ever troubled us. There, we hurried on, Cateline on my new destrier, while I led Tenebrour.

'What's the hungriest you've ever been?' I asked my companions.

'Me?' Jacques looked up.

'Both of you.'

'The winter five years ago was pretty bad, wouldn't you agree Gerard? In Burgundy.'

'Oh it was. Not that we were worried at first. Around new year, meat was as cheap as I've ever known it. You see, floods in autumn had ruined the crops. There was no fodder and the farmers were having to kill their beasts.'

'By spring the meat had long gone and we were down to the year-old hard butter they make there. Rotten, putrid barrels of the stuff came to our camp.' Jacques winced at the memory. 'You couldn't eat it without being sick, unless you melted tiny spoonfuls in cauldrons of hot water first.'

'Mind you. If you held your nose and gulped the drink down, it kept you alive.' Gerard shrugged. 'And the taste of that butter wasn't as bad as the taste of the boiled leather from our belts and shoes.'

Jacques smiled. 'Speak for yourself; my belt made a broth that would have graced the table of an emperor.'

'An emperor who was trying to poison his guests maybe.'

With never a word from Cateline, we walked at a good rate through a tunnel of ash trees. By the late afternoon, I began to anticipate catching up with the army. Surely around the next corner, or over the next crest, we would see the rearguard? In fact, it was not until about an hour before sunset that we came across a clear sign that our people were near: an elderly man – a farmer by his dress – and his wife came into view. The man was lying on his back, stretched out; she was kneeling by him.

'God be with you and how are you?' Gerard squatted down beside the couple.

It was the woman who answered. 'Not well, sir. Not well at all.' Now I was closer I could see tears in her eyes.

'Dying is he?'

'Not more than you,' said the white-haired man, opening his eyes. 'It's my knees. I can't walk any more.'

'So they left you behind?'

'Not our people. They would have found me a donkey or a cart. It was the *mutur*. Because of our slow progress, we found ourselves among them a long way back from my friends. I begged their leader,

Rainulf, to send ahead and get help. But he simply laughed and robbed us.'

'Not that we had anything.'

'But still. It was shameful, being searched like that.'

The old man closed his eyes again. The woman looked up. 'The *mutur* walked right over Michael here and laughed. All of them knowing he would die if left behind.'

'They are heartless.' Jacques shook his head.

'Can you ride?' I asked.

'You're the hero.' The farmer's eyes were open again, a surprising green. 'The young knight?'

'Guibert of Rocadamour.'

'Aye, well my lord Rocadamour, if I am put on a beast, I'll not fall off it.'

Cateline had already dismounted and with the help of Jacques and Gerard, we got the old man into my saddle, albeit with some gasps of pain on his part.

'Thank you. God bless you.' Michael's wife took my hand and caressed it.

Later, although the sun had nearly gone below the trees, the road was straight enough that we could see the campfires of our army and we pressed on through the twilight shadows.

'Who goes there?' Two of the *mutur* challenged us, bows raised.

'Gerard, Lord Rocadamour, and friends,' answered Gerard.

'Hold your ground.'

We waited, with some impatience on my part. I wanted to get to Arnulf, in the hope that his presence and lively chatter would encourage Cateline to return to herself.

Soon, Rainulf came up with five more of his men around him. Having finished with the bone he was chewing, he flung it into the undergrowth.

'You return. And you have the girl. Well done.'

'And we have these people who you robbed and left lying in the road.' I stepped forward and the *mutur* guards pointed their loaded crossbows at me.

'So you do.'

'What would it have cost you, to have sent a message to their friends?'

'Oh, about the same as it would have cost you to let us cross the Reiber safely.'

'That wasn't my policy.' I said.

'It's not the same,' said Gerard, moving alongside me. 'In your pouches were the treasure of the whole army, without we charged you for the crossing, we'd never have seen those coins again. And we didn't leave you to die.'

'Only by luck.'

'Let us through, Rainulf, we're tired and hungry.' This was Cateline, speaking at last.

With a careful look at her (defiant, hands on hips, long black hair thrown back) followed by a shrug, Rainulf nodded to his men, who stepped aside.

As we passed, silent but for the hooves of my horses on the stone, the old man – Michael – coughed up phlegm and spat at Rainulf, hitting the warrior on the shoulder.

Immediately, my hand went to my sword and beside me, Gerard's to his axe. But a wild look that had rushed upon Rainulf's face immediately subsided and he laughed, a deep heartfelt laugh.

'Well done old Viking, if I had known you had such courage, I wouldn't have left you.'

We moved on again, Jacques and I exchanging a look of relief.

'Rocadamour!' Rainulf shouted after me, as we passed the last of the campfires of the *mutur*.

'Yes?' I turned.

'Welcome back.'

Making our way through the disorganised ranks of the poor, a crowd gathered around us. A scrawny man with crooked teeth jigged from side to side in front of me, walking backwards in his desire to keep on looking into my face. A mother lifted her little son onto her shoulders, him crying, 'I want to see Lord Rocadamour'. Two bearded monks began thanking heaven that their prayers had been granted. These people, and soon very many more than these, were walking with us as we passed the stragglers of the army. Before long, I was surrounded by poor people and the sounds of their delighted laughter, their cheers, and their welcoming cries.

With a glance back at my companions, I saw Gerard was enjoying the enthusiasm of the crowd. He was smiling and acknowledged all the calls of welcome. Even more than Gerard, the old man on the destrier was delighted with himself, pleased to be alive, no doubt, and even more pleased to be at the centre of his cheering friends. Jacques and Cateline, however, seemed unmoved by the enthusiasm of the impoverished members of our army.

'Well done, by God! Well done Guibert.' We had reached our cart, where Arnulf was lying; a grey-haired woman I did not know was leading the pony that hauled his cart. 'I'd get up and hug you both, if it wasn't for my leg.'

'Thank you, Arnulf.'

Everyone was at a stand. I turned to Michael. 'Are any of your friends near?'

'Just there.'

'Call them to assist you.'

Cateline had walked to the cart, tying off the reins of Tenebrour to the back of it.

'How is the leg?' she asked Arnulf, who had gripped the boards of the cart with his arms and was heaving himself into a sitting position so that he could display his happiness at Cateline's return by hugging her closely to him.

'Rocadamour! Rocadamour!' My name rang out under the canopy of trees, quickly becoming a roar in the mouths of everyone, drowning whatever reply he might have made.

Clapping me on my back, Gerard leaned in. 'You are the talisman of the people. With you among them, they feel safe.'

Again, I should have been delighted, this was another moment that could have come straight from my daydreams – and I was pleased, of course – but my happiness was tempered by blood-soaked memories, hunger, tiredness and concern for Cateline.

'We'll talk more later,' Gerard had to shout in my ears. Then the leader of our army climbed up the wheel of our cart, waving his hands to get some quiet.

'Friends! We'll give Guibert three cheers. But then no more, for we must be on the march while there remains light enough to see by.'

Having led the people in three great roars and with a last wave to me, Gerard jumped down and pushed his way onwards toward the front of the army, Jacques close behind. Not that Gerard went far before Melinde came crashing into him, wrapping him in her arms and kissing his cheeks.

This touching sight seemed to me to express the difference between Gerard and Rainulf.

'Do you see that?' I asked Arnulf, who by straining could follow my gaze. 'Perhaps there are women who love Rainulf as much as Melinde loves Gerard, but would Rainulf allow such a display of tenderness? Or return it?'

'Rainulf? No, he's not that kind of man.'

'And yet they are very much the same, in battle anyway. And in their concern for their troops.'

Pursing his lips, in an expression that meant he was doubtful, Arnulf lay back in the cart. 'There's no honour in Rainulf, not even in matters that concern the *mutur*. Don't deceive yourself on this Guibert. Gerard, on the other hand, is a good man.'

'He is.' I lost sight of him as the crowds dispersed. 'And Jacques too.'

'I owe them my life,' added Cateline, 'and I owe you also, of course.'

'Does a lord incur a debt to the vassal who saves his life?' I responded.

'I don't know, I'm a farmer. What do you mean?' Her expression was interested, not hostile. Seeing Arnulf again had done her some good.

'I mean that when a knight swears he will be loyal to a lord and then saves the lord's life, that creates no new debt. The knight is being true to his word.'

'I see. And does the lord say nothing when this happens?' she smiled and I realised with a rush of relief, that it was the first smile I'd seen on her sweet, red lips since we'd found her. 'Does he ignore the poor knight and not even say "my thanks"?'

Without looking at either of us (he was flat on his back in the cart once more), Arnulf chuckled. 'Well,' he spoke to the sky, 'the lord might go so far as to give the knight a gift. A sword from the battle perhaps.'

'You lords are very ungrateful.'

'No,' I corrected her, 'it's just that if a lord is not careful, if he praises the vassal too much and make too much of the deed, the knight might think that his original oath had not been trusted. That only now did he believe the knight to be true.'

'Guibert. I trusted you. I knew you would come.'

'I'm not talking about us.'

Cateline didn't reply but, still smiling, dropped the saddlebags she'd been moving from horse to cart and stood before me. Then, with a shake of her head to clear her long curling tresses from her face, she stretched up to kiss me on the lips.

That night, I put my blanket next to hers and Cateline allowed me to hold her while we rested. Conscious that I loved her, I regretted my foolishness over the past few days. Instead of pretending to be cold towards her, I should have striven hard to win her affection. Perhaps now I had. With that happy thought, I felt the warm glow of her and fell asleep.

21

HE THAT IS GREEDY OF GAIN...

Five days later, the army was camped beside the river Kee. This was a truly formidable obstacle, one that made the Reiber seem like a mere stream. So wide that a bowshot could not reach the far shore, the river was fierce too. Here, the water plunged down white-foamed cascades from hills to our south and I could hear the leonine roar of the river from over an hour away. No one could hope to swim the Kee until it had lost its violence, far, far downstream.

On coming to and leaving from the Kee, the Romans had altered the direct line of their road; it angled through the forest to come to a place where a rocky island rose from the swift-flowing water. This was because the Roman solution to crossing the Kee was the same as that in our times. Despite the efforts of the surging brown water to snatch it from its guide ropes, a ferry took the passenger to the island from this, the east bank, then there was a bridge from the island across a shorter stretch of water to the west bank. The original Roman bridge had been constructed from stone and the foundation pillars still remained. But the body now was a wooden affair, albeit sturdy enough.

The main problem that we faced was not the dirty, constantly heaving waters of the river, but a man: Bishop Wernher. The bishop had built a castle – of sorts – on the island. Supposedly, this square grey bastion existed to protect the eastern frontier of the duchy.

Maybe it served that purpose, but it also served for him to take a fee from every person crossing the Kee and every boat travelling on the river. And there was nothing anyone could do about this, because Wernher was brother to King Henry.

When our army had travelled eastwards, it had taken Shalk's threat to dismantle the castle stone by stone before Wernher had relented and let our army cross without payment. Coming back, however, I knew we would not escape a heavy toll.

A small delegation – Gerard, Melinde, Count Stephen, Rainulf and myself – were waiting on the bishop in the solar of his castle, having been escorted in the ferry by Wernher's emissary (a tall, slender man with strikingly bright, long yellow hair – like that of Jacques, but thicker and worn loosely – and a flattened, misshapen nose). None of us had been allowed to carry arms and all of us were wet, not only from the spray of the river but from a sudden fall of rain that had rushed upon us when we were halfway across.

'Gentlemen … and lady,' the bishop came into the room, wiping his hands on a piece of cloth, which he threw to the ground behind him for a servant to pick up and take away. 'Welcome, I did not expect to see anyone from Shalk's army so soon. What happened?' Wernher took his seat: a modest-sized throne. But then, Wernher was a small man, so small in fact that he might have looked absurd in a great episcopal seat. What he lost in stature, he made up for with the intensity of his pale gaze.

'Shalk was betrayed by King Bratislav,' answered Count Stephen.

Gerard took a step forward, 'Were they not all massacred so? And us the only survivors.'

'And how did you escape?'

'We refused to give up our weapons and were left behind when the rest were led away to be slaughtered.' As I'd observed before, without his armour Count Stephen appeared very frail. His bent-over posture was that of an old man. Yet his voice was firm enough.

'Shalk?'

This time I answered, with a bitterness in my words that was audible even to me. 'Taken prisoner and suffocated in the chimney of Bratislav's kitchen.'

'Odd.' A suppressed smile and a glance towards his emissary. 'Was King Bratislav provoked? I have not met with any difficulty in my dealings with him.'

No one responded.

Outside, it was raining again. Here, we did not feel it: the windows of the solar were like those of a wealthy church, with crisscrossed Xs of lead holding small panes of glass.

'Well.' The bishop stood up and, still on the stage that brought his grey eyes level with ours, turned his back to us to look out of a window. 'You have how many souls wanting to cross?'

'About two hundred,' replied Gerard.

Returning to his throne, still standing, Wernher stroked his neat black beard thoughtfully. 'How many horses?'

'Fourteen.' Again Gerard. It seemed that despite his seniority in birth, years and status, Count Stephen did not seem eager to lead our side in the haggling to come and I felt the same.

'Carts with more than two wheels?'

'None.'

'Carts of two wheels?'

'A score.'

'Well, four hundred pounds of silver is all you need give me.'

Surprisingly, Rainulf now laughed aloud, a deep and dangerous sound.

'Come now, my lord; how are we to find such a weight of silver this far from home?' Turning his attention back to the bishop from the leader of the *mutur*, Gerard opened his arms wide to emphasise how reasonable he was being. 'I doubt we have ten pounds of silver between us and that if everyone surrendered all that they owned.'

'I'll pay you five pounds of silver for each of your warhorses. And one for each suit of chainmail.'

'Even at such a miser's rate, there are but six knights among us.'

'For every peasant who becomes a serf on my estates, I'll give you five shillings.'

The only other time I had seen Gerard's cheeks turn so red was when they had been flushed with the fury of battle. Now he spoke slowly, like he was mastering each word. 'Every man and woman on this expedition is free.'

'Indeed.' The bishop sat down again, after another quick glance to his emissary. 'Still, give them the choice: to freely walk downstream towards the next crossing, through forest that is home to Magyars and outlaws, or to enjoy the security of a life on my fields.'

'Does it mean nothing to you,' there was an angry edge to Count Stephen's voice which – in contrast to Gerard – he was unable or unwilling to hide, 'that these are Christian people who undertook this journey for Christ's sake?'

Bishop Wernher smiled openly and looked at Count Stephen for a moment. 'No.'

I could see the lightning in Count Stephen's eyes.

'We took a great chest of treasure from Devinium,' said Rainulf. 'Two hundred pounds or more of silver, some gold too, chalices and the like. Take this for our crossing.'

For a moment I stared at Rainulf, astonished. Why was he making such an admission to the bishop? Surely not from concern for the poor?

'Did you now?' Werner's smile was gone. 'Very well, let me see this treasure and if it is as you say, you may have your crossing.'

The bishop stood up and I bowed my head, I was the only one on our side to do so. He left the solar, a servant opening the door for him.

'Follow me.' Our yellow-haired escort signalled for us to attend him and we filed out down the narrow stairs of the tower, back out to the grey skies.

It was not possible to speak freely on the river, what with four of the bishop's men hauling on the ropes and the emissary between us. But as soon as they had left us on the bank, Melinde turned to Rainulf.

'Well Rainulf, what is your scheme?'

'If the *mutur* can't have the treasure, then no one has it and at least we get to cross the Kee.'

We all looked at the burly warrior and no doubt my expression was as suspicious as everyone else's.

'I'll bring a chest. You get your people to fill it.' Rainulf turned to leave.

'You'll not be absconding with that treasure, you know,' said Gerard. 'And even if you could steal it away, the route downstream to the next crossing is filled with peril.'

The leader of the *mutur* didn't answer.

As Gerard and his officers began to stir the army, insisting upon a return of the treasure that each person carried, a murmur of resistance grew louder and louder.

'What's happening?' asked Cateline, who had walked up to my side while I watched the *mutur* bring a large chest to the edge of the forest.

'The bishop wants our treasure before he'll let us cross.'

'The scoundrel. May he burn in hell for his greed.'

A stout, middle-aged, bearded monk – I remembered him fighting at the ambush and cheering my return last night – was stood on the bank waving a white cloth at the castle.

I went up to him. 'What are you doing?'

'I want to speak to the bishop. To evoke his pity for the sick and the poor. To remind him of his Christian duty.'

'He's not that kind of bishop. He's not concerned for the sick and the poor.'

'Nor for a reward in the next world. His mind is fixed on this one.' Gerard had joined us.

Standing tall, the monk stared at us, blue eyes shining with righteousness. *'For a bishop must be without crime, as the steward of God: not proud, not subject to anger, not given to wine, no striker, not greedy of filthy lucre.* I have to try to make him hear the words of God.'

'Try if you must,' said Gerard, 'but Bishop Wernher knows about the treasure and there will be no persuading him, but that he must have it.'

With a last, scornful look, the monk tightened the knot of his cord belt. 'For the sake of my brothers, I am determined.' With that, he seized a waterlogged ferry rope and launched himself into the river. As the rope sagged with his weight, the monk's waist and legs sank into the cold water. Hand-over-hand, he began the long journey to the island.

'Don't!' I shouted. 'Come back!'

Of course the monk did not even pause in his efforts. Around us, the clink and clatter of treasure filling the chest ceased. Everyone was moving to the bank to watch.

A cheer, though an anxious one, greeted the sight of our monk when he eventually gained the island. The roar of the rapids to our left and the thunder of the torrents flowing past us meant it was impossible to hear what the monk was shouting, but with cupped hands and head tipped up towards the battlements it was clear that he was addressing those inside the castle.

There was no visible response for some time, until the glittering reflections of burnished armour showed some movement on the battlements. The bishop's soldiers then tipped buckets of filth over the crenellations, causing our monk to fall back, arm protecting his head.

After a few more shouts, from a safe distance, the monk looked across at us, then began to make his return. I was anxious for him. The cold water would have sapped his strength on the way over and it would be a long journey back, hanging on to the rope like that, the river pulling at you.

'He's lucky,' Gerard turned his round face towards me, 'I thought the bishop might be having him killed, as an example.'

'He's brave.'

'I wouldn't know about that now. Brave is when you are smart enough to see the peril. Being a thick-minded, old monk, it probably never even occurred to him that he might be given a bolt in the heart. God love him all the same.' Gerard turned to the people crowding up behind us.

'Come on all, let's finish filling that chest.'

No one moved though, not until the monk was back, helped out of the water by a dozen hands. He was pale, shivering with cold and furious. 'That man has no right to the title of bishop.'

'Aye!' came the cries from all around.

'Nevertheless,' said Gerard, 'Wernher controls this crossing and there will be a worse cost than the loss of some coins if we travel in search of another one.'

22

THE SONS OF MEN ARE LIARS

All night, the *mutur* had stayed near the chest. And all night too, the rest of the army had ringed them, suspiciously. Not I. As I was not on guard duty, I had gone to my bed for sleep and to be with Cateline. It seemed to me that Cateline was recovering from her ordeal. Each night since our return to the army, she had slept curled in on herself, back to me. Not this last night though; her head was on my shoulder, her arm across my chest.

There was torchlight enough for me to see her closed eyes: what were her dreams about?

Despite a great many sighs from Arnulf nearby, along with the creaking sounds of his restless twisting about in the cart, I fell asleep.

When I awoke, Rainulf was crouched above me, wearing his disconcerting, blue-fanged smile. Was I still dreaming? No.

'Rocadamour, put on your armour today. And come with us on the ferry.'

'Why? What's happening?'

'Hush.' With that he got up and strolled back towards his men.

It was late in the morning that the long-haired, blonde emissary of the bishop came over to us, a large crowd – the majority of our army – watching the slow progress of the ferry across the river.

With four servants behind him and with nods to those of us he recognised, the emissary walked right up to the chest, which had been bound around the sides with rope to ensure it would not split.

The bishop's man looked at the contents, impressed.

'Quite a haul. Lord Wernher will be pleased, I'm sure.' Then, turning to his servants, 'Bring it away.'

'Wait.' Rainulf stepped between the servants and the chest. 'We want guarantees that the bishop will let us cross. Hostages too.'

'I can't speak for my lord bishop.'

'Then we'll come with the treasure and hear his oath.'

'Very well. No weapons.'

Rainulf held his arms wide, to show that he carried no axes or swords. The bishop's servants went among some half dozen of the *mutur*, who also had outstretched arms, checking for hidden daggers.

In response to a knowing look from Rainulf, I unbelted my sword and gave it to Cateline before joining the leader of the *mutur*. 'And I, also.'

Grey clouds above and dark, frightening water below. But on the strip of planks between the two, much cheer, ebullience even, in the chatter of the emissary.

'I shouldn't tell you this, but the bishop was in such a rage after Shalk crossed eastwards that he planned to imprison your leaders on the way home and ransom them. But this is better. Where did you get so much treasure? Is it King Bratislav's?'

'Devinium.' Rainulf managed a smile.

'I see. You didn't spare the churches neither? To judge from the chalice I saw.' The emissary bent down by the clasp of the chest and began to raise the lid. With a bang that rang out above the roar of the river, Rainulf kicked the chest shut. Holding his fingers to his body, as if to nurse them, though they were not hurt, the emissary gave Rainulf a scowl.

'Not here,' said Rainulf and the ferry gave a lurch as if by way of explanation for his action.

The slow haul across the Kee completed, we were taken up to the solar once more. It was a difficult task, maneuvering the chest around the tight corners of the narrow staircase. The *mutur* took responsibility for heaving it up, a step at a time, until we reached the door of the solar, held open for us by two servants.

Although this room filled the whole of the first floor of the castle, it was small for a meeting chamber, nothing like the great hall at Castle Rocadamour. The solar was, however, richly adorned. We stood on a lush red carpet; tapestries depicting each of the four seasons hung on the wall; a large banner (gold and red, with a white flared cross) stood behind the bishop's seat and the candelabra in each corner were gold leaf and reached as high as my chin.

Six solid-looking armed guards were also in the room, trying to appear disinterested but I could see how often their eyes were drawn to the large chest, now resting on the carpet in the centre of the room and made all the more prominent by the fact it lay in a rectangle of white sunlight that came weakly through one of only four windows.

Unlike yesterday, we had hardly to wait at all before the Bishop Wernher came in and he immediately made for the chest. Slowly, Rainulf opened the clasp and raised the lid.

'Not bad.' The bishop pursed his lips.

'Good enough?' asked Rainulf.

'Let's see.' The bishop nodded to his emissary who began to eagerly take out silver candlesticks and chalices. Although my view was obscured by the man's long hair, I could hear the distinctive clink of coins falling against each other as the large silver items were removed and placed on the floor.

'There's a golden crown in there too. Let me show you.' Gripping the ropes that bound it, Rainulf squatted, flexed his thick muscles, and tipped the chest up on one end. Coins cascaded onto the carpet, some of them rolling as far as me. So demanding was the effort that Rainulf's tattooed face flushed bright red and his eyes protruded from their sockets with a frightening stare.

'There's no need,' said Wernher, stepping back.

With a gasp, Rainulf flung the chest over, so that all the treasure scattered. Treasure. Swords, daggers and axes too.

'What is this?' asked the emissary.

Far, far too slowly it occurred to the guards that there was a danger to themselves and the bishop. The *mutur* had, of course, been ready and were leaping upon the bishop's soldiers with the weapons they had instantly snatched up. So too was I, having stepped over and picked up a long dagger – a dirk – while it was sliding across a bed of coins towards me.

'Guards! Guards!' the bishop began to scream, until a smack from Rainulf sent him sprawling. The leader of the *mutur* then charged the door of the hall like a bull, smashing into it with his shoulder just as a servant was escaping, crushing the man between wood and stone.

A guard was on me and I ducked a blow from his sword, stepping in close and stabbing him up through his unshaven jowls and through his mouth, finding a soft path to his brain. Throwing the body down, I turned to assist the *mutur* beside me, who was battering unsuccessfully at the shield of a tall, skillful soldier. While my comrade went high with his axe, I went low and with a good enough angle to make the most of my strength, stabbed the dirk deep, just above the iron greave armour, and into the knee of our opponent. My dagger stuck there in the bones as the guard pulled away and hurriedly I turned to the spilled treasure to find another weapon.

There was no need to panic. The fighting was already over and although two of our men were bleeding heavily, all six guards and both servants were dead.

'Christ,' said the blonde emissary, pale and shivering. 'What have you done?'

With a casual swing of an axe, Rainulf struck him in the neck, so that the bewildered head nearly came off as the man collapsed to the ground.

'Why did you kill him?' I asked, as the emissary's body gave a last twitch.

'This is no situation for taking prisoners.'

'You know what your fate will be? If you harm me?' Bishop Wernher was sitting against a wall, nursing the side of his face, which was already swollen.

'What?' replied Rainulf, closing the door to the room and bolting it with its sturdy wooden beam.

'King Henry, my brother, will hang you in a metal cage over the entrance to Aachen until you die, the ravens picking at your eyes.'

'Isn't it curious.' Rainulf was now at the chest, unwinding one end of the rope from it. 'How often men determine their own fate, through foolish words.'

'Rainulf.' I felt anxious.

The leader of the *mutur* leapt upon the bishop – a bear upon a dog – and bound Wernher's legs together. Then pulling on the loose end of the rope dragged the bishop along the floor.

'Open up! Open up!' someone, a soldier presumably, was thumping on the outside of the door.

'Smash that window,' Rainulf grunted and one of his men did as asked.

'Rainulf, don't. This is a bishop. And we've to march past his brother's villages and castles.'

'Open up!' We could hear an axe thud against the wood; the door quivered.

Wernher screamed as he was pushed through the window, not only from fear but also from pain. It was a narrow enough opening, with glass shards remaining in the lead that lined the window.

I ran over.

Rainulf and I peered out to see the bishop, upside down and spinning, sometimes knocking against the wall of his castle despite the best efforts of his flailing arms. About ten feet below Wernher were sharp-looking rocks and then he faced the danger of a short roll or bounce to a further drop into the river. It was a survivable fall if he were the right way up, but head first, it had to be his death.

'Open up!' The door was splintering.

'Sigurd, sit on the chest.' Quickly checking that the taught rope that stretched from the chest to the window would hold the bishop, Rainulf ran to the door.

An axe blade showed through the splinters of the next blow.

'Hold! I'm going to open the door.'

Silence.

Rainulf slid the bolt and stepped away, taking an axe from his belt as he moved, so that he held one in each hand.

The door creaked open and a footsoldier stepped in to the hall, many more men behind him, crowding at the entrance to look at us with angry faces.

'Stop there and listen to me,' shouted Rainulf, 'or the bishop dies!'

The soldier, a young man whose eyes were wide as he stared at the bloody carnage in the room, shook his head in amazement.

'See that rope?'

'Aye.'

'At the end of it is your lord, who is hanging outside by his feet. Do as we ask, and he'll live. Otherwise, he dies. Do you understand?'

The soldier didn't answer.

'Go on over. Just you. Ask the bishop what he wants you to do.' Rainulf gave us all a look of warning. I picked up a sword and shifted the dirk I'd reclaimed to my off hand.

'My lord?' The young soldier was looking out of the window.

Something undecipherable was screamed back at him.

White-faced, the soldier turned back to us. 'What do you want?'

'Send the ferry over for the men who call themselves *mutur*. Just the *mutur* mind you.'

'You heard him.' The soldier looked towards the door. 'Stebelo, send the ferry over. Just the *mutur*.'

There was movement outside.

'And order the servants to make a pile of supplies on the bridge: grain; food; wine.'

'And silver,' said Sigurd.

'Aye. And all the silver you've been squeezing out of travellers.'

'The strongroom is locked,' Wernher's young officer replied, speaking slowly, evidently still stunned.

Rainulf's tone was patient. 'Who has the key?'

It took a moment for the soldier to spot the emissary's body on the carpet. He pointed.

'Well, take it from him.'

'Wait.' Gathering himself, the soldier, with a worried look at the quivering rope, leaned out of the window again. 'They want your silver. From the stronghold.'

Although the bishop's voice was hard to hear, I could make out 'yes' and 'up'.

In playing games with my fellow squires, I'd sometimes been held upside-down for a minute or two. After this long, I knew the bishop's head must be throbbing.

The soldier searched the corpse and found a cluster of keys; he left the room and went down the stairs with the others. We were left alone.

While Rainulf checked his two wounded men and patted them reassuringly (despite their pain, both these *mutur* gave their leader brave grins), I spoke.

'Was this your plan?'

'Not exactly. I thought we'd climb out of a window and then set fire to the place, or something like that. Killing them as they ran out. This is better though. I never thought to get the bishop's treasure.'

'Oops,' said Sigurd and we all looked across to where he was sitting on the chest.

No longer stretched quivering to the window, the rope lay slack and unmoving on the ground.

'No!' I cried out. It couldn't be.

Rainulf and I were the first to look out. Where the rope had rubbed against the lead and glass fragments it had frayed. There was some red on the rocks close to the river and no sign of the bishop.

'O sod it!' Hurriedly, Rainulf picked up one of the candelabra and with Sigurd's help, tied off the heavy metal implement and hung it out of the window.

'You've killed a bishop,' I said, horrified.

'Aye and the devil will thank me for the new arrival.'

With Sigurd sitting on the chest once more, the room looked much as it had done. If you were observant, however, you would see that the rope was no longer as taut as it had been.

A strange sound caused me to look up. One of Rainulf's men, one of the wounded ones, was snorting, attempting to hold back his laughter. Sigurd was laughing too, in fact they all were. With tears in his wild and merry eyes, Rainulf looked from one man to the other with his savage, blue-toothed grin. For my part, I attempted to convey my dismay with what I hoped was a fierce expression. Yet clearly an accusatory glare from me meant nothing to the murderer.

'Stop,' said the other wounded warrior. 'My ribs hurt so much.'

The laughter grew louder.

From the eastern window, I could see the ferry pulling slowly back towards us, filled with *mutur*; to the west, I could see the bridge, at the foot of which was a growing pile of bags.

A group of soldiers stamped up the stairwell, led by the young commander. Instantly, every man in the solar was sober.

'We've done as you asked. Pull him up.'

'Not yet. When my men are off the ferry.'

'For God's sake! Show the bishop some respect.'

'I respect him enough not to trust him. And he'll be up all the quicker if you and your men help pull the ferry in.'

The soldier looked around at us, this time seeing each one of us properly, rather than the blood and bodies. When he hesitated, my hands clenched tight on the hilt of my weapons, thinking he had noticed the slackness in the rope. Nevertheless, I forced myself to relax, to smile at him even.

'God damn you all!' But he left again, along with his men.

When it was safe to do so, Rainulf began to chuckle once more, as did the other *mutur*. Not me, though. It was a terrible deed, to kill a bishop. Even if Wernher had not been much of a spiritual leader, the hand of every prince between here and France would now be against Rainulf. He would be hunted as an outlaw until his death.

'Hey, Rocadamour, cheer up. Don't you think this will make another great chapter to your song?'

'You think the poets like to sing about bishops being thrown from windows?'

'I suppose not. Although I'd enjoy a song like that.'

Again the *mutur* laughed. And despite myself, I found that I could not maintain a scowl in response to their smiles; in fact, such merriment in the face of our dangerous situation had a certain appeal. It demonstrated once more that the *mutur* were fearless. Sod Wernher anyway, it was his greed that had brought about this disaster.

23

FEET DIPPED IN BLOOD

When they disembarked and saw us at the window of the castle the *mutur* who had arrived from the ferry gave us cheers and waves. No sooner had the last man left the craft than the ferry began another journey towards the eastern bank of the river.

Looking at his men through a window, Rainulf smashed through the glass and lead with the head of his axe, so that he could call down to them below.

From outside the hall, from the stairwell, came the sound of the bishop's soldiers ascending towards us, their work at hauling ferry ropes finished.

Leaning out, there was urgency in Rainulf's deep voice, 'Remember Speyer!'

Below, the cheering and the catcalls ceased.

'Speyer?' I asked.

'You wouldn't like the explanation.' Rainulf shrugged, giving life to the tattoos on his shoulders. 'In short, there's going to be a fight. Get ready.'

'Pull up my lord the bishop!' The young officer was in the room, panting from his exertions. Another five or six armoured soldiers were right behind him.

'Your lord, as you rightly say, so you can pull him up yourself,' replied Rainulf, folding his arms.

'Take a hold, quickly now.' As the soldiers moved in to the hall and lined up along the rope, more came in behind them. We were outnumbered, badly. A dark, wicked expression could be seen on Rainulf's face. Although it occurred to me that I could die now, in this distant castle room I took heart from Rainulf's presence, that and the fact that half our enemies had their hands on the rope.

As the soldiers hauled in the cable, it came up easily, far too easily and soon the candelabra was clanging against the outside of the window. Their puzzlement did not last long. With loud shouts, we were at them, striking and stabbing before the soldiers could draw their weapons.

'Come on! Come on!' If the screams of the wounded and the mighty clanging sound of steel against steel did not serve to encourage the *mutur* down below, then Rainulf's roaring voice would bring them up. Would it be soon enough? There was little space in which to fight and my dirk was more use to me than my sword. Two soldiers pressed me towards a corner of the room: one was poorly trained and his lunges were easy to deflect; the other though, waited and stabbed with powerful swift jabs. I was caught in the stomach and although my mail held, I could not draw breath.

I'd have died then, with the room growing distant and a confusion of agonised howling in my ears, but for my enemies having to turn and face the incoming *mutur*. I staggered against the wall and drew air into my lungs at last. Then again. My head cleared.

Lashing hard into the nearest of Bishop Wernher's soldiers, I cut right through his leather shoulder guards and staggered him. A kick brought the man (he was young, not much older than me, with wild pale eyes) to the floor, where I could stab his unguarded throat with the dirk. Crouched, I was in a good position to thrust my sword point through the back of a soldier's leg and when he looked down at me, his head was shattered by the axe of one of my comrades.

And that was it. We were no longer fighting.

'Rocadamour?'

I stood up.

'Here.'

'Good. I thought we'd lost you.'

As far as I could tell, Rainulf was unharmed and I felt a surge of joy in that fact. For all his faults, it was hard not to love the warrior whose battle skills were bringing me home alive when by rights I should be dead. This pleasure, however, was quickly tempered by the sight of the bodies of our men. Sigurd, for one, would not rise again. And as I looked more carefully at the heaped bodies, I could see that all of the other *mutur* who had been on the ferry with me that morning were dead too.

'For some reason,' Rainulf was cleaning his weapons, 'I have grown fond of you. Despite your lordly ways.'

'And I of you. Despite your villainous ways.' My heart was slowing again and I too found some clean patches of cloth on the corpses, which I used to wipe the blood from the dirk. The sword I simply dropped. 'Yet, although you are the greatest warrior I've ever seen fight, there is something devilish about you.'

This pleased Rainulf; he gave me a crooked smile.

'Heads up lads, get the silver bagged. Leave our dead here, we'll give them a Viking funeral.'

Finding silver coins among the gore was going to be a long and sickening task and I left that hall of death. Still aching from the blow to my stomach, I winced each time I lifted a foot to climb the tower's stairwell. Were there any of the bishop's soldiers left alive above me? Mine was a slow and cautious ascent.

No one was on the roof. There, on a walkway around a pointed four-sided roof of grey slates, a fresh breeze revived me. I shivered and it was not just with the cold. If there was to be no more butchering of men between here and my return to Rocadamour, I would be happy.

Something caught my eye over by the ferry. There was a tumult, a surging of crowds. When the ferry came nearer on its return leg it was crowded with soldiers, but I could make out Gerard, Jacques and the other officers of the Milan Company rather than the rest of the *mutur*. At once, I set off to meet them.

The first man off the ferry was Gerard and taking in my blood-stained appearance, his face was grim.

'Will you tell me what happened so?'

'Rainulf hid weapons in the chest and his men surprised those of the bishop.'

'And himself? Bishop Wernher?'

'Dead. Accidentally.'

With a shake of his head and sigh, Gerard said, 'It should have been that the worst was past. That we were safe from here on in the lands of King Henry.' Then he gave me a cool stare. 'Did you know?'

'No.' This was the truth and yet I had leapt for that dirk quickly enough. A part of me had been certain that Rainulf would not give up on the treasure so easily and that part of me had been ready for the fight.

'Gerard! Over here.' Jacques was at the foot of the bridge, where the servants had left the bags before fleeing westwards.

'Dear God!' From a bag whose flap had been untied had spilled a great quantity of silver coin. 'Would they be all like that?' asked Gerard.

'All those,' Jacques pointed to a stack of more than a score of large leather bags.

'Never, not even in Rome, did I see so much silver in one place.'

'It is King Henry's treasure,' I pointed out.

'Is it though?' Gerard looked up towards the tower, Rainulf was pushing through the Milan Company towards us. 'I wonder did the king have any idea how much of a squeeze his brother was putting on those who travelled this way?'

'That silver belongs to the *mutur*!' Rainulf, angry, covered in blood and shouting was no easy man to face but Gerard simply shrugged.

'It is the property of the whole army now, *mutur* included.'

'No!' screamed Rainulf, flecks of spittle in the air, 'six of my men are dead. We fought and died for this. It is ours.'

Aware that Rainulf was not in control of himself, Gerard took a step back and raised his shield. But he did not give in.

'It will be shared among all. Now calm yourself Rainulf or die here if you be lifting that axe.'

'If it is not to be returned to King Henry, then you should give that silver to Rainulf and his men.'

Gerard glanced at me surprised, but then returned his full concentration to Rainulf.

'Why say you so?' he asked without moving his eyes from the leader of the *mutur*.

'They were the ones who dared go into that castle.'

'Aye. That was a daring deed, no doubt. But then have they not put the whole army in peril by their action? Will King Henry discriminate if he discovers what has happened here before we reach France? All share the risk, all share the silver.' There was a finality to Gerard's words that stopped me from speaking again even though I knew that it was a mistake to rob Rainulf for a second time.

Red-faced and grinding his teeth, Rainulf could not bring himself to speak either. He turned around and stamped his way back to the castle, cursing and causing the rocks to ring out with sweeping blows of his axes as he went.

Having watched Rainulf re-enter the castle, Gerard turned to Jacques. 'Let's take everyone over the bridge and make camp on the west bank, more than a bowshot from the castle. And set a guard against an assault of the *mutur*, would you?'

'He'll want vengeance for this Gerard,' I said and Jacques gave a slight nod.

'The rage will leave him. And so long as we outnumber them two to one, he won't act.'

* * *

Later, after I had washed the blood from my boots and armour, I returned to the castle. When I banged the iron knocker on the thick oak door, a black-bearded member of the *mutur* let me in without comment.

Upstairs, in the solar, the bodies of Bishop Wernher's men had gone: I'd earlier seen the splashes as they had been tossed from the roof of the castle into the dark river. The dead *mutur*, however, were laid in a line clasping their weapons.

His massive, muscular limbs sprawling over the bishop's small throne, Rainulf sat brooding, dark eyebrows almost brought together by the furrows in his brow.

'Well Rocadamour?'

'What are you going to do about the silver?'

'What concern is it of yours?'

'I would avoid bloodshed between the *mutur* and the Milan Company if I could.'

'We will get it back off them and when we do, you can have a share of the bishop's treasure. You earned it.'

'Thank you. But that silver belongs to King Henry.'

Rainulf's gaze was intense and hard to meet. 'Only a nobleman who has never gone hungry could take that view. But if you want to return your share to the rest of us, you'll hear no objection.'

'Even if he doesn't learn of the death of his brother from those servants who fled, King Henry is going to find out what happened here. And if we are caught by his troops, I wouldn't like to be carrying money stolen from his brother.'

'Fine scruples, Lord Rocadamour.' With that dismissal, Rainulf turned his attention to his fallen comrades. 'That one is Sigurd. I remember him at Corvey, climbing the outer wall. A guard swung at him over the battlements and somehow Sigurd grabbed the man's arm and pulled him right off the wall. The next is Gunrid, he had a fief from Duke Godfrey, until he gave it up saying his lord was an idle, bed-loving coward whom no man could follow. The next is Torvald, he worshipped Odin still, when his lord became a Christian. The next is Edmund, who killed a knight for lying with his woman. The next is Albric, a good-for-nothing, stubborn farmer who would rather carry an axe than work the fields. And last there is Adalbert, I've known him ten years or more. No better man with a two-handed sword.

'We were all going to be guards for the Emperor, when we got to Constantinople.'

The faces of Rainulf's comrades were uniformly pallid and had no meaning to me, though I was curious to see a glint of moisture in Rainulf's eyes. I had thought he cared for no one, least of all himself.

'And now? Where are you going?'

'Italia. South, beyond the reach of King Henry, to where the princes need soldiers to protect them from the Saracens. And maybe from there to Constantinople still, in time.'

'Rainulf, why did you ask me to come with you this morning?'

'Because you fight well.'

'All your men fight well. And you can't have been sure I would take your side against the bishop.'

Hopping on to the broken window, a finch looked at us both sideways then jumped away again into the air. A smile, sinister almost, formed on Rainulf's face, half hidden by his black plaids.

'I knew you would fight with us. And as for my reasons, my real reasons. Well, my men talk about you as though you might be King Mutur; you know this. They believed my ruse would work, when I said you would be coming with us into the tower. And then, there's something about you here,' he touched his heart, 'something the same as me.'

'What do you mean?'

'Are you afraid to die? Do you think it a sin to kill a man? No and no. Nothing matters, right? Except the company of comrades; good eating; and women. Those who live their lives for honour or Christ or a king are fools.'

'That's not me. I believe in honour, and Christ, and loyalty.'

'Is that so?'

'Of course.' Insulted, I stood up and left him with his fallen comrades, but as I left the tower I was troubled. A leader such as Rainulf was likely to be a good judge of other men. Had he judged me rightly?

24

A STRENGTH LAID WASTE

That evening, safely on the west bank of the Kee, the army ate well from the bishop's supplies. On our platters was soft bread for the first time since Devinium and with it strips of fried pork. Gathered at our campfire were a large and – as the wineskin passed around – an increasingly merry gathering. Although I had done nothing to encourage them, all sorts of lowly persons now seemed to think it was their right to sit at my fire and listen as I told Arnulf and Cateline about the battles in the solar. Nor did I mind it, as I once would have. Had they not all done their part in this expedition? Hadn't they fought in the ambush and turned the battle in our favour?

'That's a lesson in greed. That's taught the sodding bishop.' A thin, grey-haired peasant even had the confidence to comment on my words.

It felt as though I had become a part of their world as much as they a part of mine. And that too was something that pleased me. I had found that having the approval of the people was no bad thing, even if my tutors had told me never to seek the praise of the fickle mob.

Around me, many others said 'aye' and 'that's right'.

'No,' said Arnulf, sitting under the lee of the tipped-down cart, equine face shining pale in the firelight. 'That's not right. It's your greed speaking now. It would be better that we'd paid the bishop and had a free passage to France. Now, we are in great danger from King Henry.'

'King Henry can kiss my ass!' The large woman who had led our pony and cart while I had gone in search of Cateline shouted this and drew a great cheer in response.

'Is it true, Lord Rocadamour, that the bishop was going to make us serfs again and work for him?' Another poor man my father's age (perhaps a leatherworker to judge from the tools at his belt), looked directly into my eyes.

'The bishop asked for serfs. Gerard told him everyone here was free…' I began.

'That's right!' A dozen voices.

'But that did not end the matter. For the bishop demanded so much silver for the crossing that he thought you would not be able to pay and would prefer to become his serfs than risk the march downriver.'

'There's scum for you.'

'At the top, isn't it always thus?'

Outside of my hearing, had they always talked thus, the poor people on this expedition? That last comment, by a youth no older than me, would have cost him his ears if he'd spoken such words at my father's court.

'Here, now. Show some respect for Lord Rocadamour.' There was a sheen of sweat on Arnulf's brow and he spoke with some anger.

'Begging your pardon,' said the lad to me, 'of course I did not mean present company. It's just that I was a serf on the fields of Lord Theobald of Brittany and he was a hard taskmaster.'

'What are you going to do then, when you get home?' I asked him.

'Well, I'm not going back to Brittany, that's for sure. They say all men live in brotherhood at Jerusalem. I will use my share of the silver to buy passage over the sea to the Holy Land.'

This sparked a general discussion as to plans each person had for his or her return home. Some wished to buy land, or a burgess plot in a town; others a few animals. A few, like the young man, had not lost hope of reaching Jerusalem.

Seeing that the people were set for a long and lively night and feeling my stomach ache from the fighting that morning, I took my blankets from their pile beside our cart and lay down to sleep. I was soon feeling languorous, despite the increasingly loud voices around me. But then, Cateline came and lay beside me, sharing my blanket. It was a pleasure and a comfort to feel the warmth of her body alongside me and in order to let her know this, I caressed her face gently.

'When I was ferried across the Kee today,' she whispered, 'I looked at that rushing water and nearly jumped in.'

I stopped the motion of my hand.

'I used to wake up and feel joy in the coming day, especially if the sky were clear. I loved the warmth of the sun on my body, soft grass under my feet. Best of all, though, I loved the company of the people around me: my father, mother and sister.'

'Yes?'

'Now I wake up and wish that I were still asleep. What goodness I enjoy in this world isn't safe from men who just take what they want. I'm not safe from such men.'

'You are when you are with me.'

'And how long will I be with you?'

'Always.'

'You speak in kindness. But you can't be with me all the time. You have your duties. And you have your battles. One day, you will go to war and not return.'

'Maybe. But look at Count Stephen. Or my father. A lord can live a long life.'

'God send you a long life, Guibert. But I fear mine will be short.'

I held her tight then and later, tried to kiss her lips. I wanted her to wake in the morning and be glad that she was alive. Part of my own pleasure in living – a large part – was the thought that Cateline would be my wife when we returned to Rocadamour. There was something not quite right in that daydream, however. Something that was not the resistance of my father, which would be overcome, I was sure. No, the difficulty in believing in my daydreams about a life with Cateline as my wife came from my knowledge of her character. I had to admit to myself that a reserve existed in her affection for me: a reserve that now caused her to turn her face away from my lips; a reserve that had existed even before her capture and rescue; a reserve that made my heart ache.

There was something else too. A feeling that I was in a tomb and could never hope to love or be loved.

When Cateline lay with her head on my chest, listening to the beat of my heart, did she hear a melody that she did not like? Could she detect the same lack of faith that Rainulf claimed existed inside of me? Deep down, despite my efforts, had I failed to convince her that I was different to the men who had taken her by force? That I was different, too, to the *mutur,* for whom tenderness was weakness?

What could I do to make her fully trust me and want to live with me, other than bring her safely to Rocadamour and there, care for her until her joy in life had returned?

*   *   *

Dawn brought the usual rowdy outbreak of birdsong, louder even than the nearby, constant roar of the river. There were no clouds in the sky, the showers having blown over the army in the night, and I hoped that Cateline would take pleasure in the fresh, blue day.

I was standing beside our cart, whose two tugs were resting down on the ground, so that the floor of the cart formed a sloping roof. There Arnulf was stirring. He threw off his blanket and I recoiled from the sweet but terrible smell of death that was released.

'No! It was healing.'

He saw that I understood: the stench; his sweats; the groaning; his confinement to the cart.

'That was before I burst it open again, fighting the pagans.'

Squatting down, the smell was worse and I saw that Arnulf's red-stained bandages were encrusted with puss.

'We should get a surgeon.'

'It's too late. I've never known a man part with so much of his leg and live. And in any case, the foul humours have spread too far: I can't feel anything much below my ribs.'

'Christ, Arnulf. I'm so sorry.'

'Don't be. I've had a lot more from life than most men.'

'God damn it though. You and I, we would have such a merry time on our return to Rocadamour. You know how Father would have treated you. He would have sat you on his right-hand side, given you the best in everything and listened to every word you had to say about our journey.'

His eyes became moist and some colour came to his cheeks. 'Do not talk of your father, or you'll unman me.'

For a while, we didn't say anything. Arnulf lay back with a sigh and we listened to the people around us as they broke their fast, or packed up, readying themselves for the march to come. While I stood by the cart, rubbing away the tear that had fallen on to my knuckle, Cateline came over with yet more bread and bacon.

'Did you know?' I asked her.

'Yes.'

'Why didn't you tell me?'

'It was up to Arnulf to tell you.'

'And why didn't you?' I turned to him. Arnulf was not even pretending to eat his food.

'I don't know. Why darken your days unnecessarily?'

'Because... I'd have spent longer with you.'

'And less time with the bishop?' Arnulf managed a brave but frail smile.

'Lord Rocadamour?' It was Jacques.

I turned around angrily and shouted at him. 'Now what?'

Jacques took a step back in surprise. 'You're wanted for a council.'

'All right.' I pointed at Arnulf. 'Stay alive. We've more to say to each other.'

Already, though the morning was cool, Arnulf was covered in sweat. 'I'll do my best.'

Wisely saying nothing, Jacques led me along a winding route through the army to a copse where among the wild grasses were some astonishingly vivid red poppies. Seeing their colour, I couldn't help but think of the wound to Arnulf's leg that day at Devinium when I had sewed up the flaps of skin of his gaping thigh.

Present were Count Stephen, Gerard, Melinde, and Andreas. Rainulf and the *mutur* had spent the night in the bishop's castle.

'Well met, Lord Rocadamour,' Count Stephen tipped his head towards me, his curved frame bowing over yet further.

The others nodded and smiled and I returned their greeting with a brief bow of my own and a frown. It was not their fault that Arnulf was dying, yet I found myself standing ready to disagree with whatever they were about to propose.

'Well,' said Gerard, forgetting to ask permission to speak from the count, 'we have to march swiftly, lest King Henry comes. If we make good time, I think we can reach Wuttgard in three days and the French border in another three. But the question is, what about the *mutur*?'

'It's simple enough,' stated Count Stephen, who was pacing to and fro. 'We leave without them now and part ways at Colburg. That village is less than a day away where we can keep to this road and we tell the *mutur* to take the forest wagon-trail south.

'It was they who killed Bishop Wernher, not us. If there's a reckoning for it, then the reckoning should fall on them.'

'So it should,' said Gerard. 'But what I mean is, how much silver should we give them? Remembering that they took a great deal into the tower yesterday.'

'King Henry's silver? Let them have it all. That will make it all the more evident we are innocent of the death of his brother.' Count Stephen spoke brusquely.

'I agree.' After I had called out, Count Stephen turned to me and we acknowledged the rightness of our standpoint with a nod to one another.

'With all due respect, honourable gentlemen, that is not a practical proposal. Can you see the people of the army giving up the unexpected wealth they now possess?'

When Gerard stressed the words 'honourable gentlemen', Jacques and Melinde smiled. This angered me a lot. Had I not treated all of them as my equals since the battle against King Bratislav?

'King Henry won't know which coins were from that castle,' Andreas pointed out. 'I say let's just keep it all and march on. The *mutur* can have what they currently hold.'

'It's simplest,' added Jacques.

'You weren't there in the tower.' All of a sudden, a righteous anger came upon me. 'That was a brave stroke and it brought you across the river with no time lost and with a great fortune too. It's bad enough you plan to leave the *mutur* to King Henry's men, worse still you take their treasure too.'

As he looked at me, Gerard rubbed the stubble on his chin thoughtfully. 'How does this sound? If the *mutur* agree to take a different road to us, Count Stephen's road, then we'll leave enough bags of silver on the bridge for them, that when added to the treasure from Devinium it gives each of them the same amount as every man and woman in our army; as well as we can reckon.'

'Generous,' said Andreas.

'Greedy.' I replied. 'But it might be acceptable, I can't speak for

Rainulf.'

'Go then. You're the only one he'll listen to,' Gerard urged.

'And what if he doesn't accept?'

'Then we'll burn the bridge, leave them on the island and keep all the bishop's silver for ourselves.'

I shook my head, disgusted, but I turned away and set off back down the road with the message.

25

THE PATH OF AGES

I did not relish speaking with Rainulf; he was not a man who could control his anger and so before I put Gerard's offer to him, I made it clear that I had argued against Gerard and was not advocating these terms. My worries, however, were misplaced. Flanked by two of his officers, Rainulf heard me out without any obvious sign of anger.

'I suppose Gerard has kept the silver for himself?'

'Not at all,' I said, outraged, 'it has been shared among everyone, even the women got half shares and the children something.'

'Very well, tell Gerard we accept.'

With that, Rainulf ignored me and began to shout to his men that they make ready to leave.

On my way up the castle stairs, I'd noticed that the *mutur* had been busy preparing the funeral for their men. Planks, hewn from the wooden interior of the castle, had been stacked up on the entrance floor along with dozens of barrels and the whole building smelled of the tallow they had spread on its wooden floors. Soon, the tower would be aflame.

There were thirty-four of the *mutur* still alive and gathered outside the castle when I looked back from the bridge.

'Well?' asked Melinde, on my return. 'How was he?'

'Surprisingly calm.'

'I told you,' said Gerard, 'he has a fierce temper when it's on him,

Rainulf, but when it blows over, he's open to reason.'

'For my part, I shall be glad when we are a great distance from him. I've never met a more dangerous man.' These words of Melinde made me look sharply at her. I too felt that Rainulf was not to be trusted. Even here, when it seemed he had little choice, he was capable of trying to trick us somehow.

'Arnulf is dying. His leg is rotting. I had better get back to him.'

'Oh Guibert.' Melinde came over and touched my arm. 'I'm so sorry.'

'As am I,' said Gerard. 'He's a good man.'

Back at our cart, Cateline saw me coming and shook her head, dark eyes moist with tears. My heart gave a lurch and I felt tears come to my own eyes. With the cart harnessed to the pony again, its planks were flat and stretched out upon them was my sergeant, shivering, face bright white, red rimmed eyes staring into the sky.

'Arnulf?'

'I can't see,' his voice was a whisper. 'I'm cold all over. I haven't long, listen to me now.'

'I'm listening.' I reached in and took his hand, which was damp with sweat and so terribly light.

'Tell Lord Rocadamour I'm sorry for my pride. When he assigned me the task of looking after you on this expedition, I took offence. It seemed to me he was taking me from his councils to be a schoolmaster to a boy. I was cold towards him, those last few days.'

'He won't ...'

Arnulf waved his other hand. 'Hush. I was wrong. It was an honour. Tell him that. The highest honour. Remind him of Valercy, Le Puy and Nantes. Remind him of those times and say that no man in any of those battles fought more valiantly than his son did on this retreat. And that I consider myself fortunate to have ridden with you and played a part in your training. You are a hero Guibert and you will be famous. And you rescued Cateline when I was sure she was gone into the darkness of the forest forever. Incredible. Live long with her if you can. Be as famous as Achilles if you cannot.'

He let go of my hand and his own dropped heavily.

'Arnulf. I'm sorry for all the times I disobeyed you. When I tried to be the high and mighty lord and put you in your place.'

Thin and pale as they were, his lips still managed to smile, lifting his grey moustache.

'No need. I understood you, Guibert. Wanting to be a great man, like your father, but not realising how to do it. True authority is more than a birthright. Your father has the respect and friendship of his knights and it's that which means every one of us would give our lives for him.'

'You and I became friends, didn't we Arnulf?'

'Aye Guibert. From that day in Devinium when I stopped seeing you as a boy. I'm sorry it took me so long.'

We were holding hands again, when Cateline came up with a priest, one whom I'd first noticed in the battle against King Bratislav: tall, middle-aged, dressed in a dark-cowl and (remembering that slaughter), capable of great fury. Now though, he was solemn and I stood back, to let him talk to Arnulf.

'He can't see,' I said.

'Sir knight, Fulbert the priest is with you. Do you wish to make confession and prepare your soul for heaven?'

'I do.'

The priest, Fulbert, glanced up at Cateline and I. We moved away, while Fulbert climbed up on the spokes of the cart wheel, the better to lean close to Arnulf.

'What happened with Rainulf?' Cateline checked the straps on the pony and the tugs. Already, there were signs that up ahead of us the army was on the move. Soon it would be our turn.

'He agreed to take just a share of the silver and to leave us at Colburg.'

'We'll be well rid of them.'

'I suppose. But despite their uncouth manners, there is bravery to admire in the *mutur*. And we would never have escaped King Bratislav without them.'

'You are not a woman, or you could not have said that.'

While I considered this angry remark (had the *mutur* hurt her? Or did she refer to their violation of the women of Devinium?), I gathered the reins of the destrier.

'Help me mount?'

Cateline was strong enough to take hold beneath my bended leg and boost me into the saddle.

'I need a name for this wonderful horse. Can you think of one?'

'Argentus? For his silver forelock?'

'Yes. That's good. I leaned forward, patting my warhorse's neck. Argentus, that's your new name.' Then I shouted across to the cart. 'Arnulf, I must resume my duties. Stay alive and we'll talk tonight.'

It was heartening to see his arm rise in response and give something of a wave. But was there even a day left to him? I'd seen men die of rotting wounds before and once the decay had spread to the torso, they could not cling on to their lives for long.

My expectation for the day was that I would ride with Count Stephen again, at the head of the army. For all that we were in King Henry's lands, this was still a wild forest in which outlaws made their homes, men and women who would rob us if they saw the opportunity. But when I reached the front rows of the Milan Company and found Gerard, with Melinde at his side, they proposed instead that I return to the *mutur,* to give watch and warning if they did not leave our road at Colburg.

Such a duty was a necessity and I could see that I was the right one to accompany the *mutur*. They might tolerate my presence. So with a salute to Count Stephen, I walked Argentus along the road, back eastwards. Pausing at our cart, I was able to lift Arnulf's cold hand and give it a kiss. His unseeing eyes fluttered. Then I moved on, with a sad salute for Cateline as I left her.

When I reached the bridge to the Kee, smoke was rising from the castle and the *mutur* were gathering up the sacks of silver that had been left for them.

'Lord Rocadamour.'

'Rainulf.'

'Come to keep an eye on us?'

'Well, I'm not here to gaze upon the beauty of your face.'

He only grunted at this and I felt a flush come to my cheeks. This was not the moment for levity and I regretted the attempt.

When the last of the bags had been secured to their ponies, Rainulf led the *mutur* over the bridge, some of them raising their weapons in a final gesture towards the tower in honour of their dead.

'It's what you wanted, anyway, isn't it?' I asked, when we were underway and I was looking down at his thick black hair and broad shoulders. 'To go south.'

'South at Colburg is a bad route. It's slow, with no food to buy on the way. Once Gerard reaches Wuttgard he'll pass through well-stocked towns all the way to France.'

'But you'll take it?'

'I will.'

That was all we said to each other for the whole morning. Dry summer weather had resumed after yesterday's showers and we were walking through sunlight and the dappled green shadows of thousands of swaying tree leaves. Around us, this was newer forest than on the eastern side of the Kee: the trees were thinner, more spaced out, and the wild grasses beneath them thicker and covered with flowers. Butterflies were lively already and one – small and a startling blue – flitted across Argentus's head, causing him to dip his nose and twitch his ears.

My stallion had such an easy gait when he walked that I became drowsy as we journeyed, thinking back to Castle Rocadamour and how as a child I had first known Arnulf. When I was seven or eight years old, the sergeant – who already seemed ancient – began to show an interest in my riding and fighting skills. William and I nicknamed Arnulf 'horse-face', wanting to shake off through laughter the fact that we were both intimidated every time he came over to give us instruction.

The sunlight grew stronger and warmer on my back as the forest thinned out and eventually the road came out of the trees altogether, to cultivated land where yellow rapeseed alternated with strips of unripe stalks of barley and strips of fallow earth. There were farmers here too, distant clusters of men facing us, expressions impossible to see, hidden in the shadows of their straw hats.

The field patterns were marked by sinuous lines of hedgerow, in and out of which flitted starlings and finches. After the next gentle hill was climbed, we could see down to a village: a crossroads; a church with walls of stone (but a wooden roof); and a few wooden houses on strips of muddy land marked out by wattle fences and containing a pig or a hen or two.

'Civilisation at last,' I said. And this time Rainulf laughed.

We were met at the crossroads by the village priest, a balding, thin man who looked up at me anxiously, then at Rainulf.

'Count Stephen said to expect you. He says I should tell you that we've sold all the food we can spare.'

Rainulf scowled, 'The Devil rot their souls.'

'Are they far ahead?' I asked the priest.

'Not more than an hour on foot.'

'Where's the silver they paid you?' When Rainulf addressed this question to the priest, I became uneasy and Argentus could feel it. He skipped sideways and I let him take me a few paces away from the front of the *mutur's* marching formation.

'Each farmer struck his own bargain.'

'And where are those farmers now?'

'Gone back to their fields.'

'You see, the silver was ours.'

'It wasn't much,' said the priest hurriedly. 'Not five shillings in all, for some oats and a couple of pigs.'

'Even so. We want our five shillings.'

The priest looked at me, with mute appeal.

'It's not right; but if you can, you should pay him and leave them go on their way.'

Probably, the priest had been warned about the *mutur*, or perhaps he could hear the earnestness in my voice. In any event, his Adam's apple gave a jerk as he swallowed and in a dry voice, he said, 'Wait here.'

Half-running, the elderly man went to his church and came back soon afterwards, holding out his hand.

'It's all I have.'

'Not enough.' Rainulf took the few coins all the same, then spat onto the ground. 'Lads, those farmers over there have our silver. So let's have their animals.'

His men ran across to the nearby houses, levering themselves over the fences and began to chase down squealing pigs and fluttering chickens.

'Stop! Stop!' The priest rang his hands, then ran to me and grasped my leg. 'Stop them. What will we live on?'

I felt sickened. If we were in my lands, I would hunt down thieves such as these and have them hanged as an example. Not here though.

'Rainulf!' I shouted across to him. 'Your quarrel is with Gerard, not these people. Leave them their livestock.'

Rainulf didn't bother to reply.

'I'm sorry.' I looked down upon the priest's anxious, questioning face. 'There's nothing I can do or say to stop these men.'

When the *mutur* were satisfied, they formed up again and took the south road, leaving a village marked with torn fences and splashes of animal blood. There were tears in the eyes of the priest. Wisely, the farmers had stayed at some distance on the far side of the fields.

As he led his men away, Rainulf gave me a wave of one of his axes. 'Farewell, Lord Rocadamour.'

I did not return the salute.

26

WRATH, DEVASTATION, DESOLATION, BITTERNESS

Arnulf died that night. When I woke to the dawn chorus, he was white, cold and stiff under his cart. His arms and legs were so stiff, in fact, they could not be moved. It seemed irreverent of the birds to carry on as if nothing had happened and I got my hunting bow from the cart. Teeth gritted, I sought out the loudest, the mocking screech of a jackdaw, and let fly. A few leaves fluttered, but I missed; the bird did, however, hop away.

'What are you doing?' Cateline rested her arm on mine, preventing me from taking another shot.

'Arnulf's dead.'

'What good will that do?'

'Nothing.'

'Go get a spade, we must bury him while there's time, before the army leaves.'

Cateline was right of course and the tenderness of expression in her brown eyes softened my anger. Throwing the bow back in the cart, I set off up the road.

Many people were awake, including Robert, Count Stephen's *stipendiarus,* whom to judge from the fact his bandages were gone, was well on the mend. Why had not Arnulf mended too? As I passed, Robert saluted me and I gave a brief nod in return.

Jacques was awake too and gathering up his belongings; in just his jerkin and breeches, he was a slender figure.

'God be with you, Guibert.'

'And with you. Have you a shovel?'

The archer ceased his packing and faced me. 'Arnulf died?'

Tears came to my eyes and I did not find it easy to speak, I did not have to.

'We have shovels and picks. This way.'

Further on up the road, the Milan Company had a cart beneath whose covers lay a great pile of equipment for use in sieges, including dozens of iron-tipped spades.

'Gerard, you'll want to come,' said Jacques.

'What's the matter?' Yawning and also thinner in appearance without his armour (though still far more stocky than Jacques), Gerard walked over to us.

'Arnulf died during the night.'

'God rest his soul.' It was Melinde who spoke, wrapped in a brown cape, walking behind Gerard.

'I'm sorry for your loss,' added Gerard, his eyes searching mine, face full of sympathy.

This section of forest was young, the tree trunks about ten yards or so from each other, with tussocks of thick grass between them.

'How about there?' As we made our way back towards the body, Jacques pointed to a cluster of yellow, leafy chrysanthemums. 'The Romans used to cover their fallen dead with those flowers.'

I nodded and we left the road to set to work. Although clad only in light clothes and although the morning sky was grey, it was warm enough and soon I was sweating. But I dug on, wanting to make sure Arnulf would be deep enough under that his body would not be disturbed by wild dogs or other animals. Whether we rose from our graves on Christ's return, or came down to earth with our heavenly form, I did not know.

'Enough?' panted Gerard.

'A little more.'

At last I relented and we took the cold body and placed it in the dark earth. Around the edge of the pit stood Gerard, Jacques, Melinde, Cateline and myself. Beyond us stood others, men and women who had seen what we were about and come in silence to pay tribute to Arnulf. This I appreciated. It was good of them.

The priest who had heard Arnulf's confession pushed through to us.

'Say a few words about him first, would you my son?' he reached out to hold my shoulder and the strength of the priest's grip helped me gather myself.

'Arnulf. You were loyal to both my father and me. None more loyal. You were brave in battle; a great rider; an expert with sword or lance.' It occurred to me then that I had always measured myself and others by these qualities. Yet there were more important ones. 'Best of all, you were a good man. If ever I had a troubled conscience I had only to think of you and I would know what the right course of action was. The honest, true one, I mean.'

'Hear him, hear him,' muttered a few voices.

'That's all.' I stepped back from the edge: my tears were falling in the pit. Friendly hands from all around patted me on the back.

Having made the sign of the cross over the grave, the priest began to chant. 'Deliver me, O Lord, from eternal death in that awful day when the heavens and earth shall be shaken, and Thou shalt come to judge the world by fire. Quaking and dread take hold upon me, when I look for the coming of the trial and the wrath to come.'

Here and there around us a number of people murmured a response, 'When the heavens and the earth shall be shaken.'

'That day is a day of wrath, of devastation and desolation, a great day and exceeding bitter.'

Again a reply: 'When Thou shalt come to judge the world by fire.'

'O Lord,' declaimed the priest, 'grant them eternal rest, and let everlasting light shine upon them.'

Then there was silence, at least among the humans around the grave. Although the birds were becoming calmer, they still called out in large numbers. I no longer minded their fuss. The words of the priest and his followers had soothed me. Although I had listened to that psalm many times, I had never heard it used at a burial. The words were good and strong and matched my thoughts: wrath, devastation, desolation, bitterness. And in the end, the comfort of the idea that Arnulf could rest now in everlasting light.

Those of us with shovels re-filled the grave with the earth we had dug out, while in the hard ground at the head of the grave the priest hammered in a cross that had been made from hawthorn branches, stripped of bark and tied together.

Gerard thumped my shoulder. 'He was a good man. Well said.'

'Sorry.' Jacques reached around me and hugged me tightly for a moment. 'I'm sorry Guibert.'

Melinde simply stretched up and kissed my wet cheek.

Then it was just Cateline and I and, deep in the ground, Arnulf. I was crying again and squatting down, reached out a hand to the dirt.

'So far from home. So alone, here, where there is nothing.'

'As with my mother, father and, I hope, my sister.' Cateline stood beside me and stroked my hair. 'But they were all pilgrims and that means their home is with Christ. A better home than any on earth.'

'Do you believe that?'

She hesitated. 'In truth? I don't know.'

'What if he died for nothing? What if this expedition was folly from the beginning? It was me who wanted to go, you know? Not Arnulf, not my father. I had to beg and beg. And because I insisted, did I cause his death?'

'It wasn't folly to want to journey to Jerusalem,' Cateline spoke firmly. 'It may have been folly to sack Devinium, but neither you nor

Arnold had a hand in that.'

Whether she was right or not, I could not say. What mattered is that Cateline had spoken in order to comfort me. Cateline, who had suffered far greater losses than I. Standing and somewhat recovered, I kissed her on the forehead.

'Thank you.'

*   *   *

Two days later, we looked down upon a real city. Wuttgard had a cathedral, whose tall spire was topped by a cross; there were other churches too, at least three steeples that we could see. The city had a full circuit of walls, two stone bridges across the River Orris, stone buildings with two and even three stories and for miles and miles around the fields were cultivated and busy with farmers, serfs and livestock.

'Well,' said Count Stephen, 'I believe we can count ourselves saved at last.'

'I'm not so sure.' Gerard was standing between our mounts. 'What if Bishop Wernher's servants ran straight here and sounded the alarm, what kind of reception will we get?'

'Is there any alternative to crossing here?' I asked him. As always when I spoke to Gerard from my horse, he seemed older then when I was on foot.

'It's not attractive. A long walk south, maybe three days, to a village called Rittenburg that has a wooden bridge we could use. And not only is the road bad after that, but there will be a chance of a meeting with Rainulf too, since that's the bridge he'll be making for.'

'Let's go to Wuttgard then and if asked, speak the truth. We had nothing to do with Wernher's death.' Count Stephen sounded impatient. Perhaps the prospect of a comfortable journey home was filling his thoughts. I too wished I could reach Rocadamour as soon as possible: to tell Father of Arnulf's death; of my battles; and to introduce him to Cateline.

'All right, let's try it,' said Gerard, 'but I'm not bringing my men within bowshot of the walls until we've a promise of safe passage.'

We walked on under a hot sun, six knights in the van, then half the Milan Company with Gerard and Jacques their officers, then the carts and wagons and at last, emerging from the woods some half hour behind us, the rest of the Milan Company commanded by Andreas, defending the rear of the army. Our procession was a slow undulating serpent of silver, brown, and grey in a landscape that was predominantly green. On either side of us, grasses and vegetables grew along dense, curving, lines of cultivated soil.

A bugle sounded from the city and soon afterwards five riders, knights, came at a canter, one of them holding a banner showing a white swan on a red background.

'Raise my standard.'

The knight at Count Stephen's right-hand side took a flag (a black lion on a yellow field) from his saddlebag and tied it to his lance. Watching, I almost gasped aloud with pain. For I was suddenly in a world where Arnulf was riding next to me showing the Rocadamour colours. Why could that not be true?

When the riders came near, they slowed to a walk and then halted.

'Well met. I am Peter Ninefingers, Sheriff of Wuttgard.' The knight threw back his coif. His was a long face, like Arnulf's, but clean shaven. His eyes were deep set and even though the sun was nearly overhead, pools of shadow filled his sockets, making it hard to read his expression.

'Stephen, Count of Nangis.'

I had my horse take one step forward. 'Guibert of Rocadamour.'

'You return from Shalk's expedition? You had reason to turn back?'

'Alas, this is all that survive, well, nearly all. We met with disaster near Devinium.'

The sheriff waited.

Count Stephen continued, 'Provoked by the people of Devinium, some of our army stormed that city and looted it. King Bratislav couldn't forgive us, but he hid his anger well and accepted Shalk's apologies. He lured the army into placing its weapons in carts that he guarded and led them to a plain where they were massacred. Only those of us who held on to our weapons and turned back down the road survived. And that after overcoming the full army of King Bratislav in battle.'

'This is it? This is all that remains of your great expedition?' Peter Ninefingers shook his head, amazed, shocked. 'Well, you are safe now. You can camp at the same spot you used on your way east and I'll send out merchants. Do you have coin enough for your needs?'

'I believe so.'

I resisted the urge to look at Count Stephen when he gave that reply. Our people, of course, were wealthier than they had ever been in their lives, thanks to the treasure of Devinium and that of Bishop Wernher.

'The nobles among you are welcome to come to dine with me at the bishop's palace: unfortunately King Henry is busy in the north, or he would wish to hear your tale. And Bishop Wernher... well, you must have left him at Castle-On-The-Kee?'

Count Stephen licked his lips. 'It seems that I am the bearer of bad tidings then.'

'The bishop?'

'Your lord is dead.'

The sheriff turned a little pale, but said nothing.

'You may have heard of the *mutur*? A band of ruffians and thugs who joined the expedition in the hope of plunder rather than for the love of Christ.'

'I have heard of these men.'

'Somehow, when we were on the west bank of the Kee, the *mutur* tricked your lord and took possession of the castle; killing all the soldiers and – although I believe it was an accident – killing the bishop too. I'm very sorry.'

'Where are they now, these *mutur*?'

'We wanted no part of their deeds, so we insisted they march apart from us and that they turned south at Colburg. They are no doubt hurrying to cross the Orris at Rittenburg.'

'I see. And how many of them are there?'

'Some thirty-odd.'

'Forgive me, I must act at once.' The sheriff and his men turned their horses.

'Before you go, Peter Ninefingers, do the rest of us have your safe conduct?' Count Stephen called out in a firm voice.

'Those who played no part in my lord's death may camp safely outside the city. You have my word.'

27

KEEP THY MONEY TO THYSELF

That night the army was merry. Well supplied in roasted meat, wine and beer, any morbidity arising from the fact that we were camped among ghosts was quickly dissipated. Songs, some of them from my home region, rang out in the evening sky. The children formed large packs and chased each other with increasing daring underneath carts and around fireplaces, understanding that the adults tasted freedom and escape and that the dreary confined march through the forest was at an end.

Having survived disaster and, indeed, having been rewarded with treasure, did the people around me now think themselves righteous and deserving of their happiness, in contrast to those who had become meat for birds? Did they feel a sense of superiority to those vastly greater crowds of people who had once camped with us at this very spot?

The difference between being numbered among the dead or the living in my case was a matter of no great moral weight. A petulant impulse had made me stop and listen to Gerard; a desire to check Arnulf's condescending manner towards me had seen me tolerate the footsoldier as he led my horse across the square.

Yes, I had earned my place here tonight in the two battles on the bridges and above all in the ambush of King Bratislav's army. But it was Gerard to whom I really owed my life, Gerard and luck. He had the wisdom and strength of character to say 'no' to Shalk and it was my good fortune that I heard him at the right time.

Perhaps I was being harsh towards the people who were now merrymaking. Perhaps, like me, they simply considered themselves lucky and were rejoicing in the pleasure of being alive when it could so easily have been otherwise.

'Cateline, do you deserve to be alive now, do you think? Compared to those who have died?'

'Deserve? No. There were a lot more deserving people died with Shalk. Or on the way, like my parents. Arnulf too.'

'So, why do you live, when they don't?'

This question clearly interested Cateline and she stood up from the fire to come and sit before me, eyes dark and thoughtful. 'Sometimes I think I have come to the attention of an angel, who is preserving me. But at other times, I think it is a devil who has taken interest in me.'

'A devil?'

'Who wants to keep me alive in order that I suffer over and over.'

'I too… feel a presence. Or that I am being judged. But our suffering will soon be at an end. When we are at Rocadamour, we'll have a happy life. It's a beautiful castle, high above a valley that is fertile and a joy to ride through. And my brother and my sister will love you.'

'Perhaps. And if so, then it was the angel who shadowed me.'

I leaned forward to put my arms around Cateline's slender form, when I became conscious of two shadowy figures by our fire.

'Lord Rocadamour? The sheriff invites you to the palace.'

'Is Count Stephen coming?'

'He is already there.'

With a last squeeze to Cateline's shoulder, I left with my escorts; having anticipated the invitation I had made some effort to wash and to find my least dirty shirt.

By contrast with the exuberant scenes outside the city walls, the streets of the city were gloomy. Bells tolled, mourning the loss of the bishop; black banners were displayed around the square before Wernher's palace. This building was an impressive three-story rectangle, with Roman pillars across the whole of the front. Arriving through a wide doorway, I was escorted to the right, to a modest dining room, where Count Stephen, Peter Ninefingers and (as was evident from his appearance) a middle-aged, Jewish man were seated. Two armed guards were also present in the room, one at each door.

'Lord Rocadamour, let me introduce Reb Yaakov ben Reb Yekusiel. He is responsible for the supply of the fine victuals that your army is feeding upon.'

The Jewish man stood up – he was tall and looked down at me with a face whose lines were severe – and we clasped hands before sitting again. Yaakov was dressed in the traditional dark garb of his people and he maintained his greying hair in long curls beneath a cap.

Various courses of food and wine were brought to us. These were served with a respect for Yaakov's religion, it seemed, since dishes came and went rather than being left to accumulate on the table. And of course, the conversation mainly consisted of the tales Count Stephen and I gave in regard to the events that had befallen our army.

'I'm glad to have met you Yaakov,' I said when all of Peter's questions to us had been answered, 'since you can give me a perspective on this expedition that no Christian can.'

He nodded cautiously, black eyes glistening in the candlelight.

'What do you think of it? Was it just folly? Should we have all stayed at home, in safety?'

'I'll speak the truth, though it might cause offence. Yes, folly. And you were not only a danger to yourselves. My people suffered along your route. The *mutur* especially, we learned to flee from. They took everything and killed many people.'

'And if we had reached Jerusalem. Would that have brought us heavenly reward? Would that have made the journey worthwhile?'

'If a man goes to Jerusalem as a pilgrim, I believe it does him good. Many elderly Jewish men undertake that journey, wanting to study and pray there before they die. But if you go with sword in hand and the intention of killing the Muslims and the Jewish people who live there, then what kind of a God stands there ready to welcome you to heaven? Mars perhaps, or Perun or Thor? Which one of those do you worship?'

'Our intention was to worship Christ,' said Count Stephen sharply.

'Gentlemen,' said Peter, face entirely in shadow, 'let's not stray into theology.'

At that moment a knock came at the door and an agitated man in servant's livery looked in. After gesturing to our host, the servant withdrew, but not before giving me a most enigmatic, bold look. As a result, I felt uneasy.

'Excuse me, gentlemen.' Peter placed his eating knife on the table and got up.

'Well, this is the best meal I've had in months.' Count Stephen smiled at Yaakov.

'And the wine is good too, isn't that so?' Yaakov topped up our glasses.

'Very. It is nearly as good as that from France, eh, Rocadamour?'

I could barely acknowledge the count's words.

'What's the matter?' he asked.

'If the action is wicked, then life loses its savour,' muttered Yaakov.

'Let's leave.' I stood up, aghast at Yaakov's words. What did he know? The guards in the room were watching me with grim faces.

'But why?' Count Stephen waved at the table. 'We are enjoying ourselves, are we not?'

'Not I. We should never have come here. Not after Bishop Wernher was killed.'

'Yet, that was not our doing. And we have the promise of Peter Ninefingers. Sit down.'

'What did you mean, about wicked action?' I remained on my feet, looking at our Jewish companion.

'It is only a proverb.' Now Yaakov glanced at me and I saw in his searching expression something of my father, when he was seeking the truth between William and I over some childish misdeed.

Peter re-entered, with two more guards in chainmail and a frightened youth who looked familiar.

'This is one of the bishop's servants, who was with him at the castle yesterday.' Peter strode over to me, brandishing a candelabra with three candles and waving it in front of my face.

'Was this knight in the castle when the bishop died?'

'Yes, sir.'

'The other?'

'No sir.'

'What is this?' demanded Count Stephen, rising from his chair. I felt hollow and unable to move. The four guards in the room drew their swords.

'You promised us safe conduct!' shouted the count, outraged.

'My exact words were, that those who played no part in my lord's death may camp safely outside the city.'

'Lord Rocadamour had nothing to do with the bishop's death.'

'But he was there, with the *mutur*, weren't you?'

'I was. I had no idea what the *mutur* were planning and I would have opposed it if I had known. They claimed to be taking a chest full of silver over to the bishop as payment for the crossing and I agreed to escort it.' Despite my efforts to remain composed in this moment of crisis, I knew that sweat was springing forth on my brow and marking me as guilty.

'Did you see this man fighting?' Peter asked the servant.

'No sir, but he was covered in blood.'

'How did the bishop die?' Peter turned to me.

I hesitated.

'What do you know? Speak or be condemned at once.'

'A warrior called Rainulf is the leader of the *mutur*. He tied your lord by the feet and hung him out of the castle window. Then he demanded supplies and that the ferry bring over the rest of his men. Unfortunately, by accident, the rope cut against the glass in the window and the bishop fell. We didn't see the body, it was probably swept down river.'

Again Peter addressed the young man, 'Does that sound like the truth to you?'

'Yes sir.'

'Very well, you may go.'

After the bishop's servant left, there was a silence and I looked anxiously at Peter, heart pounding. What was he thinking? Was I to be executed out of hand? Why had I been so stupid as to enter a city owned by the brother of the murdered bishop?

'Lord Rocadamour, you will remain here, a prisoner, until King Henry returns. He'll want to speak to you. Count Stephen, you may go.'

'Oh, I wouldn't be too hasty to release any of them.' Yaakov spoke softly, spinning a silver coin on the table then catching it and throwing it to Peter. 'This is a shilling minted from Aachen only last month. I paid Lord Wernher a great many of these recently and yet several have come back to me tonight. The people outside your walls are using them.'

'Count Stephen, what say you to this?'

'Neither I nor Lord Rocadamour took any of the bishop's coins. We said they should be left at the castle or returned to the king. But we are not in charge of this army and could not stop the poor people from… from stealing the coins.'

'They have my lord's treasure outside with them now?'

'Some of it. Most of it.'

'And you didn't think to tell me?'

'No, I did not. For I did not wish to see another battle during this cursed expedition, but rather I wish to return home in peace.'

'Both of you will stay in prison to discuss these matters with the king. And if I know his temper, you will not be likely to leave there, except in the company of the executioner.'

With a chopping gesture of one hand into the palm of his other, Peter signalled to his guards, who pushed Count Stephen and I out of the room at sword point and then down to the cellars. There, we were put in a cell with a sturdy door and once the torchlight was no longer visible through the bars of the door, we were alone in the darkness.

'Don't despair,' said Count Stephen when the footfalls died away, 'the king will be reasonable. At the worst, he might take this as an excuse to obtain a ransom for us.'

'It's not the anger of the king that concerns me.' I was straining at the bars, which did not give in the slightest. 'It's Cateline and Gerard and the others. Unless we get out to warn them, they are going to be slaughtered.'

28

ARISE, AND LET US FLEE

Our cell was so dark that I could not see my hand before my face. By touching the walls, I discovered it was a small, dry-sided room and had no furniture at all. So I sat on the floor, arms around my knees.

'Is this your first time a prisoner?' Although I could not see his face, it was possible to hear the intention of kindliness and comfort in Count Stephen's tone of voice.

'Yes.'

'It is my third. Which, given the fickle nature of war, is not so bad.'

'What can we expect?'

There was a pause before his answer. 'We'll be given food and drink enough until King Henry comes to Wuttgard. Then, well, I find it is best to prepare for the worst. In your case, you might hang.'

'Hang? Like a commoner?'

'What you said to the sheriff, was incriminating.'

'The truth, you mean?' I said bitterly.

'Yes. It made you a participant in Wernher's death. And unless the *mutur* are caught, you will be the only man within reach of the king. He will want to make it clear that such lawlessness will always be severely punished and who else can he punish?'

'Should I hope for Rainulf's capture then?'

'That, and someone to intervene on your behalf.'

'What do you mean?'

'How stands Rocadamour with the King of France? Louis and Henry both have daughters of Duke Charles as wives. If Louis would speak for you, then Henry might listen.'

'My father serves the king for forty days each year, no more. And on his return, there is much laughter made at the expense of Louis. For the king has no authority south of the Loire.'

'I know well enough how you southerners value your independence. But if your father has done his duty in good faith, that is grounds enough to ask Louis to vouch for you. You must ask Peter Ninefingers for a messenger and send the man to find the French king with your plea. And if Peter will not allow it, you must bribe someone.'

'With what? My horses and silver are outside and soon to be in possession of the sheriff I think.'

'I'll help you, if I can.'

'O God,' I sighed aloud, envisaging the moment news of my imprisonment reached my family. It would be shameful to incur such an obligation on my father's behalf and even more shameful to be hung as a thief instead of being granted the right to a trial by combat that was my due.

Silently, we sat together in the darkness for some time.

My thoughts were spinning around, from memories of home to berating myself for foolishness: foolishness in taking the ferry with Rainulf that fateful morning and again in walking in to Wuttgard today. Perhaps I should have stayed with the *mutur* when they left the army?

'You know, earlier when I was listening to the people singing, I found I could not share their happiness. I think I had a premonition of this disaster.' For a moment my mind settled on this recollection and I voiced it, just to hear Count Stephen speak again and take comfort in his presence.

'I understand you. For it seemed to me too that the jocularity of the crowds was … inappropriate.'

'You mean, because we were camped in fields that had once held our whole army. That the dead were around us?'

'Something of that.' His limbs creaked as he changed his posture. 'But also, here we were on a retreat from a failed undertaking. We set out for Christ. So what does it mean that we few return having fought no one but other Christians? We should be downcast and humble, not cheerful and proud.'

At his words, another thought occurred to me. 'Is this God, punishing us? Is that what has happened to me?'

'Ahh. I remember being as young as you and thinking that God took an interest in my deeds. But now, I am more modest. I don't think God interferes with our affairs; he lets us reckon up our worth during our time on the Earth and judges us afterwards.'

Immediately, I felt that Count Stephen was right in this and I blushed that I had presumed otherwise, glad of the concealment of the darkness.

After another silence, I spoke again. 'I ought to hate Rainulf. But I don't.' I found I was gesturing with my hands, though Count Stephen could not see my motions. 'I understand him. If I'm angry at anyone for my imprisonment, it is myself, for walking so innocently into this city. And I am also angry at Bishop Wernher. If he had not been so greedy, we could have come to Wuttgard in peace and innocent of any harm to King Henry.'

'I hate no man. Rainulf, however… Rainulf is a man to be avoided.'

'Why do you say that?'

'You and I, we were brought up to respect certain values, such as honour and loyalty. Even a man like Gerard, despite being a commoner, has a character that holds him back from actions that would bring him shame and disgrace. Not Rainulf. He cares not about his reputation. And that makes him very dangerous to be around. His word means nothing and if it suited him to cut your throat in the night, he wouldn't hesitate.'

This gave me something to think about and while I felt that what Count Stephen said was true, there was something else in Rainulf that the count had missed. Something admirable, like the spirit of an unbroken stallion. I was on the cusp of saying so, when a patch of grey appeared in the corner of my eye. Soon after, I heard footsteps. Then the light grew bright and orange.

A bearded man's face was at the bars of our cell, eyes black discs of shadow: Yaakov.

'Listen carefully. I will help you escape. You must warn your people to flee during the night. They can do it. Peter has only footsoldiers, his knights are all gone searching for the *mutur*. But unless your people leave now, they will be butchered as soon as the light returns. Peter is full of anger and cares nothing for the lives of the poor.'

'Why are you helping us now?' asked Count Stephen. 'You were the one who alerted the sheriff.'

'Yes, and I'm sorry I spoke as I did. It was *chet*. A sin. If I had said nothing, then these people would have gone back to their homes and I would not have all their deaths on my soul.'

'What's your plan?' I came over to the door.

'Simple. Follow me quietly to a window, where my nephew waits to guide you out of the city. Then it is up to you.'

'Will you not suffer as a result of helping us?' asked Count Stephen.

'Maybe. But maybe you will hurry up and do this right and all will be well.'

The lock clicked open and I stepped out, taking the hand that was offered me. With Count Stephen on my heels, I followed Yaakov through the shadows of the cellar to some stone stairs that led up to the halls of the house. Out of that dark prison already! My heart was beating fast and the melancholy cloud that had been filling my thoughts had dissipated, being replaced with a sense of urgency. If I could only get my hands on a sword, I would rather die fighting than wait to be hung, or be obliged to place our family in debt to the King of France.

Motioning us to wait, Yaakov ascended first, raised his lantern, then waved us up. Quickly now, but with soft feet, we hurried to a nearby room: a deserted servant's bedroom. Once Count Stephen was inside, Yaakov closed the door and let out a great sigh. Rolling his eyes upwards and muttering in an unfamiliar language, Yaakov looked shaken. Count Stephen and I exchanged glances. Now what?

Placing the lamp on a table, Yaakov doused it, leaving only a faint light from the narrow window to see by. Then that too was blocked as Yaakov leaned out of the opening.

'Ready down there?'

'Yes, come.'

We lowered Count Stephen first, each of us holding one of his arms. For such a famous warrior, he was surprisingly light, frail almost. Then it was my turn. Below me a youth reached up out of the darkness to hold up his hands and support my dangling feet.

'Thank you,' I said to Yaakov before I let go of him. Without responding, he quickly drew back from the window, which closed.

'Put these on.'

The youth handed us Jewish capes and hats and, but for his short hair, Count Stephen would have been an utterly convincing elder of their community. I doubted I looked the part so well.

'This way.'

Although the episcopal palace was closest to the southern wall of the city, we were led northwards, through dark cobbled streets. It was hard to resist speeding up and even breaking into a run, but we kept to a walk. There were other people nearby, I could hear their footsteps. I could also hear voices from within some of the houses that we passed. I resisted the temptation to look around, keeping my head lowered and focused on the feet of the lad in front of me.

At last, we came to the town wall.

'This gate is in our charge. You are safe from here.'

I glanced at the gatekeeper, a footsoldier who kept his eyes away from us as he exchanged a few words with the youth. It occurred to me that I could overpower this man if I had to and I tensed my body, ready to strike if the lad's words proved mistaken. There was no need. Displaying no emotion on his face, the guard opened the gate. We were outside the city. What joy! What a reprise from my mistakes.

There was enough moonlight to see by, compared to being in that cell, it was almost daylight. As we walked away from the city, I made for a copse of trees, resisting the temptation to run until I was sure we could not been seen from the walls.

'Let's hurry now,' I turned to the count.

'Go on. I'll follow as best I can.'

Finding a path through the long rows of hedges that acted as field boundaries was not always easy. Nor was it a simple matter to avoid startling cattle, sheep, or pigs. And I was much better at it than the count, who was panting heavily.

'Don't slow yourself on my account.'

He was right and I did not stop to argue. Instead, I ran faster, along a curving route that skirted the city and brought me to the stream that ran down to our camp.

There were many fires still burning yellow and many groups of people still singing. Perhaps we had not been in the bishop's prison as long as it felt. Even so, the summer nights were short and we would need every minute of darkness to escape.

I took off my hat to show myself to a guard who was sitting by a fire that had nearly gone out. Before throwing the garment down on the ground, it occurred to me that should it be found, the hat might provide evidence against the Jewish community, so I threw it on the fire instead. Sparks flew up and these, along with the sound of the hat landing on the burned logs, woke the man, who had been drowsing against his spear.

'Who's there?' he asked.

'Where's Gerard?'

'That camp.' He pointed with his spear. 'What's the matter?'

'Get up and get ready to leave.' I ran on, to where Gerard, Melinde, Jacques, Andreas and some others were sitting around a fire. When they saw me in my outlandish garb, Jacques chuckled, Melinde looked amazed.

'We are in danger. The sheriff knows the bishop is dead and he knows you have the bishop's coins. He plans to attack at dawn. We have to leave.'

Immediately, everyone looked sombre and a hubbub of anxious cries grew up. Gerard stood up.

'Nobody panic! Silence there!'

He made me explain myself, which I managed fairly well, given my breathless condition.

'Very well. We are fortunate that his knights are away from the city. Escape is possible, but it has to be done right.' Gerard turned to Andreas. 'First of all, keep all the fires going. Stoke them up. Secondly, I want a party of volunteers to join me at the fires nearest the walls, where we will maintain our singing until near dawn. Every rider should join us there. While we do this, the rest can go on foot, but quietly.'

Having instructed his officers and assigned men to pass word of the plan to the rest of the camp, Gerard walked with me towards the city side of the camp. When we passed my cart and horses, I saw that Cateline was asleep.

'I'll be down to you soon,' I said to Gerard, before kneeling at her side. 'Wake, my love.'

Cateline opened her eyes, which were black with a hint of silver from the reflected moon. 'You are back. I thought you might stay there the night.'

'I might have stayed there a lot longer than a night. I might have been there for the rest of my life. But I've been given another chance. We've been given another chance.'

While I explained myself again, laughing when I came to the escape, Cateline looked horrified.

'What kind of a life do any of us live? When a bright and happy morning can turn so cruelly and so quickly to ruin?'

'We are not ruined yet.'

29

THE RED HORSEMAN

The footsoldiers of Wuttgard marched out of their city in fine military style soon after an overcast dawn gave enough light for the fields to become pale grey. Deploying in a long line, with a depth of three men, they then marched to the beat of a drum whose tattoo would have been the grim music that accompanied the final destruction of the remnants of Shalk's army. Except that these soldiers marched into an empty camp.

Safely out of range of their crossbows, Count Stephen and myself and four of his knights were mounted and watching the scene as the men from Wuttgard realised the deception, broke ranks, and ran about the abandoned tents. Behind us, hurrying westwards on the road, were Gerard and a dozen of his men. They had remained to keep the fires attended until the very last, giving our slower-moving people as much time as possible to get away.

Despite the difficulties of leading animals at night, our army had departed quickly enough after my alarm: there was no one in sight as far as a slight rise that was silhouetted against the deep blue western horizon, two or three miles away.

Beyond the confused body of footsoldiers was a lone horseman, Peter Ninefingers presumably.

'Will he pursue us, do you think?' I asked. 'Those men will be able to catch our carts if they are determined enough.'

Count Stephen shaded a tired-looking face against the brightness of the sun, a white disc just above the far tree line. 'The sheriff has acted in every way as his masters would have wished. He's that kind of man, a loyal and competent servant. So, yes, he'll pursue us. I hold no grudge against him for it. Yet he will have deep reservations about bringing all his men westwards.'

'How so?'

'His knights are gone in search of Rainulf, if he brings his footsoldiers after us, he neglects the defenses of the city.'

'It will be safe enough for two or three days won't it?'

'With the bishop dead? And King Henry in the north? I don't know. It all depends on what local feuds exist here. Wuttgard would be a fabulous prize for a discontented vassal.'

Although his tone was flat, Count Stephen's words encouraged me. I felt no anxiety on my own part. Armoured and on horseback, I savoured my freedom. Cateline and the other people of our army, however, were at great risk of being caught if Peter Ninefingers could commit his men to a chase.

'Here they come.'

The rider, a tall figure, almost certainly that of the sheriff, was galloping among the troops and they were forming up for a march, in a column ten wide and a score or so deep.

'Can we defeat them? If we had to?'

'I doubt it. Not unless they are caught off guard, flank or rear perhaps.'

'If we had Rainulf with us?'

'Thirty more *mutur*?' He looked at me curiously. 'They are good fighters, but would make no difference here.'

The tramp of two hundred men is a powerful sound and once on the road, they moved with alarming efficiency. It required a short trot on our part for the six of us to form a line across the road ahead of them, facing the incoming soldiers, who halted.

Hand raised, Peter Ninefingers rode up the side of the road until he was at the front of his men. 'Parley.'

'Come in peace,' replied Count Stephen.

'So it's you.' His horse was a fine blonde chestnut destrier. 'I will not ask how you escaped, what friend of yours let you out.' Peter did pause, however, perhaps in the hope that we would say something that revealed the source of our assistance. 'But I do ask you to prove yourselves men of honour and stand aside.'

Immediately, colour and energy came to Count Stephen's face. 'It is honour that puts us in your path.'

'What honour?' the sheriff looked back at him contemptuously. 'You are protecting only thieves and commoners.'

'We have a bond with these people,' I said quietly. 'They set forth for Jerusalem under our protection and we will not let them down.'

'You can't stop us.'

Count Stephen leaned forward in his saddle. 'No, but we can slow you. And leave you short of soldiers for the protection of the city.'

For what felt a long time, but was perhaps only a minute, matters hung in the balance. Then a dark and downcast expression came over the sheriff's already sour face. 'Very well, Count Stephen of Nangis and Lord Guibert of Rocadamour. You have become enemies of the King of Germany and his reach is long.'

'So be it.'

With a last, angry glare, Peter turned his steed about and soon his column of soldiers wheeled on the spot also, to face back to their city.

I tried to maintain an expression as impassive as that of Count Stephen's, yet I could not resist the smile that I felt pulling at my lips. I felt like the tide had changed direction, that the constant peril that had come close to overwhelming us was finally receding, that I would see my home again.

Having waited to witness the sheriff and his men return to

Wuttgard, our small troop of knights then rode fast along the road under a brightening clear sky until we reached the dozen of the Milan Company who were running – at a slow, steady gait – to regain their army.

Flushed red with his exertions, Gerard waved his hand in greeting and dropped his pace to a walk. He must have known at once from my expression that all was well.

'What news?'

'They do not pursue us,' said Count Stephen.

I added, 'A column of men were on the road, but when the count said that we would slow them up, the sheriff gave up.'

'God be thanked. I'm getting too old for this kind of marching.'

'As am I.' Jacques was among the volunteers and although pale rather than red, was equally covered in sweat. How could I avoid a sense of superiority in being on horseback? It came, despite my general resolution to treat all men and women as being of equal worth to me and despite my particular respect for these two friends and comrades.

The rest of that morning the men of the Milan Company struggled to catch up with their companions. It was impressive how they sustained a 'wolf trot' (a mile at a walk, a mile at a run) despite the growing heat of the day. Of course, there could be no conversation among them, whereas Count Stephen and I talked about the other, more fortunate, military campaigns of his youth. We did, however, drop well back from Gerard and his men, embarrassed to be having such an easy journey when they were sweating so heavily. At least we could carry their weapons, bows and shields for them.

After a short rest by a cool stream, entered gratefully by both men and horses, we pushed on. Some time after midday we left the cultivated fields and entered another forest which provided us protection from the sun thanks to its canopy of elms and beech. Unusually, the road here curved to avoid a large sandstone rock outcrop.

A grey pony with wild eyes was running along the road towards us, flanks covered in foam, reins loose.

'Woa!' Gerard and his men spread out and waved their arms, causing the animal to pull up, albeit the beast remained frightened and poised to jump. Count Stephen and I exchanged a worried glance and together with his four knights made up the gap to the footsoldiers.

'I know this pony; it belongs to our company, the brothers of Monthlery own it,' said Gerard grimly. 'Pass me my axes.'

While one of Count Stephen's knights calmed the pony and took its reins, to lead it behind his horse, I stared ahead to where the road disappeared from view beyond the reddish rock.

'I think I saw someone!' I called out.

Beside me, having reclaimed the weapon from my horse, Jacques was winding his crossbow as fast as he could.

'Silence!' shouted Gerard. Even Jacques stopped, motionless. And all at once, perhaps due to a shift in the wind, we could hear distant cries from the far side of the outcrop.

'Come on!' It was one of Count Stephen's knights who responded first and spurred his horse. Immediately, we other riders followed and the hooves of our steeds clattered loudly as we galloped forward.

Beyond the rock all was catastrophe: dead bodies were strewn for hundreds of yards, not only those of soldiers but also those of women and children in dishevelled clothing. Our horses splashed through puddles of blood, past broken carts and scattered bags and the discarded crude weapons of the poor. And further up in a compact formation on the road, obscured by the shadows of the trees, were our enemies. Enemies whose appearance was familiar to me, although I could barely believe it.

The *mutur* stood facing us, ready to fight.

'Halt!' Count Stephen gave the order and we reigned in our horses.

My heart was pounding. There was no sign of Cateline among the dead, nor of Tenebrour or my pony. The *mutur,* what were they doing here? Had they really ambushed our army and killed children for the silver they carried? What I was witnessing was utter insanity. Yet deep in my soul, I knew that the *mutur* were capable of this horror.

Our people, so nearly safe. Slaughtered by those who had once been their companions. Somewhere nearby, the Devil was laughing and laughing and laughing.

I counted twenty-six *mutur* altogether, seven at the front with spears. Just to the side of the road (two on my left, one on the right) were three men with raised crossbows, at an uncomfortably close distance. How had I ever admired these butchers? Had Rainulf planted the seeds of my misunderstanding when he talked of my becoming King Mutur? Was it his deviousness or my own inexperience of men? In either case, my eyes now saw them in their proper light, as the Devil's warriors.

'So there you are. We did wonder.' Rainulf stepped forward from his line, plaids swaying. His boot and leggings were soaked in blood. 'Well, count, what's it to be?'

'What do you mean?' Count Stephen's voice was quivering with anger.

'I mean that I'd like to know whether you feel that your honour is challenged and are determined to fight us? Or will you leave us reclaim the silver that is our due.'

'*Lifestealer* here is going to cut your evil head from your body.' He raised his sword high and all three crossbows focused on the count. 'I would have fought you for what you have done to these poor people. Let alone the fact that you have murdered Robert, my knight.'

Shocked, I looked back to where Count Stephen was pointing: an overturned cart had spilled Robert face down, his body hacked with deep wounds.

'And what about you, young Rocadamour, do you still wish to be

King Mutur?'

'Rainulf,' I would not let him goad me and I kept control of my voice. 'You once claimed that I was like you. I am nothing like you. You are a devil and if Count Stephen does not kill you first, my lance will send you back to hell.'

'Wait!' Gerard shouted from behind us. I did not turn but remained poised on my stirrups preparing to attack the soldiers ahead of us. As the footfalls of our friends came closer, I tightened the straps of my shield and adjusted the position of my scabbard.

'The man himself,' spat Rainulf, clenching his axe so firmly his knuckles were white.

'What have you done?' Gerard screamed.

Rainulf gave a sinister grimace. It was the most wicked expression I had ever seen. 'I've outsmarted you, Gerard. That's what I've done. I've ambushed and destroyed the Milan Company.'

'Children, clergy, women... What need for such butchery of innocents?'

'Innocents?' Rainulf shrugged. 'Everyone now dead on this road mocked us at the Reiber, with Prince Slavniak bearing down on us. Everyone here too, took and carried the silver that my men won with their courage and lives in Bishop Wernher's castle. It was you who brought about the deaths of women and children when you gave them a share of our treasure to carry and so made them part of the conspiracy against us.'

'Melinde. Where is she?'

'Her head is there, in the ditch. My men didn't want her, she was too old for them.'

I looked down at Gerard: his eyes slowly closed and opened.

'Rainulf.' Gerard no longer shouted; he walked up the bloody road. 'I have no more words for you. But my axes want to speak. Meet me now, one against one.'

'Certainly old man.' Rainulf hefted his shield and a spiked mace, before momentarily turning to his men and calling out for everyone to hear. 'Don't trust them. And if Jacques raises his bow an inch, shoot him.'

'It's not fair,' I said to Count Stephen, 'Gerard is exhausted. Let's charge them now.'

'Fair or not, it is for Gerard to choose.' This was said loudly enough, but then he dropped his voice and looked to either side. 'Afterwards, whatever happens, we charge.'

30

HEAVEN DEPARTED AS A BOOK FOLDED UP

Two small armies. A stretch of forest road strewn with the recently dead like a scene from hell. And two men. Much the taller, much the stronger and much the more wicked was Rainulf. Until now, I had not realised what hatred really was: that you could taste it as a sourness between your clenched teeth. Rainulf was a heartless butcher of decent people and he had deceived me, played with me and made me think there was a kind of nobility in his fierce independence. By contrast, Gerard was a man I could love. He was brave, of course, and an experienced fighter. More, he was a commander who could understand a crisis at a glance and give orders that meant the survival of his followers in the face of impossible odds.

Until now, perhaps. Because I had just seen grief and rage fill his mind, to the extent that his one desire was to cut down Rainulf by his own hand. As did we all on this side of the battlefield.

It seemed to me that if we were to triumph, six knights and twelve exhausted footsoldiers against twenty-six *mutur*, then we had to fight as one and that Gerard should be part of a line of men following up the charge of the knights. Instead, he was out in front of us, an axe in each hand, a shield across his back.

They met at the half-way point between the armies, some twenty yards away from each line of soldiers and immediately, with no more effort than if he were swinging a stick, Rainulf swiped at Gerard with his heavy spiked mace. Both of them knew it was a feint and Gerard did not commit himself to the counter-attack. That had to be Gerard's strategy, to dodge the mace and rely on the swiftness of his axes to find an opening.

Another waft of the mace, this time downwards from on high and with a swerve Rainulf smashed Gerard's foot into the ground. Even as the shocking blow had landed, the leader of the *mutur* leapt back like a cat, avoiding the sharp edges of Gerard's iron blades that lashed out at him in return. A great cheer went up from Rainulf's men along with several individual cries of encouragement; our side was silent.

Now Rainulf wheeled around Gerard, to test his mobility. My heart sank and if it were possible, my jaws tightened even tighter. There was no doubt that Gerard was in great pain and unable to use his left foot. Again, a strike of surprising speed from Rainulf and this time the mace caught Gerard's shoulder. As his opponent staggered, Rainulf deflected Gerard's one good axe swing with his shield and with a roar of triumph smashed Gerard's head apart.

At exactly the same time, Jacques was flung backwards, his blood spraying into the air. All three bolts had hit him in the chest as he'd raised his crossbow to try to save Gerard.

'Charge!' shouted Count Stephen. 'Revenge for the fallen!'

It was heartening that the remaining ten footsoldiers of the Milan Company gave a loud yell in response and ran behind us as we knights spurred on our horses.

Those of the *mutur* who had survived the journey to face us on this day were not so many in number, but they were a compact group and showed no sign of wavering as our horses hammered the road with iron hooves. I let go the reins, leaned forward and wondered, as Argentus rode towards an undaunted spearman, which way he would duck his head.

Astonishingly, as we neared the enemy line, I felt the weight of my destrier shift and he swerved to the left, leaving the road and the battle. What kind of warfare had he been trained for? One where I threw something from my right hand perhaps? But being left-handed, all that faced the enemy in this position was my shield.

Wasting crucial moments, I had to gather the reins and guide Argentus through the trees and around the back of the enemy troop. The screams of horses and the cries of men wounded in battle were heartrending, but neither Argentus nor I were discouraged and soon we broke from the undergrowth to ride at soldiers who held swords and axes rather than spears.

This was more effective, my destrier had at least been trained to kick at such opponents and I rose and fell in the saddle to assist him. Again, I did not feel fear now the fight was on. And while an incandescent rage filled me, it did not rule me. Rather, I channelled it into every thrust of my lance. As soon as the shaft of my lance was shattered, my fury poured into my sword as I cut down at heads, shoulders and hands.

In my earlier battles, I had not been wounded. This time I registered two hard blows from the weapons of the enemies around me, but strangely I did not feel them until the press around me had loosened and I saw that I must ride at a crossbowman before he shot me. It was after I had killed the archer that I looked down at the blood pouring from my left thigh, which barely had the strength for its duty. My right shin too had been scoured nearly to the bone, the greave having been torn away by a club, and my right arm was numb to the shoulder from the blows I'd caught on my shield. Yet I could still hold my seat and Argentus was in a battle fury himself, foaming at the mouth and carrying me from opponent to opponent with little direction needed from me.

At last, there were no more enemies around me. Nor were there friends. Everyone was dead or writhing in their own blood. Except, that is, for Count Stephen, who was on foot, falling back, always falling back, as Rainulf advanced with swing after swing of that deadly mace.

This was no duel and although the ground appeared to be swaying like the branches of the trees above, I urged Argentus past the corpses and the dying men and horses to help the count.

Before I was half way to them, Count Stephen surprised both Rainulf and I by dashing in unexpectedly as Rainulf raised his mace. With incredible speed and precision, the count thrust *Lifestealer* between the bones of Rainulf's lower arm.

With a cry of pain, the leader of the *mutur* dropped his mace and would have pulled his wounded arm away except that now the count had continued his run forward, moving somewhat to the side to keep Rainulf's arm outstretched and caught on the sword. At last, at enormous cost – severing his hand almost entirely – Rainulf whirled about and managed to fling off the count, who staggered several paces up the road.

'You are a dead man Rainulf.' Count Stephen simply regained his balance and waited. The blood pouring down the arm of the leader of the *mutur* was bright red and was splashing on the ground.

Looking up and down the road, seeing nothing but the dead or twitching bodies of his comrades, Rainulf gave a snarl from between clenched teeth.

'Thus ends the story of the *mutur*; wasn't it magnificent!'

'No,' said the count. 'It was squalid.'

Frowning, Rainulf looked around him, perhaps for a weapon to take up in his left hand, because he shook off his shield, which fell to the ground with a clang. But his face was as white as that of a corpse, the black tattoos making a striking contrast. And he staggered as he tried to walk.

'Rocadamour. For your honour's sake. Bind my arm.' Rainulf's voice, usually so powerful, had fallen to a near whisper.

Even had I wanted to – and I did not – I couldn't help him. It was all I could do to avoid crashing to the ground as I slid off Argentus and discovered that I could not walk. It was while crawling then, that I saw Rainulf collapse and lie looking towards the man who had killed him. Soon, the blood ceased spurting from his wound and his good hand ceased to scrabble for his mace. Perhaps at the end, he just wished to hold it, so that he had a weapon on him should he find himself in Valhalla rather than hell.

'Is it just your thigh?' Count Stephen was already winding a tourniquet around my upper leg. My wound was similar to that which had killed Arnulf, but lower and not quite as deep.

'The shin too, of the other foot. Not bleeding as much but I'm worried about rot.'

'I see. Hold this, one of my men has clean bandages.'

'So do I, in my saddlebag. Needle and thread too.'

Deciding against stitches, the count bound both my wounds very tightly indeed, then relaxed the tourniquet. By now, both legs were throbbing and the pain was bad and growing.

'I have to leave you a moment and check if any of my men live. I'll be back.'

'Go.'

As I lay on my back, looking at the dappled branches above me, I wondered about Cateline. Tears came to my eyes too, for Jacques and Gerard.

'Guibert?' A small dark-haired girl, perhaps five-years-old came into view.

'Aye.'

'Cateline's dying. She wants to speak to you.'

'Where?'

'Just up the road a little.'

Determined not to pass out, I threw off a great wave of darkness as I rolled over onto my front and began to crawl. There was enough push in my legs that I could make progress through the dirt and blood and gore.

'What are you doing!' Count Stephen was shocked. 'Lie still.'

'Cateline is wounded. Help her.' I could hear the croak in my voice. Then footsteps as the count ran up the road.

'I'll tell her to wait for you.' The girl was gone too.

It was harder, somehow, on my own. Every push was so painful that despite my desperate anxiety to see her, I began to make excuses to myself that would justify ending my efforts. That Cateline was fine, the girl didn't understand. It would be well enough to wait for her. Or even that my motions were pointless, because she was already dead.

I kept going, until I could see them through a shimmer of heat from the road. They were at a cart, all three of them looking at me; Cateline was seated, leaning against a wheel. The count hurried back to me and with his help I was able to crawl those last few yards.

'O Guibert.' And she gasped with the pain of speaking. Slumped against the cart, Cateline had a crossbow bolt embedded deep in her stomach and she sat in a pool of dark blood six yards across. In one of her white hands was the dirk I had taken from the bishop's castle and in the other a sharp butcher's knife.

'Cateline.'

'I wouldn't let them touch me.' Again she groaned with the effort of talking. 'Are they dead? Is Rainulf?'

'Yes. All dead. Rainulf too, killed by Count Stephen.'

'Good.' Her smile was grim. And it was the end. The light went out of her beautiful eyes and a moment later her head fell forward, dark tresses swinging in a light breeze as though she were still alive.

31

CONVERSATION FROM A CHILD

'He's awake.' A girl was sitting in the same cart as me. For a moment I did not know who I was. And I was nearly happy. Then my memories returned in full.

'Woah.' A horse snorted, the cart stopped and Count Stephen was beside us, seated on Tenebrour.

'How do you feel?'

'Sore.'

'Any fever?'

'I don't think so.'

The count nodded and gave me a wan smile. 'Have some water.'

Eagerly, the girl held a skin up for me and I drank deeply.

It was evening, near sunset and we were still in the shadows of a forest.

'Is it the same day?' I asked.

The girl looked at me astonished (curiously, she had one brown eye and one green eye). 'Yes. Of course.'

'What's your name?'

'Marguerite.'

'And what happened? Before we arrived.'

But Marguerite said nothing, only stared at me with her huge mismatched eyes.

Count Stephen shook his head. 'The poor innocents. They fled from Wuttgard straight into an ambush. The *mutur* were hidden at that outcrop. It was hopeless, given the confusion of their march and the fact we knights were absent. So the *mutur* were victorious and were gathering silver from the bodies when we arrived.'

'Who else lives?'

Silence.

I closed my eyes. 'The silver. Where's the treasure?'

Count Stephen pulled a sour face. 'I left it there on the road. There has to be a curse on it.'

'All of it? After everything … ? Not even something for the girl?'

'Nothing. The treasure is what destroyed our little army and I could not stand the sight of one coin from it. And don't worry about the girl, I'll see her cared for when we get to Nangis.'

I sank back into the cart and looked at a tranquil azure sky, where an early star was visible between the gently swaying branches of a maple. High in the sky, a larch crossed my view, giving depth to the air above, while nearer, a bee flew past in a series of swerving lines. From the light scents of rose and lilac, I could tell that there were rich clusters of flowers near to us. The plants and creatures of the earth and air cared nothing for the affairs of men, cared nothing for the fact that they no longer shared the world with Cateline, Gerard, Jacques, Robert or any of my comrades of the retreat.

A sigh escaped me. 'Are you taking me to Nangis then?'

'Until you are well enough to ride. After that, if you still want to, I'll send you on the way home, with an escort as far as the Loire. Or you can stay on with me, I'll make you lord of four castles.'

'Thank you. Let's see if I live first, shall we?'

With an exchange of smiles at that, the count signaled for Tenebrour to walk on and soon – painfully – our cart jerked into motion. Around us, I could hear the hooves of several horses and I pulled myself up, hopeful. There were no other riders, however, just a line of horses with the count and Tenebrour at the front, then my pony and the cart, then four other ponies and lastly Argentus.

This pitiful sight was all that remained of Shalk's vast army. The thought made my head swim.

We did not travel much further before Count Stephen decided to stop for our camp.

'There's a stream over on the left, which will do us for water. I'll hunt for some meat, while there is still light. You'll be safe enough here.' He said this, looking up and down the shadow-covered road. But perhaps he was not so sure, for instead of riding away at once the count dismounted and taking a crossbow from the cart, wound it, loaded it with a bolt and gave it to me. 'Just in case.'

When he was gone, Marguerite jumped down from the cart.

'Wait.' It was an effort to pull myself up further into a corner, so I could put my elbows on the sides of the cart and lift myself to see the girl. All was well; she had spotted some blackberries, many of which were ripe.

After filling herself with the fruit, with purple smears around her mouth, Marguerite returned to the cart and saw me watching her.

'Do you want to know what I call them?'

'What, the blackberries?'

'The horses,' she rolled her eyes, contemptuous at my stupidity.

'What do you call them?'

'This one,' she pointed to my pony, still harnessed to the cart, 'is Dancer. Then Whitey, because of her mane. Mary, because my sister would have loved her. Then Margaret. Then Judith. Then Sampson.' She counted them out with her finger.

'Argentus. The stallion is Argentus. It sounds like silver, for his forelock, you see.'

'Is he your horse?'

'Yes. The pony – Dancer – is mine too.'

'Was he really called Dancer?'

'No. But I like it. I'll call him Dancer now.'

'What was his name?'

'My sister called him Tristan.'

'Tristan.' When Marguerite repeated the name, the pony pricked up his ears and looked at us. 'He understands!' she cried with pleasure. 'Tristan, Whitey, Brigid, Mary, Margaret, Judith and Argentus. Can I help feed them?'

'I'm sure Count Stephen would welcome your assistance.'

It was nearly dark when the count returned and in the meantime I had given Marguerite one of the cloaks from beneath me. Although the summer day was warm and the night cool rather than cold, she wore only a thin dress.

'A coney, a dove and a wild pig!' Count Stephen was very pleased with himself. 'I'll get a fire going, then look after the horses.'

The girl sat up in the cart and stared at me with her intense eyes.

'Marguerite would like to help with feeding the ponies.'

'Good. I shall be glad of it shortly.'

Count Stephen's efforts with the cooking, however, were surprisingly slow and inept. After stacking up branches in a large pile, as though a fire were already underway, he spent several minutes with the flint, lashing plenty of sparks towards wood that was admittedly dry.

'God damn it!'

'Here, help me out of the cart.' Many was the night that I'd made a fire while out with my fellow squires in the countryside around Rocadamour.

'I'm sorry Guibert, I wanted to let you rest, but it's been years.'

With his thin but strong arm to assist me, I staggered over to the wood and laid myself along the road beside it.

'Marguerite.'

'Yes?'

'Help me can you? Get pine needles if they are dry, or cattails or dry moss or down from birds. Also bark, if its really dry too.'

While Count Stephen led the horses one-by-one to the stream to drink, I pushed over his stack of wood and selected just the driest twigs and laid them flat upon each other. With some well chosen tinder from Marguerite, I was able to catch a dozen sparks from the first strike of the flint on some moss and blow them into flame.

'Here girl,' called the count, 'you can help with that one…'

'He's called Tristan,' Marguerite interrupted him.

'Tristan,' the count smiled. 'Fill this nosebag for Tristan. Half full, from this satchel.'

While the count was entirely professional in his care for the horses, brushing them down and arranging their feed, I could see he was at a loss when he rejoined me in order to prepare our meal.

'I'm afraid that I'm out of practice. This is the first day in twenty years I've been without a vassal or a servant. Do we set up a spit?'

'Let's just get that big pot out and broil the meat with some carrots. It will be easier.'

In the end, after a long time in the near-boiling water of the pot, the food was passable, but my bowl remained full after the others had finished.

'Eat something Guibert, your body needs the meat.'

'I have no appetite.'

The count came closer, his grey eyes vivid in the firelight. 'I've seen men with wounds far worse than yours live. And I've seen others with lighter wounds die. There's luck comes into it. But there's also spirit. Those who want to live, who have a desire to live, a reason, they do better than those who have lost heart.'

'You are right,' I realised it as I spoke. 'I don't know if I want to live after today.'

'You say that now, but remember, after every battle a warrior feels the same, even if he is on the winning side. And when people you care for have died in that battle, you have so much more reason for sorrow. This is a darkness of the soul that everyone feels and it will pass.'

'Will it?'

'I promise you it will. Now, think of your father awaiting your return and eat up.'

There was no savour in the food, or at least, none for me. Yet I could not argue with the count, I felt that he was right. And I did think of my family, that helped too.

Much later, with the logs on our fire settled and barely glowing, I was drifting off to sleep when Marguerite lay her head on my shoulder and put her arm across my chest.

'Guibert?' she whispered. 'Are you awake?'

'I am.'

'Can I sleep here?'

'You can.'

* * *

Unknown to her, Marguerite played a considerable role in my recovery. I, at least, still had my family. So how could I lose heart when she who had no one kept going with a lively spirit and a real joy in simple pleasures, such as the sight of a large purple butterfly? Neither Count Stephen nor I were accustomed to talking to little girls of the noble class, much less the children of farmers. Yet in our clumsy efforts to converse with her, we learned that Marguerite's parents and two sisters had died on the journey, her father and a sister called Mary in that final battle with the *mutur*. Strangely, though, for most of the time she was much the happiest of the three of us.

For my part, despite the count's words, it was impossible not to mourn: Cateline and Arnulf especially, but also Gerard, Jacques and Melinde. And all the people who had gathered around my fire and shared their rough wine with me. They were good people and my world felt so empty without them. Count Stephen was downcast too, probably because of the death of his knights, but also because of anxiety. We were still in King Henry's lands and no doubt in great danger.

Those first few days after the ambush by the *mutur,* the count pushed us hard. Each time the pony pulling the cart showed signs of being unable to sustain a trot, he put a fresh horse in the harness. And we never stopped for any length of time, except when it was too dark to go on.

With no footsoldiers or poor people to hold us back, we moved swiftly enough. On our third day together, however, we were overtaken by a rider galloping westwards. There was no doubting the look of amazement on his face as he passed, curiosity too. Nevertheless, his business must have been pressing because he didn't slow down to talk to us. Count Stephen rode with even more determination after that, at least until our evening camp.

Thereafter, we daily came across increasing numbers of people using the old road, in both directions. And as we got closer and closer to Clairbourg and the border with France, we met dozens of farmers bringing fruits, greens, beans, corn and cheeses to that great city. These farmers were a great relief to the count, as for a few coins they were happy to sell us prepared food, sparing him the need to hunt or – even more arduous for him – to cook.

It was a glorious summer's day when we reached Clairbourg, with a clear blue sky and the triple fleur-de-lys fluttering from every tower. All three of us were delighted with the sight and with the relaxation of our fear that someone – outlaws, or King Henry's men – would assault us on the final stages of our journey.

Once under the huge portcullis, Count Stephen made for the keep, where the castellan, Duke Robert, was a cousin of his. There, with a roar of incredulity from the duke and soon after, the bustle of servants rushing to help us, I carefully lowered myself from the cart to the cobbles of the keep's central square.

Eyes sparkling in the sunlight, face lit up with triumph, Count Stephen came over to me and clasped my right hand in a surprisingly strong grip. 'Our woes are at an end now Guibert. Rejoice with me.'

'That I do, count. I really do.'

32

THERE IS NO COVERING
FOR DESTRUCTION

When you live five years with a horse, you understand his moods and I knew that Tenebrour was increasingly impatient to be home. With snorts and prances and tosses of his head, he would catch my eye, as if to say 'let's hurry.' For these were familiar lands, they were my lands. The scents from the woods and fields were right; the colours of the ripening grains and grapes were right; and even the few clouds that there were in the sky seemed to be drifting over us at a height and with a shape that seemed exactly right.

Poor Tenebrour, I would not indulge him and allow him canter to his stable. For one, Argentus behind us was heavily loaded. Having gifted Tristan to Marguerite at Nangis I had then to sell the cart, for I was not going to risk the spirit of the destrier by harnessing him to it. It was necessary, therefore, for the horses to take turns with the burden of my equipment.

There was another reason, too, that I did not hurry. Without having planned it, I found that the landscape was helping me recover my childhood memories. This was important to me, because unless I could recover something of the youth I had been, I doubted I would ever again truly feel joy in being alive.

A nearby oak tree had been a favourite for a whole group of my friends, the reason being a long, low branch upon which we could sit. It had served as a practice mount, of course, with each of us eager to take our turn as the brave knight holding his seat while under attack from the sticks of treacherous churls.

If I were here at the tree alone, or with Timeous, my squire who had died of a fever on the outward journey, I'd enjoy sitting still, making no sound, until in every direction the crickets began to hum. Then too, I might spot a frog making its awkward, stealthy way towards the pond that lay in the hollow of a copse to the northeast. And if I were lucky, a hawk would appear from the south (where they nested in the steep rocky face of the hills) and hunt out of a blue sky, diving with exhilarating speed upon its prey in the nearby fields.

Here the road passed a large farm belonging to one of our tenants. And although I never knew his name, I had met the farmer once when running through his yard in pursuit of William. There, I had been absolutely terrified when the farm dog came racing out of the house, barking as if to bring the sky crashing down. It was a sheepdog and today I would not fear its kind. Then, however, the slavering canines of the dog seemed about to tear out my young throat as I was backed into a corner, arms across my body, quivering with fear.

The farmer had come out of the house, given a derisive laugh and called off the dog. 'Lord Guibert, is it?' And he simply shook his head.

William came over, wide-eyed, while a blush that I knew was turning my cheeks red was still upon me. I made him swear never to talk about the incident, not even in jest and when he thought we were alone. For I was ashamed of the fear I'd displayed. In my heart too, I swore private revenge upon the farmer. Foolish child that I'd been. Today I was smiling at the memory and if the farmer had been in view, I would have waved to him.

As the road began to climb away from the river, up towards the castle, several people from the village recognised me and ran towards me. I waited for them. First to arrive were a group of children and soon afterwards came their parents. These were seven of the twenty-two burghers of Rocadamour village, and the group included the brewer and her husband, both looking older than I remembered, though I had only been away a matter of months. One of the two village butchers was there also, in a red-stained apron. Although everyone was smiling, when they reached my horses they turned shy.

'Welcome home, Lord, we feared you dead.' It was the butcher who spoke first.

'Welcome back!' with the first of them having spoken, greetings came from all around.

'You heard Shalk's army was destroyed then?' The two weeks I had spent recovering in Nangis must have been time enough for the news to travel south.

Her face growing more solemn, the brewer answered. 'The priest spoke about it Sunday last, saying it were a terrible judgment from God.'

'Well, I've returned and must let my family know at once. I wouldn't have them suffering with worry for a minute longer than they have to.'

'Aye, that's right lord, ride on up.' The butcher saluted me with his cleaver.

With farewells and heartfelt cries of thanks for my delivery sounding at my back, I set Tenebrour in motion once more. And this time I did not prevent him stepping up from a trot to a canter.

Long before reaching the castle I could make out the guards over the gatehouse. And each time the road turned to bring the castle closer into view there were more figures on the battlements. After the last turn, reaching the final stretch of straight road up to the portcullis, I could see dozens of people staring out at me from between the machicolations, including my mother, father, William and Alice. A bugle was sounding repeatedly and, faintly, the bell of our family chapel was ringing wildly.

'Slow now, Tenebrour, let them see us.'

We trotted under the gatehouse, my head tipping back to see the joyous smiles of my family for as long as possible.

All around the courtyard our knights and footsoldiers were sending up a clamour, hammering their weapons against their shields. Cook came out from the kitchen with his servants, all banging on their pots to outdo the soldiers. Stableboys took my horses after I dismounted. Tenebrour was eager for the company of his old friends, Argentus, however, was looking around at all the cheering, noisy people with some anxiety in his eyes.

'Fear not,' I patted the neck of my destrier and smoothed his silver mane.

Then the gatehouse door was flung open and Alice charged into my arms, causing me to wince with a stab of pain from my wound.

'O Guibert. My prayers were answered.'

'Welcome home my son.' Mother hugged me as best she could with Alice in her way, her eyes glistening.

When Alice finally let go, Father stepped forward and held both my shoulders, behind him I could see William grinning like a fool.

'Guibert. This feels like the day you were born to me, come again. Welcome home.'

'Thank you sir. It's good to be home.'

Then it was William's turn. 'By God I missed you Guibert. And in truth, I didn't think you'd come back.'

One after the other, my father's men – my men in due course – came and welcomed me. By now all the castle's servants were outside, forming a large ring around our group. There were many smiles and those of the servants who knew me best called out their delight in my return.

'Arnulf?' asked Father and the pleasure of the reunion immediately faded, as I'd known it must.

'Died in the night beside me, of a wound to his thigh that became rotten.' This was painful news to my father and all his vassals and I could see it on their faces.

'Timeous and Radolf?'

'Timeous died of a fever not two days after we left France. Radolf volunteered to be among the first across the Reiber and was with the vanguard when they were ambushed and killed to a man by Prince Slavniak.'

By now everyone had ceased their merry noise and all were straining to hear my answers.

My father shook his head solemnly. 'It's a miracle you are standing here before us. What a shame that miracle could not have brought our friends back too.'

'Amen,' said one of the knights.

'Come inside, Guibert, and take a drink,' he raised his voice, 'and tonight after our meal we will learn everything.'

On my way into the keep, my mother took hold of my right arm and my sister my left. Enough of my heart had survived the expedition that my body filled up with the sweetness of their love.

That night the feast hall was as full as I'd ever seen it, more so even than after my father's victory at Mont Morency. The leading men and women of the village had walked up to the castle to attend at the lower tables, while those servants whose duties allowed it were permitted to stand beside the walls and listen. Of course all the soldiers were present, with the knights seated in front of the top table, their squires attending them.

It was a busy room, with platters arriving and being taken away and a constant hubbub of conversation whose tone was celebratory. This was understandable: the heir to Rocadamour, their future lord, had returned to them. Yet I recalled the words of Count Stephen, when he looked at the happy crowds outside Wuttgard and said they should be more modest. Our expedition had been a shameful failure.

More swiftly than usual – for I'm sure that everyone in that room wanted to hear my story – the courses came and went. Until the moment came when my father stood up. Silence from one and all, from the far end of the great hall to near.

'Tonight we give thanks to God for the safe return of Guibert,' he paused.

'Amen!'

'And I invite him to tell us something of his experiences.' With a nod to me, Father sat down again.

Knowing that this moment would come, I had prepared for it during my convalescence in Nangis by telling my story to a scribe, who had written down my words (and had asked my permission to keep the manuscript in order to help write a history of the deeds of Count Stephen). I'd practiced my tale in my thoughts too, while riding towards Castle Rocadamour. What I wanted to do was tell everyone – from my father to the lowliest serf present – about what I had seen. This was not a song such as the one composed by the murdered poet, to praise valour and encourage nobility, this was something else: an unflinching account of catastrophe and greed.

With a steady voice, my words came easily enough and in the right order. For the first part, I spoke of the journey to Devinium and the death of our squires. Then, with servants quietly refilling goblets with wine, but hardly anyone else stirring, I described the cruel deceit practiced by King Bratislav upon Duke Shalk. When it came to my decision to stay with a commoner called Gerard, I did not claim any great wisdom, but told them the truth, which was that I was simply asserting my right to independence from Arnulf.

For perhaps three, maybe four hours, I told everyone in that hall the story of the retreat. As it grew dark the wall torches were lit in their brackets and the candles on the tables. Still, I held their attention. Even when there was a tear on my cheek, my voice did not waver but grew louder and more bitter as I came to the final ambush of the Milan Company by the *mutur* and to the death of Cateline.

Finally, with the arrival of Count Stephen, Marguerite and myself at Clairbourg, I was done.

'Dear God,' someone nearby muttered.

Before I sat down in the hushed hall, I looked around at my family. Unable to face me, tears were streaming down the face of Alice. William, unfortunately, seemed to have understood nothing and his expression was one of rapture and awe. My mother, on the other hand, must have realised exactly what I was trying to say, because she was appalled (mouth open, face pale, food untouched). And my father was looking back at me with an expression I'd never seen before.

Father knew – of course he knew – what it was like to cut through iron and flesh and bone with all your strength and anger, to dismember another man and run through the spray of his blood. He knew also what it was like to see a friend die, whether from having their face smashed open by a mace, their body pierced deeply with crossbow bolts, or from the inexorable rot of a wound.

This knowledge he had not tried to teach me, it had been necessary for me to learn it for myself. We locked eyes and recognised one another and acknowledged one another. If the ghost of Achilles were to greet dead warriors after a life spent at war, then as he welcomed them to hell, Achilles would have shown exactly the same expression as my father wore now: a combination of comradeship, respect, and black, black horror.